Scared
Scriptless

ALSO BY ALISON SWEENEY

The Star Attraction

Scared Scriptless

A Novel

ALISON SWEENEY

HYPERION

New York

Hyperion
Hachette Book Group
237 Park Avenue
New York, NY 10017
www.HachetteBookGroup.com

Printed in the United States of America

RRD-C

First Edition: June 2014

10 9 8 7 6 5 4 3 2 1

Hyperion is a division of Hachette Book Group, Inc.

Library of Congress Cataloging-in-Publication Data

Sweeney, Alison, 1976-
   Scared scriptless : a novel / Alison Sweeney.
      pages cm
   ISBN 978-1-4013-1105-6 (pbk.) — ISBN 978-1-4013-3091-0 (ebook)
1. Television broadcasting—Fiction.   2. Television actors and actresses—Fiction.   3. Man-woman relationships—Fiction.   I. Title.
PS3619.W4424S33 2014
813'.6—dc23

                                     2013048191

I dedicate this novel to everyone who works (past, present and future) at Days of our Lives. *The cast & crew who tirelessly create the enduring and captivating world of Salem—and to everyone who has ever watched and been swept away by it.*

Scared
Scriptless

Act One

Act One

Scene 001

"I can feel the arrhythmia in his femoral artery."

"He's going into cardiac arrest."

"We're not going to lose him!" Intense eyes meet mine over the patient lying on a makeshift hospital bed.

Momentarily startled by the urgent gaze, I quickly recover. "Yes, he's in V-fib," I say.

"He needs another four hundred cc's of propofol." His eyes remain glued to the monitors all around us.

"But you said the max his body could handle was two hundred...," I reply.

"I know what I said, but if I can't finish the surgery, everything we've done for him will be worthless. He'll die if he wakes up now."

"Doctor, his body isn't responding to the treatments. What makes you think the surgery will make a difference?"

"Nothing."

I glance up at the seemingly cavalier reply, but his face is anything but casual. His expression shows the tension, the responsibility, and, most importantly, the concern he has for the patient under his care. "But I don't have another choice. We're a hundred miles from the nearest hospital. At this point my instinct is all I've got to go on."

For a split second, I am caught up in the moment. It's so easy to actually believe we're in a surgical tent in a dusty Middle Eastern desert. Then I shake my head and remember that we are, in fact, on a sound stage at Hogan Chenney Productions in Studio City, Los Angeles. That's a testament to Billy Fox's acting talent; even in rehearsals, he gives it his all. If I weren't holding the script in my hand, ready to prompt him with the next line if he needs it, I'd totally buy that he really is about to save this man's life.

"Nailed it," I say, with my best *School of Rock* impression. Billy breaks character to grin back at me. There is, also, a weird backward dance with guitar, but I skip that part since there are other people watching. "As always, you've got it word for word." I am a details person, and nothing makes me happier than an actor who knows his lines perfectly.

Billy's stellar performance is one of the reasons *The Wrong Doctor* has become a hit show, fan favorite, and Emmy nominee in its very first season. Of course, the rest of the cast and crew and the terrific writing have all contributed to our success. I like to think that I played a key role myself, in my job—which I love—as Script Supervisor for the show. Today is our first day shooting the second season, and the energy and excitement on the set is palpable. The pressure's on too. We have to deliver the same high standard as last season, which is why we've been rehearsing this scene so many times.

The U/5 actor—so named because he gets less than five lines of dialogue—playing the patient lying on the table peeks up at me. "Are you rehearsing the scene again? Can I take five?"

"Of course," I answer. "We're going to be relighting for another five to ten minutes. Be sure to let the AD know you're leaving set, okay?" Given his deer-in-the-headlights look, I add, "Frank. That guy right over there." I point helpfully. "Are you okay?"

"Yeah, I just need to use the restroom." His gaze shifts to Billy and is immediately infused with hero worship. "But if you need me to stay, Mr. Fox...you know...for an eyeline...I don't have to go right now."

Billy, who's been making notes on his script, glances up at the hapless guy. "No, thanks, dude. No problem. I got this." He smiles casually and goes back to methodically reciting ER phrases. Real doctors have incredibly hard jobs, but actors playing doctors don't exactly have it easy. All that technical jargon has to be letter-perfect and usually requires a high-paced, tension-filled, commanding delivery.

Billy stars as Dr. Jason Lucas, a hotshot LA plastic surgeon who gets arrested for a DUI and is sentenced to do community service for Operation Smile, an organization that sends doctors to the third world to fix cleft palates. The steamy locations also require Billy to be sweaty and shirtless a lot. Between the action-packed edgy drama and the eye candy, there are lots of reasons our show has become a fan favorite. Billy has kept his shirt on during these rehearsals, much to the disappointment of the interns.

"Okay, Billy. You're good?" I have to be super careful about the dialogue for this scene because the director wants it all in one take for the "master shot." Since it establishes everything that happens, it's the most important angle of the day. We'll then go in and shoot close-ups, but I think he'd rather use the one camera angle if he can get it, so Billy has to get his lines perfect in one take.

"Femoral artery, arrhythmia, cardiac arrest...yeah, I got it," Billy says while continuing to study intently.

It's my job to micromanage these sorts of specifics. There are plenty of actors who cringe when they see me coming. If the actor doesn't know his lines well, I'm the one who calls him on it. In other words, I sweat the small stuff.

"Just remember, Billy, four hundred cc's and a hundred miles away." He nods absently as Bobby, the prop master, steps in to go over the specifics of the fake needles that he'll be using.

I head back to my director's chair and get settled in for the next take. I open my large spiral notebook, which is always (always, always) by my side and helps me keep meticulous track of every detail of my work and personal life, in list after list. Some might call it compulsive, but I call it organized. With a few seconds of downtime before we shoot the next scene, I look at my recent lists: *Groceries: Animal crackers, PB Cheerios, granola bars.* I quickly jot down *oranges.* A girl can't live on cereal alone. Below that, there is a list of ideas for presents for my mom's upcoming birthday: *"Real Simple* subscription? *Slow Cooker?* Inspired by an infomercial I watched way too late last night, I start to add *panini maker* to the list when Frank, the assistant director (best AD in town), cuts into my thoughts. There is so much happening on a set all at once... the lighting guys are set-ting up a ladder on the floor, the sound mixer is testing various mic packs, a couple of grips behind me are in some sort of hacky-sack play-off while waiting for the all-clear before moving the delicate camera equipment into its new position. I can zone out whenever I need to, despite the chaos. But when I'm on, I'm on.

"Maddy!" I hear my name through the chaos.

"Sorry, Frank." I immediately dump the list in the side pocket of my chair. "What's up?" I look up at him. "What's all over your shirt?" He may be a first-rate AD, but his competence on set is matched only by his ability to spill things on himself... and any-one else in the vicinity.

"Oh shit, must be mustard from my In-N-Out," Frank says, scratching at the yellow stain.

"When did you sneak away to In-N-Out?"

"Oh, you didn't hear? Hogan brought an In-N-Out truck to set today. Burgers for the crew as a 'back to school' treat." He hands me an unwrapped burger. "I got an extra. You want?"

"That's okay, I'll try to grab one later—" Before I can even finish my sentence, Frank is unwrapping it. My stomach growls looking at the delicious string of cheese and special spread, which no doubt is two seconds away from landing on his jeans. I do love burgers, and without question there are times I eat them just as a silent form of protest against all the girls here in LA who wouldn't dare touch one. It's the same rationale as to why I wear flats almost exclusively—and not even designer ones.

It's not at all surprising that Hogan Chenny, or as Frank calls him, "the Big Guy," got us all In-N-Out today. As head of Hogan Chenny Productions (HCP), Hogan is head writer, creator, and executive producer for *The Wrong Doctor* and an all-around prime-time drama icon. Given his success and his reputation for being a hard-ass, a lot of people are intimidated by him. The fact that Hogan stays in his office most of the time contributes to his Oz-like reputation, but he's also the classy kind of guy who gets In-N-Out for the crew, just because. And although few people are aware of this, I know firsthand that Hogan has a softer side because he has been a family friend since I was a little girl. He was a regular at my family's ski lodge up in Wolf County, California. When I worked the lifts after school and on weekends, Hogan and I would often chat about movies and TV. He introduced my brothers and me to the old classic '80s dramas *St. Elsewhere*, *Hill Street Blues*, *L.A. Law*, and all my favorite old movies that I am constantly quoting.

As a self-professed type-A person, I grew up with a plan: attend University of California–Davis, move home to Wolf, work at my dad's resort, marry my high school boyfriend Brian, have kids ... yada yada yada—but things didn't quite work out the way I'd planned. Instead, right after graduation, Hogan offered to help me (just that one time, I might add) get a job as a production assistant, so I could "give TV a shot." It was the ultimate entry-level position, but I was willing to do the grunt work for every department.

I'll never forget getting off the plane at LAX wearing my Marmot fleece and Merrell boots. It was like landing in another world. While it was hard to get used to the traffic, the smog, and being a natural dish-water blonde in a sea of highlighted perfection, from the very first day, I loved being a PA on *300 Madison Avenue*, a drama about the residents of a luxury apartment building. Turns out my passion for organization, eye for detail, and willingness to work fourteen-hour workdays were essential skills when it came to the chaotic beast that is television production. That was ten years and twelve shows ago, and now here I am as script supervisor on *The Wrong Doctor*.

"So what do you think, Maddy? Are we gonna actually make some TV now?" Frank asks, shaking me out of my trip down memory lane.

"I hope so. I'm pretty sure that's what we all came here to do," I deadpan.

Frank and I are a little frustrated that Ernesto Diaz, the director for the season premiere episode, keeps insisting on so many rehearsals before actually shooting anything, which risks putting us behind schedule. And speak of the devil, Ernesto appears out of nowhere. I send up a quick prayer that he didn't hear our disgruntled exchange.

"We changed the angle of the opening sequence," he announces, all business. "Cameras need to see it one more time."

Meaning we're doing yet another rehearsal. I groan internally, and through the monitor I see from the flinch on Billy's face that he has the same reaction to the news of yet another rehearsal.

Ernesto suddenly takes off, charging back toward the set. I quickly redo the perpetually messy knot of hair on my head—a nervous habit. I can feel strands of my stick-straight hair slipping free as I grab my script and give chase. One thing about my very un-Hollywood-like athletic frame, I am built perfectly to dodge set pieces and leap over moving cables. It's no sweat to navigate through the backstage "jungle" and ease into the "surgery" tent set as unobtrusively as possible. I sense Frank appear next to me and know that we're both having the same thought. This is going to start getting expensive if we don't start reining Ernesto in. This is our first time working with Ernesto Diaz. Normally the directors who come to *The Wrong Doctor* have done TV before and understand the balance between creativity and finances. Ernesto seems to be getting swept away with the former at the expense of the latter. It's clear that Frank and I are going to have our hands full keeping him on time and on budget this week.

"All right, let's get ready to shoot one," Frank booms to no one in particular. The camera crew takes some final measurements as Bobby puts all the props back in the start positions for the scene. Ernesto is still in deep discussion with Billy. I mosey over to listen in, see if maybe I can subtly help us stay on track.

"I feel this scene is pivotal. This is the moment Lucas realizes he cannot save this man..." Ernesto continues to gush over the plot point. After Billy has made several "I agree" type noises, he glances at me helplessly. I make my move.

"Billy, here's that line you wanted to see again." I slip in next to him and hand him my pages, pointing to a line that he has gotten right in every rehearsal. Ernesto watches us for a second.

"Good, good. This will be good." He pats Billy's shoulder confidently and marches off.

"Well, Maddy, I just want you to know, we're all counting on you." Billy quotes the immortal words from *Airplane* as he hands me back the script. He can't be any more specific than that since the mic under his shirt picks up every sound, but I know exactly what he means.

"I picked the wrong week to quit sniffing glue," I murmur darkly. I hear Billy snicker as I return to video village. Sometimes "video village" can be quite the who's who, especially on a hit show like ours, but if any network execs or producers decide to stop by to watch the action on the monitors today, they're in for a tight squeeze. There's barely room for Ernesto, the sound guy, our producer/writer, and me. Those of us with "need-to-know" status are all huddled together in the tiny area carved out for us between huge set pieces, slipping our headsets on to hear the dialogue as Ernesto yells, "Action!"

We do several takes, as I make notes of the action and specifics in each of the wide shots to later match in the close-ups to guide the editors in postproduction. Billy picks up the needle on his second speech; the nurse moves the tray away from the bed before she exits; the U/5 has the blanket pulled up to midchest area. I snap a picture of the screen with my digital camera to make sure I can replicate the exact placement of the blanket.

It's vital, if tedious, that I keep detailed and specific notes since it ultimately means the difference between the audience losing itself in the story or being distracted because they notice, consciously or subconsciously, inconsistencies in the filming. Not on my watch!

After filming the scene two more times, Ernesto mercifully calls for a ten-minute break and I take the opportunity to wander over to the nearby craft services table. "Crafty," as we call it, is set up behind the Dr. Lucas's Prison Tent set. Billy Fox/Dr. Lucas will spend much of this season trapped in this cramped prison after having been kidnapped by Islamic extremists in last season's cliffhanger finale. I glance over at his sad little cot as I round the corner. Good thing this is only TV because movie star Billy Fox, with his perfectly mussed hair, wouldn't last one day in the desert. Taking in the boring offerings at the table, I am debating if I can make it to the In-N-Out truck and back before rehearsals start again when Craig Williams steps next to me.

"How's the afternoon going, Madelyn?" He reaches for an apple.

"Good, good." I try to stifle some of the unexpected awkwardness I feel by faking extreme interest in the pretzel bowl. Craig is the executive in charge (EIC) of production at HCP, which means he oversees the budget and personnel and is involved in creative decisions for *The Wrong Doctor*.

"I love how Ernesto followed that single-camera angle from the tunnel into the terrorist cell. If he can nail it, I bet that makes it on the season preview for the show. It looked amazing. And we need a killer sizzle reel for the network to promote season two. They can run promos of just that shot and the fans will freak out. It'll go viral."

"I know, I love that shot too. He's really committed to making that work. It'll be great." I make sure to infuse my tone with enthusiasm. This is not the time or place to express doubts.

"Well, it's already two-thirty. He better end up with something to knock our socks off after spending all day on two pages of material. According to the call sheet, there are five more pages to shoot today." Although it doesn't stop anyone from asking questions all day long, the call sheet has all the information the cast and crew need for that day of production, from the time everyone is expected to arrive on set to what pages of material we will be filming and in what order. "Will you get those all done by the time we wrap?"

Craig drives me and practically everyone else on the crew crazy at times with this micromanaging, but we all put up with it because we know how much pressure he is under.

"Yep, don't worry. We lost a little time this morning, but we can make it up this afternoon. Frank and I are sticking to our guns here. We don't want to fall behind our first day back in production."

"I tell you what, Maddy. Let's talk more about this tomorrow night. A PA will call me to let me know when you wrap, and you can just come straight to my place. I'm making you my infamous pineapple grilled salmon." He winks at me as he walks away, before I can even respond.

And this is #702 on my list of why it may not be a good idea to date your boss.

Scene 002
Ext. Wine store, Studio City--evening

Exactly twenty-four hours later, after a mad dash home to shower
after we wrapped (late of course), I am wandering the aisles of
Monte's Wine Emporium near my apartment in Studio City, trying to find the perfect bottle of wine to go with Craig's salmon.
Beyond my standard glass of Pinot Grigio, wine is not my area
of expertise, so I am a little overwhelmed as I walk through the
Argentines. *Robust notes of cherry?* I'm so out of my comfort
zone here. Back home, we Carsons usually drink beer or a whiskey concoction my dad perfected in Vietnam (supposedly) and
that my older brother, Mike, christened "Waxy Sour" because of
the strange film it leaves on your tongue after a glass or two. So
I am really out of my element evaluating tannins, but I finally
settle on a Malbec recommended by none other than Monte himself and head back to my car and onto the windy canyon road
taking me to the city side. As I sit in traffic—another thing about
LA that I will never get used to—I find myself mentally reviewing
the pros and cons list I made last night about dating Craig. Since
tonight is the third time that we've gone out and I am going to his
house for the first time, where he is making me dinner, I think it's
fair to use the term "dating."

Pros: Craig is the right age—thirty-seven, two years older
than me. He's already at the executive level at HCP, code for "job
security," meaning he's not in one of the many Hollywood jobs
that are completely unstable and unreliable. He has East Coast

manners. Small-town people like my parents (and me, I'll admit) love that old-school gallantry. I can count on one hand the number of guys in LA who have actually opened the car door for me. I'm not saying he has to run around the hood to open the door, like Alex P. Keaton from *Family Ties*, but it's nice to feel looked after.

Cons: He has a bad habit of name-dropping and often uses industry expressions like "Let's put a pin in that." He gets manicures on a weekly basis—on any given day, his nails look nicer than mine. And also, the biggie: He's my boss. Yes, the hierarchy in the entertainment industry can be a bit fuzzy, but at the end of the day, the week, or the shoot, I turn those time codes in to him. When we're paying the crew overtime, I get chewed out just as much as the much-higher-paid directors.

As I turn onto Sunset Blvd, I go right back to the plus column, which is headlined by two words: "dry spell." It's like being in the ocean and dying of thirst with the guys in LA. I know, ten years is a long time. That's not to say there wasn't a fling here or there. I dated a sound guy for a while and had a yearlong romance with a guy who gave tourists paragliding lessons. But given my main rule, established from day one—NO ACTORS—dating in LA is hard. I'm around *a lot* of actors and even more would-be actors. Their reputation for being vain, insecure, and needing attention—a deadly combination—is not unfounded. Billy Fox is an obvious exception to that, but even he has his moments. Before you go getting ideas, there is absolutely nothing going on between Billy and me. I'm happy to admit that most of the preconceived notions I had about him when we first started production turned out to be false. Working together on a set bonds people quickly, and only one season later, I know he's one of my true friends in this town. But every time I see his picture in *US Weekly* with another gorgeous supermodel, I'm equally happy that's all he is.

The truth is—and I think a therapist would probably be quick to point to this as a reason for my dry spell—I have a bad habit of still measuring every guy up against Brian, my high school/college boyfriend. Does that always happen with first loves? Brian has long since moved on and married a lovely girl from our hometown. And I am happy for him—I am!—I just wish there were more guys like him in LA. Guys who have calluses on their hands from something other than lifting kettle bells at the gym.

Wanda—yes, I named my trusty GPS after my favorite John Cleese movie—announces the turn into Craig's neighborhood, which is marked by a wooden sign that reads GABLE ESTATES. The twisty road keeps going up into the hills above the Sunset Strip, which according to the map is "Beverly Hills Adjacent." Taking in the mini-mansions around me, I suddenly have an eerie feeling that I am trespassing. The gorgeous brand-new houses are mixed in with older hillside homes similar to what I was surrounded by as a kid up north, but it's mostly a lot of huge estates hidden behind tall fences. Compared to my tiny but adorable studio and my modest childhood home that my dad built himself in thirty days (or so the story goes), it's clear that I am not in Kansas anymore. I've been in LA for a long time, but it's sometimes still hard to wrap my head around the differences in culture, taste... excess. I wonder which will be Craig's—the rustic cabin style or the mansion. Then the guessing is over as his house falls into view: a gorgeous Mediterranean-style version of the latter. My friends back home imagine that my lifestyle involves designer clothes, a membership to the beach club from the original 90210, and daily convertible rides up the Pacific Coast Highway. My life is so far from that scenario that it makes me laugh every time. Yet here I am pulling up to an actual gate and intercom.

Before I buzz the intercom, I do a quick check of hair and makeup in the rearview mirror. After deciding to wear my hair down tonight, I have to stop myself from reflexively reaching for the hair band next to my watch to pull it up in its usual knot on my head. The tiny mirror shows only parts of my face at a time, but no question the mascara really does accentuate my almond-shaped brown eyes. All the sports and outdoor lifestyle as a kid seems to have left me with a permanent farmer's tan, but right now, I'm grateful that the smooth rich tone means I didn't have to attempt slapping foundation on my face, which I feel sure would have left me looking clown-like. Makeup in general is not my thing. What little I know, I've learned from watching the talented makeup artists work their magic on so many actors over the years. So I feel only a little bit self-conscious reapplying the rosy lip gloss that my friend Stella, *The Wrong Doctor* makeup artist, gave me. One last deep breath, and I hit the call button.

"Hello?"

"Craig, hi. It's me." I barely get a few words out before a loud buzzing noise interrupts me and the gate starts to open, allowing me to pull past an overgrown bougainvillea onto Craig's circular driveway. Craig is standing outside his front door, and I must admit he looks great in a navy T-shirt, cuffed linen pants, and bare feet. It's weird to see him wearing something other than a power suit. I suspect he's thinking the same thing as he takes in my Gap T-shirt and tie-dyed maxi skirt.

"Maddy, hi. How was traffic?" he asks, giving me a kiss on the cheek.

People in LA are obsessed with talking about traffic and discussing the best routes to get anywhere. If you don't believe me, check out "The Californians" on YouTube, a *Saturday Night Live* sketch that is twice as funny if you live in LA because it's not that far from the truth.

"It was fine." I return the kiss—he even smells different than he does at work. "It only took me forty-five minutes or so. Here . . ." I rather inelegantly hand him the bottle of wine.

"A Malbec, perfect. Let's head to the deck." Craig ushers me to his gorgeous backyard, which is surprisingly homey and warm, with lanterns dotting the lattice and big black iron planters overflowing with flowers. No question he had a professional decorator and landscaper comb every inch of this place. It's perfect. I sip from the large glass of wine he poured me as he promises no shoptalk for the evening. It's a new rule, since our first two dates involved quite a bit of talk about work, so much so that until he kissed me good night I wondered if they *were* actual dates. A few minutes ago, though, Craig insisted I taste the sauce he was finishing up and he spoon-fed it to me, so I think we're safely in date territory.

"So, babe, if we're not going to talk about work, I guess it's time we get personal." He places a piece of delicious-smelling steaming fish on my plate. "Are you ready to hear my childhood sob story?" He laughs and takes a bite of quinoa salad.

"Is it a sob story?" I ask.

"No, actually. I basically grew up in Pleasantville." Craig's story isn't that different from mine. We both grew up in charming small towns. Craig's family apple orchard in upstate New York sounds idyllic. He shares ridiculously exaggerated stories of his youthful escapades growing up on the farm. It reminds me so much of my own childhood: growing up in the mountains, the crisp winter air, the snow on the ground, and a town full of people who know my name. I had Craig pegged for a much different past—prep school, fraternities, and blondes with pixie cuts, which is part of the reason I was so surprised when he asked me out. We both had been lingering after a preproduction meeting for *The Wrong Doctor*, discussing the details of a complicated chase scene we were prepping for season two. Abruptly he asked me to join him for dinner after we wrapped for the day. I was so taken aback, I just mumbled yes and then wished I were the type of girl who had sexy shoes under her desk. Except I don't even have a desk, since I spend all my time on set. A pair of trendy wedges may have spiced up my outfit—a plain black button-down and dark jeans—but the Chuck Taylors had to do. At least I'd tossed them in the washing machine after our last location shoot out in the salt mines in Simi Valley, which do a great job impersonating the Middle East desert. I am five foot eight, so any heel would put me eye-to-eye with Craig's five-ten frame, so perhaps it's better that he has yet to invite me to Mr. Chow's or The Ivy, two of his favorites. I was way more comfortable at the wine bar down the block from the studio, anyway.

"...so my haul that week was literally twice every other worker's." Craig is laughing and I realize I've been thinking about where to keep a nicer pair of shoes instead of listening to his story. *Focus, Maddy!* I nod to give him the impression I've been hanging on every word.

"And I'm a little embarrassed to admit, my tendency toward the dramatic got the better of me by the end. I poured the last basket of apples all over my dad's desk in the front office. Red Delicious, Galas, and some Fujis were rolling all over the place. I glared at him, but all I said was 'Good-bye, Dad. See you at Christmas.' And I walked out. I didn't even slam the door. I closed it gently and then I headed cross-country, and that was that. Once I actually moved out here, rather than just threatening to, they handled it okay." Craig refills our wineglasses and I realize it must be almost 11:00 p.m. and, more importantly, that I have a really nice time when I am with him. One more for the plus column.

"So how did your parents handle you moving here?" he asks.

"Better than yours, it sounds like." I smile, remembering. "I'm from a small town in Wolf County, up in the Sierra Nevada Mountains. I always thought I would stay there, but then I got an opportunity in TV. Actually, my parents loved the idea of me coming down here. And it's not such a long drive, so I go back as much as I can. My dad and my older brother, Mike, manage the ski resort in town. They fight like those guys on *American Chopper* sometimes, but they love each other. And they're cut from the same cloth—they're total snow junkies."

"Do you miss it?"

"Definitely. I miss grabbing my skis and hitting the slopes right after it snows. I miss getting to drive the snowcat in the dark, grooming the bunny slopes. But like I said, I get my fix every few months when I visit."

"Do you ever think you'll move back, or are you a Valley girl now?"

"Gag me with a spoon!" I do my best Valley girl impression, earning a laugh from Craig. "But yeah, I always did feel like I would move back, get married, have kids, work for the family business...but now, I don't know...my life is here."

"So, what's next for you, Maddy? What do you want to be when you grow up?"

"I thought we weren't talking shop," I say half-jokingly.

"We're not. I'm talking about hopes, dreams, wishes.... What's your heart's desire? What would you do if you could do anything?"

I take a minute to think about this. I'm not sure I'm ready to put all my cards on the table with Craig yet. Reason #37 not to date your boss: How am I supposed to open up, allow him to get to know me, when any hint that I want to "produce someday" or "try directing" might make the higher-ups worry that I might jump ship, or worse, give me that *one* opportunity that I'm not sure I'm ready for. I go with a conservative answer. "The truth is, I can't really imagine doing anything else. I love what I do. It's corny, but true. Well, you get it, right? I think we all feel that way, everyone from Bobby, the prop master, to that new twenty-year-old sound kid holding the boom. Almost everyone I've ever met on a set for that matter. We're all part of the magic. We're telling the story. And I love it, especially when it's great. When we know what we're doing is going to really impact the audience, make them laugh, cry, or scream at their TV...that's when it's really good. That's what keeps us coming back to work in between. When it's below freezing on an all-night shoot or the actors are being difficult, or we worked twenty-hour days five days in a row. I keep signing on for another season, another show because I love knowing I'm part of something special. It would be hard to give that up."

I must be more tired than I thought, I think, embarrassed by my sentimental monologue. I know that when I start to get sappy, I've either had too much to drink or I'm exhausted. In this case, probably a bit of both.

"Cheers to that, Maddy. Well said." Craig clinks his wineglass with mine. "Well, for the record, I think you have a bright future at HCP. Maybe you'll produce or direct one day." What is he, a mind reader?

Not sure if I am talking to my boss or my date, I go for the safe reply. "I'm happy where I am, with what I do. I like to think I'm not dramatic enough to be a creative type. Always talking about 'my art.'" I smile, hoping I don't sound totally obnoxious.

"I'm surprised you're not more ambitious, Maddy. You're talented."

Okay, now it does feel like we've switched into performance review mode. "Thanks...So, Adam starts Monday. We have him shooting the fight scene on his first day. So much for settling in."

Breakout daytime star Adam Devin is joining the cast of *The*

Wrong Doctor after a six-year stint on *Days of Our Lives*. Craig picked him up before anyone else could snag him. He and Hogan consider it a big coup, and I don't disagree. As if our show doesn't already have enough eye candy, they recognized the brilliance in casting Adam in a new starring role as Ahmed, the sexy but dangerous leader of the terrorists holding Lucas. On Monday we're scheduled to shoot a complicated fight sequence in which one of Ahmed's lieutenants gets gravely injured and requires Lucas's medical aid. It's perfect for our demographics. The male audience loves our show for the tense situations, complicated story lines, and, the obligatory gritty graphic fight scenes. The female viewers will swoon over Adam's sculptured muscles and dark good looks. And Hogan has written this incredible scene for Billy, where he wrestles with upholding his Hippocratic oath or helping these criminals.

Craig mentions the fact that Adam practices martial arts enough to do a lot of his stunts himself. It's exhausting work, but the shots are so much better when you can minimize the use of a disguised stunt double. Of course, we have to balance that with the safety of our actors. After all, if someone sprains an ankle or breaks something, that'll shut down production for weeks, so we have to always err on the side of caution. Anyway, I take Adam's Tae Kwon Do skills with a healthy grain of salt—actors tend to put all sorts of things on their résumé, "special skills" that mysteriously disappear when they get the job.

I can only imagine how the girls on set are going to swoon on Monday, but I'm withholding judgment until I see his performance. Good looks and fighting skills aside, our show has won critical appeal because of our talented cast, not their cut abs. Billy Fox may have been *People* magazine's Sexiest Man Alive last year, but Adam could give him a run for his money. Luckily the two of them are buddies. Apparently they did a few modeling jobs together years ago and became fast friends, so fingers crossed we won't have a battle of the alpha males on set. Which will definitely make my life easier, because Billy also happens to be directing Adam's first episode on Monday, marking Billy's first time in the director's chair.

"Adam will be great. Hogan and I are excited about the arc this season. We realized we're a little guy-centric; we need to make sure we stay balanced. Keep those wives and girlfriends watching too."

At one point I would have found this conversation sexist, but after ten years in the business, I've realized that it's not. Yes, I'm sure there are chicks who love action sequences as much as the guys do, but no matter what the demographics and focus groups indicate, we can never forget that really, we're appeasing the network first. They want to know they've got their bases covered before hitting the airwaves. And they're the ones paying the bills.

Speaking of bills, I sneak a glance at my watch, not sure exactly how to exit this dinner without the forced intervention of the waiter bringing the check. I certainly don't want to overstay my welcome; besides, the shoptalk that we unsuccessfully tried to avoid has reminded me that I have new pink pages to break down before Monday. Every week, the script is sent out for the next episode we're shooting. Whenever the writers make changes to a script that's already been published, we change the colors of the pages so people know which version is most current—pink, then blue, then green, and so on. The actors are supposed to memorize their lines and understand the overall arc of their character in the episode. The costume designer reads it to develop a concept for what each character will wear and how many different outfits they need. The prop master accounts for any specific items we'll need—anything from a cell phone to an AK-47. I go through and make detailed notes on everything—action, dialogue, props. I'm batting clean-up for every department to protect the continuity of the storytelling.

Dealing with the pink pages tops the weekend to-do list, which

I carefully marked in my notebook today, along with *(2) hike with J.* I am getting up early on Sunday to meet my friend Janine, who works in editing at HCP. We planned earlier this week to go for a walk in Fryman Canyon. The Los Angelenos call it "hiking," but I can't bring myself to do that. It's really a walk—a nice one for being in the middle of a big city, but a "walk" nevertheless. And yes, even recreation goes on the "to-do" list, which also includes *(3) Call Mom; (4) Office Depot—(see Office Depot List); (5) Bug Matthew and Mike about Mom's b-day.*

"Craig, I've had such a lovely night." And it's true. "But I better go..."

"I did too, Maddy." We walk to the door, and my heart starts thumping. Do I kiss him good night? Even though we've shared a few nice kisses, things haven't escalated yet. It's still so new for me. I just don't feel comfortable in this part yet, particularly since he is my boss. I wish I had a writer's stage direction spelling out for me exactly what to do.

Suddenly, Craig leans forward, taking the decision out of my hands. He kisses me gently on the lips but pulls away before I have a chance to decide if I want him to go further. We walk silently up his driveway to my car parked on the street, his arm around my shoulders keeping me warm. He's really taking things slow, and I like it.

"See you next week." He opens my car door for me, and I slide past him to get in, taking in one last whiff of his delicious scent. He stands in the driveway as I pull away. At the first red light I hit on Sunset, I pull my hair up into a bun and am that goofball smiling to herself. I've always been one of those annoying people who actually looks forward to Monday—to a productive workweek, with my organized "Things To Do" list neatly updated every Sunday evening. Now, with flashbacks of Craig's vivid blue eyes dancing in my head, I realize I have one more reason to anticipate the workweek.

Scene 003
Ext. Studio parking lot--day

As I pull into my assigned space on the studio lot Monday morning, I triple-check my tote bag. Script? Check. Timer? Check. Notebook? Check. This is why my brothers make fun of me and my supposed OCD, but I never forget stuff. I'm not that person who leaves their cell phone right by the front door. That would be my worst nightmare. That's why I triple-check, so I always remember. But today, more so than most days, I want to be completely 100 percent on top of my game. I don't normally get butterflies—that's more an actor's thing—but I'm actually a bit nervous for Billy's directorial debut today.

No question Billy is an A-list star with the top-grossing action movies of the past two summers, but last season he started shadowing the directors on *The Wrong Doctor*, asking questions, studying their choices, and so on. He played it off casually, saying he was curious and loved a new challenge, but I can sense how much it means to him and I know how hard he's worked to get his first shot in the chair. All of us on set are really psyched for him. It's nice to see someone you really like take a chance like this. The crew doesn't often get credited when big-time directors are up there onstage accepting their Emmys, but I can tell you, not one director won a golden statue with a crappy crew behind them.

When I walk onto the set (exactly fifteen minutes early, as planned), Billy looks like he's already been here for hours. He's always pretty intense when he's acting, and I can tell he's a little nervous now.

"Good morning, Herr Director," I say in my most absurd German accent.

"Frau Blucher," he replies with a glimmer of a smile. A *Young Frankenstein* reference is a good sign, even if he turns immediately back to the script.

"Okay, Captain, I'm ready. Hit me with what you're thinking for today." I pull out the call sheet and we talk about each scene we're shooting. Frank sees us and joins the huddle. Victor, the director of photography, wanders in a minute later, coffee in hand, to lean over my shoulder. Our DP can make any director's vision come to life; actresses swoon for Victor's lighting, and his technical comprehension of cameras and angles all are part of his magic touch.

All three of us are impressed with Billy's approach and methodical plan for the day. We break up the preshoot meeting as the actors in the first setup arrive. Adam Devin walks over to check in at makeup. It's the first time I've seen him in person, and I have to admit, he may be even better-looking than on TV. He's grown out his hair and a scruffy beard for the role. I check my watch—6:58. He also gets points for arriving right on schedule. I was shocked the first time I witnessed an actor being so unreliable that a PA (not me, thank God) was sent to wake him up after calls, texts, and e-mails had failed to get through to him.

Once, when I was still a PA on *300 Madison*, one of the female leads was a no-show as of two hours past her call time. A bunch of us sat around alternating between taking bets on if and when she would actually show up and calculating how much her lateness was costing the production company. The key grip won $200 when the actress strolled in four hours later. I estimated that the lost hours cost $50,000. The director leaned over and told me it was more likely four times that number—$200,000—and she'd merely muttered some excuse about "traffic" as she stumbled into the makeup trailer, never removing her bug-eyed sunglasses. After several such incidents, it wasn't a surprise to anyone when her character got a rare disease at the end of the season and had to go to South America for "alternative treatments." Turns out there was no cure for the disease...or her unprofessionalism. Even on a hit show like *The Wrong Doctor*, which thankfully has a generous budget, every dollar needs to be accounted for—preferably onscreen—especially nowadays, given that the tough economy has affected Hollywood as much as every other industry. Lots of older crew guys have tons of great stories about the "glory days" when there was tons of money to throw around and the crazy excesses of not just the actors, but also everyone in Hollywood. Let's just say an In-N-Out truck isn't even in the same ballpark. These days, the studios and executives don't have the money or patience for anyone who doesn't respect the schedule. Hopefully Adam isn't just making a good first impression on his first day.

"Please get the first team out to set. We're going to block." Frank's voice echoes over every walkie nearby, and within a minute Adam and the other actors appear, ready to rehearse. I stay close by, ready to help Billy if needed and make careful notes of what is planned for the scene.

"Let's just run through the dialogue once," Billy says to the actors.

I zero in on my script, red pen in hand, making notes and watching Billy work with the cast. Immediately I notice that Adam has a casual way of reading the script. He always has the intent, but he ad-libs a lot too. Ad-libbing is one of my least favorite habits in an actor. First of all, it's a pain in the ass for me since my job is to make sure each actor follows the script precisely.

Second, they never seem to remember exactly what they said so that they can repeat it verbatim on subsequent takes. Third, it annoys Hogan and the staff writers when things are paraphrased. I make a note to mention it to Billy. As director, it's his job to address it. The first day has been organized so that Billy can get the hang of things, shooting scenes he's not in. Tomorrow he's going to be doing double duty, directing and acting in the sequences. It's not unheard of, but it definitely creates some new challenges to deal with. But that's tomorrow's problem.

The first scene we're shooting actually comes toward the end of the episode. It's technically complicated because of the cramped quarters on set and because the action sequence requires so many different camera angles, so we want to do it first and get it out of the way. In this episode, Lucas and Naveen (an Indian medical researcher held captive by the terrorists) hatch a complicated plan to steal a walkie-talkie from one of the guards, with disastrous results. Hogan wrote the scene so the audience can see how little Lucas and Naveen really understand about how serious their predicament is. If handled properly, it will really jack up the tension and reveal just how dangerous the bad guys are, especially Ahmed, whose sadistic charms are introduced.

Billy calls "cut," and the actors who have "died" in the attack are resurrected for the break. The makeup team inspects gory bullet wounds to see whose need a bit of refreshing with the mix of corn syrup and red food dye that mimics blood. I see Adam shake his head for a moment, as if snapping out of character. Then he looks over at Billy, who is staring at the monitors, looking pleased. "Good?"

I think Billy speaks for all of us when he says, "Yeah, Adam, you rocked it." Frank looks at me from a few feet away and nods. We're all impressed. Usually it requires many more takes for an actor to nail a scene, particularly on the first day.

As everyone takes five (or in this case, fifteen), I check my watch—we're looking good on time. I review the copious notes I took during the scene to make sure I didn't miss anything. I also took detailed continuity pictures with a small digital camera I keep close at hand. I have a visual record of every prop and how the actor is holding it and every movement they made in the scene. The actors work with the director before the cameras are set up to figure out the blocking, meaning the movements that feel natural for the scene. Once it's set, they have to match the same movements in every single take. All of the pictures help back up my own memory and provide evidence, should I need it.

I know they mean well, but I've developed a sort of motto that has seen me through lots of sticky moments: "Never trust the actors." I suppose that sounds harsh, but I was burned once in my first job as script supervisor. Talk about learning the hard way. It was a short-lived show about cops going through the police academy. The postproduction producer and director called me down to the edit bay and showed me how the most climactic scene of the shoot wasn't editing together because the lead actor had been holding the gun with one hand in the wide shot and with two hands in the close-up. I remember so clearly the star being so charmingly convincing, "Darling girl"—said in his gorgeous Italian accent, which somehow transformed into a credible Bronx accent for the show—"I've been doing this for decades... everyone knows I hold my gun like this." The crew around me chuckled, and I backed off... and then I paid the price since I was the one who got chewed out. So now it's (A) write notes, (B) take pictures, and (C) never trust the actors.

I flip quickly through the pictures. The last one shows Adam looking off-camera with a half-smile on his face as he tucks a gun into his back waistband. My thumb hesitates for a second on the power button. He looks, well... hot.

"Not you too?" Billy startles me, and I almost drop the camera.

"What are you talking about?"

"You're swooning over Adam." He playfully punches my arm. I have yet to tell Billy about my dates with my boss; Craig and I have an understanding that this should be kept pretty quiet, for now at least. Anyway, I most certainly was not swooning, but I know from years of dealing with my brothers that if I get all defensive, Billy will never let up. So instead, I dramatically fan myself and pretend to drool over Adam's image on the screen, knowing Billy won't miss the sarcasm.

"Maybe you're immune to him, but I think Michelle is going to get me off schedule by jumping in to fix Adam's hair every two seconds. I'm on to her."

"You know how it is, Billy. Let them have their kicks. I'm sure Adam isn't complaining."

"I'm impressing you today, aren't I? It's okay. You can tell me." He says it with a laugh, but knowing him as I do, there's a touch of insecurity there too. Even hotshot actors appreciate positive feedback.

"You're doing great." I wait a beat… "Finish the episode on time and I'll be impressed. Until then…"

"I know, I know… Never trust the actor." He smiles as he walks away and calls everyone back to set.

Scene 004
Int. Crew craft seating--day

"I noticed you and Billy seem to get along really well." That's Craig's hello as he sits down opposite me during our catered meal break.

"What do you mean?" I hesitate before biting into my ravioli.

"Nothing." He takes a bite of the seafood gumbo I passed up (some things you just don't eat from the catering truck if you have any common sense). "I've never seen you play favorites with directors before." He swallows. "But I suppose not all of them are *People*'s Sexiest Man Alive. Are you a closet Foxaholic?" He snickers. Thank God he's kidding. Or is this a hint that Craig is a little jealous of Billy's celebrity status? Craig may not be leading-man good-looking—he's not as tall as Billy, or even Adam, and he's lean, not muscular—but with his adorable floppy hair and his bright blue eyes, he can certainly hold his own. I decide to act as if this is all in good fun, which I hope it is.

"Yes, you've got me. I have to sleep with my 'Foxaholic for Life' T-shirt under my pillow since I can't wear it to work." Billy gets a ton of grief from the crew because his fans call themselves Foxaholics. It brings us such joy to torture him about it.

"So, Friday was fun...," he says, and although I welcome the subject change, my eyes reflexively dart around the room to see who's in earshot.

"Maddy, it's okay. We're adults; we're allowed to date," he says as if reading my mind. "But I understand that you don't want to call attention to 'us' on set, so we'll keep a low profile." He smiles understandingly at me and takes another bite of gumbo. Here I am, having lunch with a guy I'm dating, and any chance of impressing him disappeared about nine hours ago. I tug at my dark red oversized CAL sweatshirt, but nothing will make it actually formfitting. Knowing it doesn't make a difference, I find I'm vain enough to force myself to sit up a little straighter.

It's going to be important to stay practical about this whole thing. I don't want it to get awkward at work if something goes wrong. But the thing I appreciate about Craig is that he seems very practical too. And to be sure, nothing is going to get in the way of his career. So as far as office romances go, this one is relatively low-risk. I hope.

"I had a great time," I say, taking in his disarming smile. We spend the next few minutes catching up on our weekends, and somehow I've already polished off my ravioli. One of the weird side effects of working in TV is that you eat very quickly. My plate is clean ten minutes after I've sat down, and I have a ton of work to get to before the crew's union-mandated hour-long meal break is up. Craig is only halfway through his lunch, and I can't help but conclude that it's a telltale sign he's never actually worked in the trenches.

"Will you be done by eight tonight?" he asks. I know Craig always has his eye on the budget; so do I. That's why they love me in the offices, but I'm surprised he's this nervous about Billy.

"We'll be done in twelve," I assure him. A twelve-hour day means no overtime. It's what you always aim for, and based on what I've seen so far, I think Billy's going to bring us in on time.

"Oh, that's great. But I wasn't asking for work. Tonight is HBO's Upfront Party at Barker Hangar. I heard Spago's is catering. Join me?"

I don't know if I ate the ravioli too fast or if it's the thought of walking a red carpet with Craig, but suddenly my chest feels very tight.

"Maddy, it'll be fine. No one else from the crew will be at this party, and it's not like they're going to post our picture together on WireImage, right?"

It would be just my luck to get caught in the background of a celeb's picture on the popular industry website. It makes me cringe just imagining myself caught in some awkward pose, but my parents would still tape it up on the fridge for everyone back home to fawn over. My few run-ins with the famous red carpet did not go over well. So I avoid them whenever possible. It fits in nicely with my No Actors policy, and it helps me avoid any and all media, particularly the paparazzi, with no trouble. Not that they're coming after me—they most decidedly are not. But even if you have self-esteem the size of Texas, it's hard not to take a hit as the photographers practically mow you down to get to some passing celebrity behind you. But this relationship is so new, I just don't want to get into why I have reservations about going to an event that every wannabe is frothing at the mouth to get in to. So with an inward girding of the loins, and with his promise to be discreet, I accept his offer.

"Great, pick you up at eight, Ms. Carson."

Scene 005
Int. Maddy's bedroom--evening

Shit. Shit. Shit. The clock says 7:48, and I am crawling around under my bed in my underwear looking for the matching shoe to the one pair of black heels I own. Ugh. Why did I even agree to go to this thing? All of the producers and network executives schmoozing and "being seen"? Just thinking about how out of place I'll feel makes me want to crawl into bed. I'm sure there are thousands of women who would love to be in my shoes tonight, but I can imagine a hundred other things I'd be more comfortable doing, like cleaning out my Tupperware drawer, which I am embarrassed to admit was actually my plan for the night.

I am not normally one who revels in self-doubt and insecurity. I have a degree and a respected career. I am, as my father says, "a smart cookie." But if I have to try and "glam it up," stealing Stella our makeup artists' description, I completely fall apart. And now I have three minutes for glamming. I grab a pencil skirt from J.Crew.

I try to picture the outfits I see Molly from wardrobe style the female cast members in. I can recall every item of clothing our cast has worn in all fifteen episodes we've shot so far—a completely useless skill unless you are a script supervisor, in which case it's perfect. I decide that the gray cashmere T-shirt sweater my mom gave me for Christmas will go acceptably. I throw on the clothes and then smother myself in one last cloud of hairspray to keep my newly flat-ironed hair in place. One of the upsides to being tall is that I don't have to balance on high heels all night. I slip on ballet flats and do a final check in the mirror. I am dabbing on lip gloss when the doorbell rings. My pulse picks up a bit and I convince myself it's from seeing Craig, not nerves over the party.

"You look spectacular." Craig smiles as I open the door.

"Thanks. You look great too." And he does. Tonight he is wearing a very trendy Paul Smith suit. This suit seems more his personality than the conservative ones he wears at HCP. The cut emphasizes his lean torso, and the brightly colored shirt brings out the darker blue flecks in his eyes.

"Ready to go?" Craig checks his watch as I lock the front door.

"Are we late?" I ask. I'm already self-conscious enough; I have a split-second vision of all conversation between Angelina Jolie and Steven Spielberg screeching to a halt as I step over the threshold.

"There's no such thing as being late in Hollywood." Craig laughs as we get into his car. "I just want to be sure we're there before Billy leaves."

"Why? Is Billy leaving early?" I had hoped there would be another friendly face around tonight.

"Yeah, Billy's publicist let me know he has another event. What's her name? Sophie Atwater? Tough bi—"—he coughs—"chick. She doesn't give an inch, that one. Anyway, she said he has to leave by nine o'clock, and I want to introduce him to a few people before that."

I go to check my watch and am staring at the freckles on my skin for at least a second before remembering that in an effort to be feminine I'd taken off my trusty, never-leave-home-without-it black divers watch. It has two timers on it and is waterproof up to 100 meters. I love that watch. My dad gave it to me for my six-teenth birthday, and I've rarely been without it since.

"You okay?" Craig asks.

"Oh yeah, sorry. I just realized I forgot my watch. Well, not really forgot because it wouldn't have gone with this outfit." Did he really need to know that? I'm such a dork. "I'm just not used to being without it. My dad gave it to me."

"Aha. A daddy's girl. I should've known," he teases.

I'm hit with a pang of homesickness for my dad and add to my mental to-do list to call him tonight. He always gets a kick out of hearing about my "glamorous" life. Since I am actually wearing a skirt tonight, this will impress him for sure.

"Yeah, we're very close. Everyone in Wolf County knows him. He's like the honorary mayor. In fact, at one point he thought he might run for actual mayor, then remembered he hates meetings, which is why he never worked in corporate America. 'You only go around this merry-go-round once, Maddy-girl. I'm not going to waste it counting paper clips.' "

"He sounds like quite a character. Working on the ski slopes seems like a nice life. My fingers always freeze when I try to type e-mails on the lifts in Aspen."

"Please! To my dad, a 'blackberry' will always be a piece of fruit. To text he has to scroll through a-b-c. The reception up there is so lousy, they're just happy to get a call through."

"Well, then we have that in common, don't we?" Craig laughs.

It's nice that even though there are a million differences between his hometown and mine, he's made an effort to find some common ground.

Talking with Craig as we drive through the pretty downtown streets is unexpectedly comfortable. It helps that I am melting into the buttery seats of his obviously very expensive car and my favorite Adele song is playing softly through the speakers. Maybe we can just drive around all night instead of actually arriving at the party.

"So, are you headed up to Wolf for the holiday weekend?"

"Yep," I say, feeling a flutter of excitement. "My brothers and I are throwing a surprise party for my mom's sixtieth birthday."

"Sounds like fun. Who all is coming?"

"Oh, everyone in town. If you think my dad's a character, the rest of the town is loaded with them, believe me."

I start in on a story about my parents' closest friends who are totally into taxidermy. By the time I get to the part where I get back at my younger brother for stealing my ski poles by scaring him with the bear skin rug, complete with head, while he's making out with his girlfriend, Craig is holding his side, he is laughing so hard.

"I swear, he still flinches when he sees bears in movies." I snicker at the memory.

"I love that story. And I love hearing about you as a little troublemaker." He winks at me, and I smile back at him. "Too bad we're here. I want to hear more."

I look up and sure enough, we're pulling in to the valet.

"Oh, that's nothing," I say as we get out of the car. "You should hear the stories my parents tell me these days. If anything, it's gotten more eccentric since I left."

"Really?" Craig seems to hesitate for a second. "Well, I'm looking forward to having one of those Waxy Whiskey things with your dad, for sure."

For once the pinball machine feeling of pushy photographers jostling me on either side to get a clear shot of a passing celeb doesn't faze me at all. Instead, all I can think as I smile and try not to blink too much at the flashes is, *He wants to meet my parents?*

Once we're inside the ballroom, Craig heads for the bar as I sit with that thought for a minute and take in my surroundings. The room is an airplane hanger. Big. The main dining room of the restaurant has been cleared of tables and filled with gorgeous hanging white curtains that billow everywhere. Elegant crystal chandeliers hang low, creating an intimate setting, even though the ceilings have to be a hundred feet up. Potted ficus trees twinkle lights, and there's a huge turnout. Celebrities I recognize casually sit in an arrangement of sofas and divans (that's what they call the sofas without a back, which I only know from listing set pieces for the art department). Network executives gather around an approaching waiter holding a tray of hors d'oeuvres. Of course, every woman in the group shuns the offering. You don't get bodies like theirs by eating Kobe beef sliders with blue cheese. Having just told so many Wolf County stories, my dad's voice is in my head as I look around. *"This is slicker than a whistle covered in spit."* Sometimes he sounds just like Dr. Phil.

The young starlet, Lola Stone, suddenly stumbles by in snakeskin stiletto platform heels twice as high as seems safe, laughing loudly. I worked with her on a show a few years ago. Even after endless efforts from the executive producer all the way down to me drilling her lines with her over and over in the makeup trailer, nothing seemed to help her remember them. It was hardly a surprise to read the tabloid headlines about her alleged coke addiction. I wonder if she would remember me. She does look quite glamorous, as does everyone. I fiddle with my iPhone, trying to make myself look important and busy while I wait for Craig to return. Thankfully, he's back in a minute or two with a drink that is so bright pink, it looks like it could glow in the dark.

"They have a signature cocktail tonight," he says, handing me the frosty martini glass with an expectant look on his face. Normally, I don't really drink anything but wine or beer, but Craig seems anxious to make this night fun, and I'm feeling jittery, so maybe a fruity cocktail is perfect. It's just so... bright.

"Thanks, I—" But before I can even finish my sentence, Craig is looking over my shoulder.

"Sorry, Maddy. There's Hogan. I should go say hello. You'll be fine, right?"

"Sure," I say, much more confidently than I feel. I can always hide in the bathroom if I feel awkward.

I watch for a minute as Craig chats with Hogan. It's a weird feeling, wondering if they are talking about me. Also, it's hard not to think about the fact that Craig clearly did not want me joining him as he spoke to Hogan. But given that I've kept our family's long relationship with him under wraps, I guess it's understandable that Craig doesn't automatically include me. It looks serious, and Craig is my boss, after all. Whatever they are talking about, Hogan seems deeply concerned about something, and that's probably not good.

"Hey, Maddy. You look beautiful." Billy's familiar face appears in front of me, and he leans in for a Hollywood cheek-to-cheek air-kiss. He has a gorgeous blond bombshell at his side. "Maddy, this is my date, Felicity. Maddy is the script supervisor on the show." The light in her eyes evaporates the second she realizes I'm not some big-shot producer who can get her discovered.

"Hi. Nice to meet you," she says automatically, blatantly looking over my shoulder. "I didn't know they invited the whole crew to events like this." Ah, so she's not as dumb as she looks. Her zinger cuts me deeper than I'd care to admit.

"Whoa, whoa...," Billy says, putting his arm around her, an arm that seems like a tree trunk in comparison to this girl's slight shoulders. "Sharpen your claws somewhere else, Felicity. Maddy is one of the good ones." She smiles dismissively at me and her eyes return to darting around the room, looking for someone better she should be talking to. He smiles at me and rolls his eyes apologetically.

"No damage done. This isn't really my scene. Um...so... Craig actually asked me to come with him tonight."

A surprised look crosses Billy's face. "Oh, he did, did he? We have a lot to talk about, missy." But before he can interrogate me any further, I hear a strong voice coming from behind me. "Billy! What's up, man?"

Saved by the...Adam? I don't have to turn around to recognize the deep, scruffy voice of our new star. Adam Devin has squeezed in and now I feel that he is just behind me. When I turn to face him, we are way too close for comfort.

"Hey, guys, fun party." He gives Felicity the type of quick once-over that girls totally notice but pretend not to.

"Good evening, Adam. I'm glad you're enjoying yourself." Why am I being so weirdly formal? Billy shoots me a funny look.

"Yeah, it's a good time," Billy says. "But I have to leave soon, so I'd better go kiss the ring now." Before I know it, Billy and Felicity are off to find Hogan, leaving me alone with Adam. At a loss for conversation, I decide to at least be productive.

"How are the training sessions going for the stunts next week? The script breakdown looks intense."

"Good. But, please, no work talk tonight. How about we enjoy the party? You look like you could use another drink. What is that anyway?" he asks, taking in my nearly empty glass.

"I have no idea. A pinktini or something."

"You girls and your fruity drinks. I'm a whiskey guy myself." Before I can protest that I am, in fact, not a fruity-drink girl by any means, Adam curses.

"Sorry, I just didn't know Lola was going to be here." We both look over at the bar where Lola somehow seems even taller, and even drunker, than when I saw her last. I'm not surprised these two have crossed paths.

"I can't go over there yet." He looks genuinely uncomfortable.

I can't help it; I bite. "What's the deal?"

"Well, let's just say Lola and I aren't on the best terms, and I don't want a something-tini thrown in my face tonight."

Typical, I think. I don't even like Lola, but it seems obvious that she's the victim in this story.

"I don't want to even ask what you did."

"You just assume it's my fault?" Adam says with a smirk.

This conversation has taken a weirdly personal turn. I don't need to know about Adam's love life. Before I can even open my mouth to acknowledge that I may have jumped to a conclusion about him, never mind bring myself to apologize for it, Adam saves me the trouble by launching into their backstory.

"As it turns out, she had a very specific agenda when she dated me. Lola Stone is only interested in one thing: the guy who can get her to the next level. When I realized our relationship was mostly about our next press appearance together, I decided it was time to move on."

We both turn back to look at her at the bar. In her fire-engine-red dress, she looks like Jessica Rabbit.

"See Jordan over there?" I stand next to Adam as I scan the room. "He's at the other end of the bar." He nods his head, as if I could miss the four-time Oscar-winning director.

"She's going to scope him out for her next mark." We both watch Lola sipping her drink as her eyes slowly troll the room. "She's like the Terminator, sizing everyone up and cross-referencing their image with their IMDb résumé and then weighing the cost/benefit ratio." I can't help but snicker at his analogy. "See? Target in sight." Adam quietly makes an alarm sound effect to complete the visual. I swallow a giggle. (I am so *not* the giggling type.) We both witness Lola's eyes settle on the handsome African American man, who looks thirty-five instead of his actual age of fifty-five. "She's going to make her way over to him, find a way to touch his arm, and then brush her hair behind her ears. It's her classic opening move."

By LA standards, this doesn't seem so bad. I'm sure there are at least twenty-five other young actresses in this room trying to catch Derek's eye as well.

"Even if she is, a lot of people here would say she's just networking, making harmless business connections..."

"Okay, I hear you. Let's make a bet. If she's just making industry connections and it all seems totally aboveboard, we'll hit your go-to trendy hot spot and I will buy you a round of your favorite fruit-tini. If she crosses the line into inappropriate, I win and it's whiskey at my favorite dive bar."

Trendy hot spot? Fruit-tini? Who does Adam Devin think I am? Yet, somehow it seems harmless enough to play along. And I am oddly at ease at this party now, sipping my goofy drink next to Adam Devin, of all people, watching Lola sashaying toward the director. Craig steps into my line of sight, clearly heading in our direction. I wonder just how long I've been talking to Adam.

"You're going to lose," I say as I wave at Craig, who has stopped five feet away to say hello to another HCP exec. In the split second before Craig arrives at my side, Adam leans in and whispers in my ear.

Focusing back on Craig is harder than it should be, but luckily he's not really paying attention anyway. "Hey, babe. Sorry about that. Let's do a lap around the room." Craig's arm slips around my waist and without waiting for an answer, he is already steering me forward. His words barely register. What is still ringing in my ears is Adam's husky voice saying, *"You're wrong, Maddy. Either way, I win."*

Scene 006
Int. Conference room at HCP--evening

Matthew: What time do you get in Friday, sis?

Me: I'm going to hit the road first thing in the a.m. I should be up there by noon.

Matthew: What did we get Mom?

Me: WE?? *I* got Mom a panini maker.

Matthew: I totally forgot to get something. Can't I just go in with you?

Me: Mom's birthday has been the same for all 24 years of your life. Forgetting is not a good reason. You still have five days. Go buy her something nice.

Matthew: Um, like what...?

I send him back the little emoticon of the scream face and then ignore his texts for a while. Yes, not everyone has birthdays color-coded in their calendars with a ten-day and five-day reminder like I do, but Matthew's classic youngest child syndrome drives me nuts. Somehow he always thinks things are going to work out for him with zero effort. And infuriatingly enough, they usually do. I'm sure he'll show up at our mom's surprise party Friday with a semi-funny card from Ralph's, and she'll love it just as much as the top-of-the-line panini maker I bought her.

I can't bother to be annoyed or distracted right now, though. It's 7:42 on Monday night and I am still at work, desperately hoping we'll finish soon so I still have time for a run tonight. But the correlation between the number of days I intend to run after work and the number of days I actually get to do so is about 1,321 to 1—and tonight is no different. A run would be especially good right now, given how antsy I've been all week. I've been replaying Adam's weird flirtation at the party last week. Luckily, he didn't have any scenes to film the rest of the week, so I didn't see him on set, but when we're back from the Labor Day hiatus, he'll be here. Why am I even thinking about this? And what about Craig being so strange all of last week? On the way to the HBO party, I was pretty sure we were going to proceed to the next level in our relationship, since he was definitely giving the signs. But afterward, he made some vague comments about the "pressure being on," dropped me off at my place, and has been MIA ever since. The only time he's reached out was to cancel the plans we'd made for Saturday night. He was really apologetic about it and we rescheduled for this Wednesday so we could see each other before I head home, but still...that's also weird.

I heard from a PA in the offices that a lot of closed-door meetings have been going on this week. That could explain things, but I wish he wouldn't shut me out. I know there are things that go on above my pay grade that he isn't at liberty to discuss, but it's awkward because I just don't know how to handle it. On one hand, I want to be supportive, so perhaps I should text him to let him know I'm thinking about him. On the other hand, that could make him wonder what I know and if people are talking about these closed-door meetings. So I have no idea how to proceed. Gah. Reason #521 why you shouldn't date your boss!

Maybe I should just sit back and appreciate the distraction of working late tonight. And with that thought, my phone vibrates. Janine ran out to grab us some sushi since we have at least another hour of work ahead, and I just can't eat one more meal at Crafty.

While the crew is on a ten-minute break, I sneak away to Janine's offices in postproduction. I see she's knee-deep in organization—this team runs like an intense machine. They have to edit together the episodes from all the different camera footage we provide, mostly using the notes I have created as a guideline of what the director had in mind. As I walk in, Janine is unwrapping our takeout with one hand while typing on her iPad with the other and talking with the phone tucked between her shoulder and ear—multitasking at its finest. I turn my back to her so she knows I'm not trying to rush her. I casually review the notes she has written with huge multicolored pens on the whiteboard that makes up one whole wall of her office.

The first thing I notice is the scheduled dates she has circled with huge red arrows pointing at them. I follow her scribbling to see that the editing team has an incredibly tight set of deadlines for getting initial cuts of the episodes to Hogan.

"My backup plan is to quit and retire to a little casita in Mexico." Janine's comment is such a non sequitur to her phone conversation. I turn back around and realize she's actually talking to me now.

"Why do you have such a quick turnaround?"

"Hogan had a big meeting with the post team before production started. He felt that the network took so long giving notes on the episodes that we didn't have enough time to incorporate their changes as well as *his* changes to their changes." We both smirk. Basically, Hogan is a control freak. He wants to edit according to what the network wants, then have enough time to show them why he was right and still be able to go back and fix it as he wants it before it airs. I don't blame him; after all, it's his show. But since they moved up the premiere date for the new season, it just adds to the pressure the editors feel to get the episodes cut (edited) and in Hogan's hands ASAP, if not sooner.

"Craig's going to have a conniption about all the overtime that's going to require for my team." Janine dips her spicy tuna roll into the ponzu sauce.

"He'll make it work. I'm sure Craig understands why Hogan wants extra time with the episodes. And if it helps, you can tell him that the earlier we get notes about added scenes or pickups, the easier it is for us to squeeze into the current production schedule. So that will save money."

I have had to resign myself to it: no matter how meticulous we are (I am) during filming, there are always going to be scenes or little parts of scenes that we have to go back and film again. Sometimes it's as frustratingly unavoidable as a glitch in the camera or the digital file it was saved on, and the editors discover that some of the material is just unusable. I hate when it's a creative choice or something we could have avoided through better preproduction planning.

"Oh, God, remember episode four? Hogan decided weeks later that he hated that guy's wardrobe in the South American sequence and wanted a complete reshoot. You and Frank spent hours figuring out the least expensive way to add three days of filming to the production schedule before cooler heads prevailed."

"It wasn't cooler heads." I put up a hand so I can swallow my bite of shrimp before continuing. "Hogan would have done it. You saved the day by selling him the idea of focusing on the other camera angle, and Craig talked him into being okay with the close-up shots so that you never really saw what the guy was wearing."

"What who was wearing?" I turn around to see Billy in the doorway, loaded down with DVDs.

"You're going to watch dailies at"—I check my watch—"nine-thirty?" I know I shouldn't be surprised by Billy's work ethic at this point, but, well, I am.

"Yes, Maddy, that's what directors do. They sit up all night and obsess over the dailies." He smiles. "You think actors are bad about obsessing over our performances...I plan to apply that same level of neurosis in my first time as director. Isn't that what you called me once, neurotic? Oh, and narcissistic."

"Ouch!" Janine says.

I blush with embarrassment, thinking back to the days before Billy and I were friends. He had caught me in the middle of an inappropriate rant about him and another actor, after they had a hissy fit about how loud the crew was during their rehearsal. In retrospect, he was obviously stressed out that day and tense about his performance. And the crew was talking a lot since the director had made some big changes. Even Frank apologized to Billy about it afterward. I definitely got the diva vibe from him that day and didn't hesitate to say it. Obviously, we got past it. He was professional enough to know he overreacted and cool enough to call me on my crap and then let it go. I'm glad it happened, honestly, because I don't think we'd have as good a relationship now if it hadn't. But it's still embarrassing.

"I would say 'I'm sorry' again, but you threatened to never say a line of dialogue as written if I apologized one more time. So for your own professional reputation, Billy, I'll refrain."

"It was the only threat that I knew would work. 'I hate ad-libbing' is going to be your epitaph, Maddy."

"You say that like it's a bad thing." I take the teasing about my obsessively by-the-book reputation in stride because I'm used to it, and because I kind of like it. As far as obsessions go, I'd say it's a pretty healthy one.

"Speaking of us neurotic actors...guess who was asking about you last night? Adam!" He says his name with a goofy smile, before I can even begin to guess. Not that I would have gotten that one right, in a million years.

"What do you mean, he was asking about me?"

"We met up to shoot some pool over the weekend, and I believe his exact words were 'so what's Maddy's deal?' He must've learned that smooth talk on the soap," Billy snickers. I am too uncomfortable, not to mention caught off guard, to begin to formulate a reply. Oblivious, he continues. "He said he talked to you at the HBO thing and you seemed cool." He does an exaggerated impression of Adam's tough Brooklyn accent.

Cool? Ha, cool is the last thing I feel. Especially at this moment.

"Well...so what did you tell him?"

Billy raises his eyebrow and looks pointedly at Janine, who goes back to shuffling cards around on her desk like she's at a blackjack table.

"Oh, she knows...," I tell him, reading from his look that he's wondering if Janine knows about Craig and me. I finally confessed all to her on our hike over the weekend, mainly because I needed her to help parse out his message canceling on me. "But no one else does, so let's keep it that way. Okay?"

"No problem," Janine agrees quickly before saying, "But I gotta say, did not see that coming. Craig and Maddy. I mean, I would never have called it..."

"What? He's nice." I am a little taken aback that Janine and Billy both seem so shocked by the idea of Craig and I dating.

"Oh yeah, totally. You guys seem so different, somehow. But hey, opposites attract. Isn't that what they say?" Janine fills in quickly.

"I was actually feeling like we had a lot in common. We both—"

"Okay, well not to interrupt the girl talk here," Billy pipes in. "But I told Adam I thought you were seeing someone. Know what he said?"

"I have no idea, Billy. This is all very ninth grade," I say, with my best above-it-all huff.

"Well, for the record, he said 'too bad.' I'm not saying you should date him. I'm just saying... well, you've got a lot of options out there. That's all." Does Billy have a problem with Craig? Is that what I'm reading between the lines?

I get a little defensive on Craig's behalf. "Adam's an actor. On this show. He dates supermodels. And did I mention he's an actor? And I have a ru—" The word "rule" is still forming on my lips when Janine and Billy recite like grade-school students, in unison, "No actors!"

"Oh my God, you guys are the worst. New topic," I say, eager to get off the subject of my romantic life, which frankly has never been something to inspire more than three minutes of discussion.

"Fine," Billy concedes, much to my relief. "What are you guys doing this weekend?"

"I'm heading out to Burning Man," Janine announces.

"What?" Now it's Billy's and my turn to speak in unison. I guess I shouldn't be too surprised that Janine's free spirit and self-expression would be drawn to an event like Burning Man. From what I've heard, it's like Woodstock, without the bands. It makes sense that Janine, one of those rare homegrown Hollywood people, would be drawn to this mecca celebrating the individual within a communal environment. Most people in this business came from somewhere else to pursue the Hollywood dream. But Janine has the unique confidence that you get only from being born into the business; her parents are world-class editors who have worked on some of the biggest features with incredible directors. She was probably taught to speak Avid before English.

"What? Don't look so surprised. Burning Man is an experience. I'm going to be off the grid for three days." She sighs with pure bliss. "Being one with nature and art... not to mention hot, artsy guys," she adds with a laugh.

Billy and I exchange a skeptical look. Janine going to Burning Man is like me standing in line to go to a Vince Camuto sample sale. But then that's why I love her—just when you think she's going to zig, she zags.

"That's hard-core, Janine. And I thought she was the granola one," Billy says, pointing at me.

"Well, I *will* be wearing fleece this weekend...," I say.

"Off home to the mountains?"

"Yep." I'm unable to hide my smile. "We're having a big surprise party for my mom's sixtieth birthday. She has no idea I'm coming up. I told her I had to work."

"So you're off the grid too. Should I not even bother texting you? Are you going to come back with hairy pits, smelling of patchouli?" Billy teases.

"Ha-ha, smarty pants. I do plan to shower while I'm home. It's going to be heaven. Hikes, hanging out by the lake. I'm going mountain biking with my brother."

"Sounds like a nonstop workout." Janine groans. "No thanks, the toughest thing I'm going to be doing is figuring out where to put my next henna tattoo."

"I can just picture it—all weekend we're going to see Maddy's Facebook posts: 'Hiking. nine a.m.' with some postcard-perfect Instagram updates every five minutes." Ever since his publicist made him get on social media, Billy has been obsessed. "Meanwhile, I'll be here, with these," he says, gathering up the stacks of DVDs he left on the table. "Have fun, ladies."

"He really is so hot," Janine says with a sigh as soon as Billy is out of earshot.

"Watch who you say that to, or this week's love of his life will scratch your eyes out." I start grabbing up the rest of my sushi. "Okay, I have to get back to work. And I know you don't need any more distractions. Thanks for dinner—next time I'm buying."

Just as I'm settled back in my chair on set, ready to polish off the rest of my tuna roll, my phone buzzes. Must be Matthew again, bugging me about Mom's gift. I wipe off my fingers to reply to his text, grinning already that I've got him begging. Matthew's weakness is he hates being ignored. Instead it's a message from a number I don't recognize.

> I hope you don't mind, Billy gave me your number. I wanted to make sure you have my numbers so I can collect on our bet. —Adam

I stare at the screen for several seconds. And then I turn my phone off and stash it in my bag so quickly you'd think it was on fire.

Scene 007
Ext. Pacific Coast Highway--dawn

_____

"I will wait,
I will wait
for you."

I belt out the lyrics of Mumford & Sons as the song blares through the speakers of my car. To my right, the dawn sun is casting a yellow glow over the Pacific and empty highway stretches before me. It's beautiful. There's something very peaceful about being on the open road at 6:00 a.m. And if the traffic stays light, I'll be home in plenty of time to get to the restaurant for my mom's surprise party at 1:00 p.m.

The flat California desert disappears into gorgeous green hills and farms, the farther north I drive. I love how different the views are every hour on this drive. It's always a surprise to see what's around the bend. Likewise, with my iPod on shuffle, I have no idea what music is going to play next. One minute I'm listening to Michael Bublé croon his latest and the next I'm transported back to ninth grade, head-banging to Trent Reznor. But the best part of this windy six-hour drive is that it leaves plenty of solitary time to think, which this morning mostly consists of me replaying my rather strange date with Craig last night.

We met up for drinks at the Mexican place near my house, but just like last week he seemed distracted—there, but not there. As I munched on the nachos we ordered, I mentally added to my list of "possible reasons why Craig is so distracted": *#7. He doesn't want to date me anymore; #8. Family issues; #9. He has a secret wife he never told me about, like on the* Dateline Exclusive *I watched way too late last night.* The possibilities were endless. As it turned out, it really wasn't anything especially surprising. At the end of the night, as we're standing at my door, he turned to me and said, "Look, Maddy, I know, I've been distracted the last week. I'm sorry. It's not you. It's just, well, things are a little crazy right now. Hogan is talking about needing to bring in some new blood. He's talking about making some changes on the development side."

I couldn't help but make a face—changes at the top make everyone nervous.

"Don't worry about me. I'm fine." He took my hand and started playing with the braided string bracelet my mom made me the last time I was home. Luckily it's a pretty tame version of her many artistic endeavors, so I'm happy to humor her and wear it, although jewelry is not usually my thing.

"Then why all the secret meetings?"

"Ah, so people are talking."

Damn it, I wasn't supposed to reveal that, but he didn't press me for details.

"The good news is that Hogan is excited for the future of HCP. He isn't just coasting on the success of *The Wrong Doctor.* He wants more. I just..." He hesitated, and probably out of habit more than worrying that the random strangers at Casavega care about our conversation, he leaned in closer. "I want Hogan to give me a chance to run Development too." He gave my hand a squeeze. "I know I can count on you to not say anything to anyone about this. I want to get my ducks lined up and then go to him with a proposal."

On the one hand, I was thrilled that he confided in me. On the other hand, I'm uncomfortable thinking that he probably never would have told me his plan if he knew about my relationship with Hogan. I kept meaning to tell him about it, but how do I do it now? I don't want Craig to think I actually have any influence over Hogan, because I don't. But I don't know how to tell him now without him thinking I've been keeping something from him.

As if I have conjured him with my thoughts, Craig calls.

"Morning, Maddy." Craig's voice rings through the Bluetooth speaker of the car. He still has his morning voice, which I decide I like. Very much. It's kind of husky and understated, without his usual polish.

"Hey, you. Did you just get up?" The clock on the dash reads 7:48.

"No, I've been up for about twenty minutes. Just watching last night's *Sports Center.* How far are you? Did you really get up at five-fifteen?"

"Well, five, actually, and I was on the road by five-thirty." Yup, I have this super annoying habit of waking up about ten or fifteen minutes before my alarm goes off. Almost every morning. It hurts because I could really use the extra ten minutes of shut-eye. But I know if I set my alarm for ten minutes later, I wouldn't be able to sleep for worrying that would be the one morning I wouldn't do it. "I got to see a beautiful sunrise, and I'm making good time."

"And I haven't even made coffee yet. You inspire me, Maddy. I need some of your energy."

I don't know if it's energy, per se. I do think it's that I was raised getting up early to hit the slopes when they open, or to get on the lake for the best conditions or before the crowds. And now working in TV, we're either up at "Oh-dark-thirty" or we don't start until 10:00 p.m. and we're filming all night, and I'm back in bed well after the sun comes up. The good news is that I can sleep anywhere, any time. The bad news is, never for long and very restlessly. I'm always afraid there's going to be a problem with someone on the crew or cast, so I have to leave my phone on all night. When we're in production, I'm like a doctor—always on call. One of the best parts of going home is the naps. I can't wait to sneak in a few, under my mom's quilted afghan (another of her hobbies) on our old couch.

"So, you're back in town on Monday, right?" Craig asks.

"Yep, I'm sure next week is going to be crazed after the holiday weekend, but maybe we can do something next Saturday, in the morning? We could go for a walk up to the Griffith Observatory." Given Craig's anxiety levels these days, he could use some time in nature, as opposed to some overcrowded brunch spot in Santa Monica, which is what I imagine he would suggest.

"Aren't you going to be hiking at home? You want to go again?"

"Well, it's not really a hike, more like a nice walk, but don't knock it till you try it, mister."

"Oh, yeah, sure. Okay. I'll hike with you. It'll be fun. Listen, that's my other line. Have a great time in Wolf. Text me when you get there."

"Okay, I will. Have a good weekend, Craig."

Apparently he's already disconnected because Adele's voice comes through the speaker as the iPod comes back on.

My car eats up the miles into the Sierras. Through the desert I have to set the cruise control to avoid speed traps. But now that I'm into the mountains, I like to actually drive this part and pay attention to the terrain. Soon enough, my exit appears and then I see the cheesy wooden sign that says WELCOME TO WOLF COUNTY, POP. 4500. The knots in my shoulder muscles automatically ease up a bit. I'm home.

Filled with giddiness and nostalgia, I make my way across

the main road through town. The strip is dotted with inexpensive motels and fast-food places that were built when I was a kid. The town hit a boom in the '90s when tons of fancy houses were built near the slopes, and all these hotels cropped up to satisfy the weekenders. But it's starting to look a little run-down already.

When I get to the intersection of Main Street and Old Forge Road, I am shocked to see that Terry's craft store, Crop Till You Drop, is boarded up. I went to school with Terry's daughter, Jill. It was open when I was here last April. I guess it didn't survive the off-season this year. That seems to be happening more and more frequently with all of these beloved mom-and-pop shops. The economic downturn has hit Wolf County harder than I'd thought. I make a mental note to call Jill while I am home and check in.

It's just after noon but I can't go home yet and ruin the surprise—my mom has no idea I'm even coming—so I decide to pay Brian a quick visit first. I pull off onto Pine Cove Road, a street I know as well as my own. I rode my bike here after school pretty close to every day, until I saved up for my first car—a used Jetta I was ridiculously proud of—and then I drove over pretty much every day. I pull up in front and knock on the door. I hear a dog barking and then what sounds like a stampede. Twin four-year-olds appear at the door, still squabbling over who gets to open it this time.

"It's my turn, Luke."

"Ow! Stop it! It was your turn last time!"

"Hi, Luke. Hi, Liam." I kneel down and hug Brian's children close. Behind them is Brian's wife, Lily.

"Maddy, you're early! I didn't think we would see you until the party! Come on in." She pulls both boys off me. I look around the warm, cozy living room that looks as if a cyclone has just passed through.

"Lily, so good to see you." We hug, and Lily smells like milk and honey. In the TV version of my life, I would surely despise Lily, the woman who scooped up my ex months after we broke up. And there was probably a week or so, ten years ago, that I did. But then I realized (or rather, my brothers didn't hesitate to spell it out for me) that I left Wolf and Brian. What was he supposed to do—pine away for me for years? Well, okay, that would have been nice for my ego, but the more generous part of me wanted Brian to be happy. And the truth is, Brian had waited for me. We did the long-distance thing for a while, still thinking that I would eventually return and we'd settle back into the life we'd had before. But when I got offered my first major promotion, script supervisor for a network show, we both realized there was no going back for me. To be offered this job, working on a network show? It was a huge opportunity. One I wanted.

"More than you want a life back here?" Brian had asked.

"Yes. More than that," I admitted. What else could I say? He deserved my honesty. But I knew I had to let him go. Fast-forward ten years, and I am standing in the kitchen he and Lily inherited from his parents, which Lily has given a makeover straight out of *Real Simple* magazine.

"I love what you've done, Lily. The mosaics on the backsplash are amazing."

"Oh, thanks. I did them all myself," she tells me as she hands me a bottle of water from the fridge dotted with the twin's artwork.

Of course she did. Lily does things like make mosaics and apple pies and organic baby food. But she's so damn sweet, you can't hate her for it.

"Come on, let's go out back. Brian has been out here all day working on that damn dirt bike of his," she says, rolling her eyes affectionately. The first time I heard Lily curse was when I knew she and Brian were going to work out. The sweetness is sincere, but she's feisty too. "He's going to be so happy to see you."

We head to the backyard where the twins run to Brian, screaming, "Daaaadyyyyy" at the top of their lungs. Lily hands him a beer and kisses his forehead. Taking in their easy affection, I look around at the swing set, the trampoline, the white picnic table, and Weber grill perfect for a family of four. It feels like I am stepping into exactly the life I thought I wanted back then, and I feel a quick pang of nostalgia thinking about the road not taken.

"Well, look what the cat dragged in!" Brian comes over, wiping the grease from his hands, right onto his T-shirt. Same old Brian.

"Hi, friend." We exchange a good squeeze, and somehow I don't mind that I might end up with motor oil on my T-shirt. Brian immediately starts quizzing me about the drive, work, and my life. I know it's just a matter of time before he says, *"And the men, Maddy? How are they?"* with a raised eyebrow. Now that he and Lily have settled in so well to married life and parental bliss, they are both determined for me to find the right guy. It's sweet, but annoying. I do love telling him the stories of what guys are like in LA. We have laughed until we cried over the ridiculous things that are considered "normal" in Hollywood. But he's still on me about the men I date and refuses to believe there aren't any "real" guys in the entire city. Hopefully I can ward off the romantic inquisition until after I have had a few glasses of wine at the party.

"So is your mom going to be surprised?"

"Hopefully. The plan is for Matthew to call her to say his Jeep broke down in front of Pete's Tavern, and ask if she can come pick him up. When she does, we'll all be there. You guys are coming, right?" I take in Brian's greasy shirt, realizing I am not the only one who needs to freshen up soon. Although for Brian, freshening up is trading one concert tee for another. I can't help but think of Craig's $125 Burberry T-shirts.

"Of course, we wouldn't miss it. We can all head over together. I just hope no one saw you pull in here. You know the phone tree would spring to life immediately once someone spotted our local celebrity."

"Oh right, my celebrity status. Don't worry, daaahling . . . I'm still the same old Maddy From the Block," I say with a Rita Hayworth old-Hollywood lilt. "Anyway, I am glad I got to see you before I face the wolves." A little local Wolf Humor, but not that far-fetched. Once I'm at the party surrounded by my parents and their friends and everyone who's been "auntie" or "uncle" to me, I will be deluged with questions about my life and demanded to tell my Hollywood tales.

After many fantastic stories from Luke and Liam about four-year-old life in Wolf, I make my excuses and head out. Mike, Matthew, and I agreed to meet at Pete's Tavern at 1:00 p.m. to go over everything. Since reception is so spotty up here in the mountains, I know better than to keep them waiting. Sure enough, they are standing on the street waiting for me as I pull up to the coffee shop, and my heart soars at the sight of them—my brothers, loyal, irritating, lovable protectors. Mike envelops me in a bear hug before I can even get out of the car, as if it had been decades since we'd seen each other, rather than a few months. Which, I'll be honest, I love. My older brother doesn't express himself a lot, but when he hugs me tight and says, "How ya been, kid?" I know he means "I love you, I missed you, and if anyone is not treating you right, I will kick his/her ass."

Matthew is next, looking charming and adorable with his long floppy hair. He's just moved back home after a year in China teaching English, followed by two in Portland, bartending and substitute teaching and, "you know, rocking out"—whatever that means. Now he's back in his old bedroom, strategizing his next step. He loves teaching and is amazing with kids, who worship him and his effortless coolness. He's waiting to hear if he got a placement at our alma mater Brook Haven High (home of the Wolverines, obviously). It'll be hysterical that he'll be working alongside a few of the same teachers who had us way back when.

"Okay, guys, we have to get to it." I feel myself going into what they call "Maddy mode." "I never got a final head count for the party. How many people do you think are really going to show up?"

"This is Wolf, Maddy, not some Hollywood *gala*. Everyone is coming." Mike is not your sugarcoating type.

"Oh God. I sent out so many e-mails. And the Andersons asked if their cousins could come, which means an extra five people. I said yes without even thinking."

"We're going to need a bigger boat," Matthew deadpans. My parents think I'm bad—Matt is a movie-quoting machine. He was by my side when Hogan started indoctrinating us in TV/film history. No doubt it's annoying to anyone who doesn't get it, but we don't care. We crack each other up. So, I can't help but laugh at the classic *Jaws* reference but quickly get him focused on the task at hand. "The party is in less than an hour. Does Pete have the final numbers so we have enough food? Is everything else ready?" My brothers have assured me they could handle all the party details since they were right here, but thirty-plus years of experience makes me a bit skeptical. Reflexively, I reach into the car to grab my notebook.

"Everything is set. But I know you won't relax until you see for yourself," Mike says. "Go on in. I'm going to pull your car around back so Mom doesn't see it." Matthew and I file into Pete's

Tavern, a dive bar and Wolf County landmark since forever and Carson family favorite since we came of age. Pete Jr., the second-generation owner, is the warm grandfather figure everyone loves. He has the perfect white beard to play Santa in the town Christmas fair every year, although I suspect all the kids know it's Pete. Mike, Matthew, and I always did, but we were happy to go along with it.

Despite playing warm, jolly old Saint Nick once a year, Pete is a lovable grump, so I am not at all surprised when all I get is a head nod from the other side of the bar. "Maddy, you're home."

"Yep, Pete. Thanks so much for having us." I look around at the rustic setting. It's like a warm sweater to me, but it's also not very festive at the moment.

"Would it have killed you guys to get more than a few balloons? Some flowers? Maybe a centerpiece?" I am getting a little exasperated; a party is taking place here in thirty minutes. Dare I ask if they remembered to pick up the cake? I knew I should have demanded they reply to the checklist e-mail I sent with more productive responses than, "There goes anal Maddy" jokes.

"Flowers? Why? No one's died." Matthew doesn't look like he's kidding. I don't bother to explain; I just grab my purse and dash out.

Twenty minutes later, I've managed to race to Forever Flowers and the grocery store to grab a few bouquets and ribbons. I channel Bernie, our expert set designer, whom I have seen turn a dark and smelly back alley into a Paris café. I feel like Mary Poppins on crack, rushing around the room, assigning tasks to my brothers and Pete. Soon the room exudes birthday cheer just in time for guests to start streaming through the door. Bernie would have been proud.

Within ten minutes, my arms are tired from all the warm

embraces of friends and neighbors. Everyone comes in for hugs and *how are yous*, and I feel like a cross between a visiting dignitary and a shy teenager.

My phone buzzes just as Mr. Tanner is telling me about his niece's latest baton-twirling recital:

The Eagle Has Landed.

"Shhhh, everyone, she's here, she's here!" Everyone manages to stop talking just in time to scream, "SURPRISE!" when my mom walks in.

The look on her face is priceless, and then she locks eyes on me.

"Maddy?? Oh my God, Maddy, what are you doing here? This is too much." And she's in tears. Good tears.

"Hi, Mom. Happy birthday!" I give her a Mike-size hug. I love her smile and the way she is touching my cheek with the back of her hand as if to see if I am really there. Meanwhile, my dad jumps in to grab me around the shoulders and pull me in to his chest. I tuck in under his chin and it's a perfect fit.

"Daddy." I squeeze him tightly around the middle and then pull back. He's a big teddy bear; the whole mountain man persona suits him well.

"I can't believe it all worked out without her figuring out the surprise!" he says with such pride. My parents are sort of notorious in town for not being great secret-keepers. "For weeks, I've been so nervous I didn't know whether to scratch my watch or wind my butt."

Looking at his neatly kept beard, the workman's shirt, and Wranglers, it's hard to imagine that he once routinely wore suits to work from nine to five and was working his way up the corporate ladder in accounting for a Fortune 500 company. Then he met my mom. She's five years older than he is, and he loves dragging out the part about how he had to convince her that the age difference didn't matter, while Mom rolls her eyes. The romantic story we heard from infancy is that they came up here for a summer getaway, fell in love with the place, and never left. Secretly, I've always admired how brave they both were to take such a risk. Clearly, that risk-taking gene is recessive. I had to be pushed out of the nest, and no matter what fantasies I have for my life, deep down I am not the type to willingly take that kind of leap of faith.

My mom is over the moon with the party and being surrounded by all of her favorite people. She backs up his story, claiming she had no idea this surprise party was even happening. I find that hard to believe because my dad has not successfully kept a secret from her, well . . . ever. But if she's faking it, she's doing a great job.

Earl and Louise, my parents' best friends, immediately step up and hand them champagne glasses.

"To Helen!" Louise sings out. Everyone echoes her and the cheers fill the house. I clink glasses with my parents and my brothers (Mike's drinking his champagne out of a beer mug) and take a sip.

I wish that Hogan could have been here for this. We had been secretly texting all week as he tried to rearrange some sort of important meeting to make it. But since he couldn't get out of it, I'm glad I didn't let my dad know it was even a possibility. I would hate to have gotten his hopes up. They usually only see Hogan in the winter months.

"Mom, Dad, Hogan sends his love. He really wishes he could be here to celebrate."

"Oh, of course, sweetheart. What fun that would be, but I understand. He has so much going on. He e-mailed me a birthday poem this morning. I swear, that man can write anything."

"He says you two are overdue for dinner." Hogan and I get together every few months—stealthily. Hogan doesn't think it's a big deal that we are practically family and always reminds me that I earned my success fair and square, but I am still leery of people knowing about our relationship and feeling like there's any whiff of favoritism. We've both just been so busy now that shooting has started that we haven't found time to get together. And honestly, another reason I haven't been so eager to book dinner is that I will have to tell him about Craig. Unless Craig already told him—which I doubt, because one whiff and Hogan would've been on me like white on rice. I don't know how Hogan is going to feel about it, but I guess I am going to find out soon enough. For now, I put the thought out of my head so I can focus on the party.

I look up in time to see my dad dipping my mom on the dance floor. They look so young and in love. I know how lucky I am to have these parents, this family, this community. Mom and Dad have each given Matthew, Mike, and me countless pieces of relationship advice over the years and have refrained during any heartbreak my brothers and I experienced, or whenever we marveled at how they did it when our other friends' parents were getting divorced. My dad always said, *"Remember, honey. A leopard doesn't change his spots. People are who they are; they don't change too much. Your mom always loved me for who I was, and I loved her for that."* Or from my mom: *"Make sure he loves you just a little bit more than you love him. And surprise him with lingerie at least once a year."* I could have gone without that last tidbit. But as I see my parents dance into the night and as I cry through my father's moving toast, all I can think is, *I'm so glad it's worked for them.* I also try to imagine Craig dipping me on the old parquet dance floor under a moose head strung with Christmas lights, but somehow my brain can't process an image that includes Craig *and* a moose head. I text him a picture of the moose:

Me: Bongo says hi from Wolf County.

I laugh out loud when seconds later he texts back.

Craig: Does that thing bite?

Scene 008
Ext. Mountaintop bonfire--dusk

The next night, my brothers and I are at a clambake at Wolf Lake, clinking beer bottles to toast a wonderful surprise party. Matthew can't stop replaying the iPhone video of Mom blowing out her candles and accidentally blowing a bunch of frosting into Dad's beard. Tonight is another perfect night, cool and crisp. My legs are a little sore from hiking all day, but a good kind of sore. And once again, I'm surrounded by old friends. I didn't know who was going to show up, when Molly, a friend from high school who now works as a waitress at Pete's, sent out the Facebook invite— and the answer was everyone. Or at least everyone who went to Brooke Haven High School between 1998 and 2008. The only difference is, back in the day, we would have had beers and joints (well, me just the one time), and now there's beer and... kids running around. Brian's twins are currently having a heated sword fight with two long sticks, and I am hoping that no one loses a cornea tonight. Snuggled together on the other side of the fire, Brian and Lily seem unfazed by their boys' antics. Actually, Lily seems much more concerned with finding the perfect song on her iPod to play on the Bluetooth speakers they brought. Mike's best friend, Jacob, claims that he should get to pick since he won the afternoon's hacky sack game and that that's always been the rule (a rule no one remembers). Eventually Springsteen fills the air.

No one is talking about scripts, schedules, or screen tests. No one is looking over anyone else's shoulder to see if someone more important is in the room. The women are eating and wearing faded jeans from the Gap. Once again, I try to picture Craig sitting here with us, and the image just doesn't compute. Craig channeling his inner mountain man would be really entertaining...or a disaster. But he did say that he'd love to visit, so maybe I'm not giving him enough credit.

Being with my family and old friends this weekend, I've felt very far from home, and at the same time right at home. And sitting in front of this campfire, I have one of those moments of feeling totally and utterly at peace in my skin. The kind of moment where you didn't even realize how wound up you were, until the feeling of calm settles on you. I take a deep breath, enjoying the cool mountain air and the sharp scent of firewood.

"What's going on in that busy head, Sis?" Matthew leans in next to me as he pokes a stick at the fire.

"Nothing." I laugh. "You'd just tease me for being sentimental."

"Well, since I haven't seen you in what seems like forever, I will allow your sentimentality only this once." Matthew does a mock stern voice.

"It's just nice...you know? Being home. That even though we've been away so long, leading whole other lives, we come back here, and everything just falls into place. It's like nothing has changed; we're still in high school, coming up here every weekend. We're so lucky. Most people don't have this."

"I know what you mean. But don't you think it's great that you get the best of both worlds? You get to have your life in LA, pursue your dreams, and Wolf is always here. It's the rock." We both keep looking at the fire. My brother is not usually this deep.

"I'm jealous that you're back here," I say. "You had your adventures, and now you're going to live near Mom and Dad, inspire the next generation of Wolverines...maybe finally date someone longer than two months." I playfully punch his arm.

"Well, yes to the first two for sure," he says, laughing. "I can't promise the last one, but I'm psyched to be home. And I'll be closer to LA now, so I can pop down and visit. You can take me to lunch on Rodeo Drive." He jokingly pronounces it "rodeo," as in bull riding and cattle calls. At least I *think* he's joking.

"Sure thing, we can do that. I love you, baby brother."

"You too, Sis," he says, getting up to grab more firewood. "And you know, Maddy, you could always move home too. I mean, it's not unthinkable."

I sit quietly pondering that for a while and wonder why, even though I love it here, it's never occurred to me to move back to Wolf. Can you really go home again? And can I give up my career? I stuff these thoughts away, happy to let the music, fun, and beer sweep over me.

Hours later, the crowd has thinned as some of the families with young kids have gone home, but the dancing is still going strong. Everyone is laughing and getting crazy. I sit in a lounge chair, sweaty from my classic '80s dance moves, catching my breath. Brian squats down next to me, watching the chaos. He smells like campfire and musk, a smell I would bottle if I could.

"Hey, you. Where are the kids?" I ask.

"Lily took them home. They didn't even move when we put them in the car seats. They're going to sleep well tonight."

"That's good. You and Lily are such great parents, Brian. I don't know how you do it."

"I know, right. How did that happen? One minute, we're kids playing around this very campsite, and the next, we're bringing our own kids here. It's freaky. How did we get old enough to have kids? Sometimes I still feel I'm acting the part of Dad. Cool Dad, of course," Brian says, laughing. "Hey, wanna go for a walk?"

"Sure." I look back at the rowdy crowd. "Let's go."

When we finally get far enough away from the cars and the fire, Brian pulls out a mini flashlight.

"It's a full moon tonight. What's that for?" I ask.

"I thought you might get scared since you're a city-folk type now."

"Ha-ha," I say as we head into the night. "Do I really seem different now?"

"A little. I mean, it has been ten years; it's going to change you. It's meant to change you a little, right?"

"Yeah, but when does it get to be too much?"

Our conversation stops as we get to the darkened lodge and the lift rising up the mountain in the distance like a shadow.

"Should we go up?" He turns to me, smiling mischievously.

"What the hell. For old time's sake."

I get the keys from my dad's hiding spot. Thankfully, that hasn't changed. And within minutes, Brian and I are riding up the mountain on the bunny slope lift.

"Do you know how much trouble we would be in—today, never mind when we were kids—if my dad ever caught us doing this?"

"Some things never change." Sittting on top of the tarp protecting the seats from the summer sun, isn't as comfortable today as it was when we were kids. But we sit together, heading up the darkened hillside, and there's just an easy silence. This is one of my favorite things about being with Brian; we don't have to talk.

Finally, after a moment, he leans into my shoulder. "So, Maddy. How's life?"

I take a minute to answer because I know Brian really wants to know.

"I'm good. It's good. I'm still loving working on *The Wrong Doctor*. This season is going well, but it's hectic."

"Lily and I can't wait for the new season. Any insider scoop for us?"

"No spoilers from me. Besides, that would ruin it. I will tell you, we have a great new character. This guy Adam Devin. Lily watches *Days*, right? He's on it."

"Oh, man, first you have Billy Fox and now this Devin guy? You just want to torture me while my wife swoons over your friends."

"Well, they're not exactly my friends. Well, Billy is for sure. But I barely know Adam. I am sure he's like all the rest, though. I will be happy to remind Lily that she's way better off with you. You can catch a fish with your bare hands. Adam would need two prop guys and a stunt double to pull that off," I add with Wolverine and ex-girlfriend loyalty. "You guys should come down and come on set one day. It would be fun."

"God, Lily would love that. With the little guys, it's hard to imagine getting away to LA. But we'll try. I'm glad you're still loving your job, Maddy. Any idea what comes next? Maybe your own movie or show? I mean, you have all of these good ideas. I remember all of the stories you used to tell me as we sat in our tree."

"We were fourteen, Brian. All those stories were about lost love and teen angst." I laugh and cringe simultaneously at the memories. "Besides, LA is a very different place; that's not how the world works. There are the creatives and there are the worker bees. I'm a worker bee and that's fine. I love my job; it's what I want."

"Yeah, I just don't like to see you get into a rut. You left Wolf to achieve something big and amazing. I don't want you to lose sight of that."

"Does my life really sound that boring to you?" I ask, trying to keep the edge out of my voice.

"Not at all. Your life is amazing. Are you kidding? Lily is always looking for you in *US Weekly* and *People* magazine. She swears you must be just off-screen in every shot."

"Please assure her that I am not."

"We just want you to be happy. I know how hard it was for you when your parents forced you to take time away from Wolf after college."

"They didn't *force* me..." They sat me down and lectured me until I relented. I was so cocky at twenty-two, thinking I knew best—I was willing to take their dare, to live somewhere else, just to make sure Wolf was what I wanted. Within a year of living in LA, I realized why they went the tough-love route. I would never have taken the chance otherwise, and now I wouldn't trade my life for anything.

"I don't think either of us pictured you working in Tinseltown," he jokes, to lighten up his sudden serious turn. "I know it meant so much to you to prove yourself to Hogan and your parents. I just hope it's still what you want."

When was the last time I actually stopped to think about what I really want?

"It is, Brian."

"And what about your love life? All work and no play, as they say." He flashes me the same huge grin that melted my fourteen-year-old heart. I knew this was coming, but for some reason, I just don't feel like telling him about Craig. It's so new.

"I see your plan, Brian. You did this on purpose. You got me up here on a freakin' ski lift so I'm trapped, and then you interrogate me. I can throw you off this thing, you know."

"You didn't answer the question, Maddy."

I just look at him and roll my eyes. "I know."

Saved by the bell, my phone rings, and it's my dad calling.

"Hey, Daddy, how are you?"

"Good. Where are you?"

"Oh, um...just at the campfire...talking with Brian." Brian

and I look at each other and crack up that we're still sneaking around behind my dad's back all these years later.

"What's that loud noise?" Oh God, the lift motor—of course he can hear that.

"I don't know. The reception is really bad up here. I'm losing you." I stagger my words so it seems like I'm cutting in and out. Unbelievable how easy it is to revert to a teenaged mind-set.

"I feel like a monkey trying to do math, trying to use this damn thing. Your mom and I are headed to bed, so we'll miss you when you get home. We're zonked after today, so we just wanted to say good night and make sure we're on for lunch tomorrow before you hit the road."

"Yep, lunch sounds good."

"We were going to go to Crazy Eights Café, but now your mom wants to make lunch with that sandwich thingy you got her."

I am touched my gift was such a hit. "That sounds great."

"Good, because your mom and I want to have a check-in."

In Carson family lingo, a check-in is a talk about some sort of family business, like where our vacation would be or when my brother decided to go climb Kilimanjaro. Once when I was seven, Mike, Matthew, and I called a check-in to discuss getting a pool in the backyard. The answer: no.

"Is everything okay, Dad?"

"Yeah, all fine. We just want to have time with our girl."

But something about the way he says it is unconvincing. As Brian and I make our way back to the campfire, I have a nagging feeling in the pit of my stomach.

Scene 009
Int. Maddy's bedroom--morning

I press snooze on my alarm clock for the second time. I can't even remember the last time I did that—needed an alarm clock, let alone pressed snooze. I am going to be late today, something that also never happens. But I am dealing with no sleep and a little bit of an emotional hangover after the family check-in and the long drive. I meant to hit the road right after lunch and get back by midnight, but I didn't leave until 7:00 p.m., much to my parents' objections. They kept insisting I stay an extra night because driving in the mountains so late at night isn't the best idea. But then neither is missing a day of work when we're already getting behind in the shooting schedule. It was tough to leave, though. My mom, already a sentimental person, was feeling especially so after the birthday party. One thing led to another and soon enough, they dropped the bombshell that they are thinking of selling the ski shop and retiring. To some place warmer. Like Arizona. I can no more imagine my parents in Arizona than I can imagine—well, me in Arizona. They are mountain people. Wolf County is a part of our family.

But apparently business has been really slow, and they, along with other businesses in Wolf, have been struggling for the last couple seasons. Or as my dad put it, "It's slower than molasses running uphill in July, around here." Something they've effectively hidden from me until now. Even during lunch, I got the feeling they were holding back, and their forced cheer made me feel even worse. They assured me no immediate decisions would be made in terms of selling the lodge or the house, but they just wanted me to know it was a possibility. "It might be about time for the third act, Maddy."

I just sat there stunned. I can't even imagine a life that doesn't include my parents living in Wolf and running the resort. It's almost incomprehensible. After lunch, instead of hitting the road, I insisted that we go through the books, as if I could find some obvious mistake or accounting error. Turns out, the situation is pretty serious. Not dire, but definitely stressful.

The whole drive home last night, all this morning, and now on my ride into work, my mind keeps racing with ideas to rev up business. I'm going to call Mike later tonight (for now my parents have kept Matthew in the dark, since he's just decided to move home) so we can put our heads together. But first, I have to get through today's shoot, which is going to be insane.

As I walk on set, Frank greets me and looks at his watch. He's clearly had his morning coffee because a good deal of it is down the front of his shirt.

"Wow, Maddy Carson isn't early. I was going to start calling morgues when you weren't here at seven on the dot. I assumed you must have gotten whatever Adam has..."

"What are you talking about? What's wrong with Adam?"

"Stomach flu. It's bad. The day is blown."

Adam can't be sick. We have an intense schedule today to make up for the holiday weekend. This is not helping my mood or stress level.

"He's not really sick, though, right? What do you bet he was on some three-day bender and just can't find his way off some rapper's yacht? Were there girls screaming in the background when he called in?"

"Um, no. Maddy. He's here. In his trailer." My face still hasn't released its disbelieving expression. "You don't believe Adam's really sick, go see for yourself. But don't breathe in there. What-ever he's got, believe me, you don't want it."

Frank steps over to talk to Rian McCourt, this week's director, to start rearranging the schedule. Frankly, I am still skeptical that Adam is really too sick to work today. But then why did he bother to come in? Maybe he's pulling some diva move regarding contract negotiations or something. Happens all the time. McCourt waves me into the discussion.

"Maddy, we can't scrap the whole day. We'll have to shoot around Adam. I have a shoot in Brazil next week."

"I . . . I totally understand your situation," I say calmly. Except I don't. McCourt's not here next week? This is his episode; he has to finish it. I glance at Frank. This could turn into a nightmare quickly. "Adam's in every scene today and tomorrow. Maybe we can try to get some of Billy's stuff done this morning and then move some scenes from Thursday to today?"

"Except the set for those scenes isn't built yet. Even if they worked twenty-four-seven, they won't have it ready until Wednes-day at the earliest," Frank offers.

McCourt flicks his pen at the monitors in frustration. It pings off and we all watch it roll away. Then he storms off with a terse, "I need a cigarette. I'll be back." And this is what I mean by the diva moods. McCourt's dramatic exit means that Frank and I are left to strategize a viable option while he has a smoke break. I need to call Craig, as he should be alerted to any setbacks that could potentially cost the production major dollars. But given the stress Craig is under, I hesitate. Maybe we can find a solution first.

Suddenly I hear Yoda's voice coming from my cell phone: *"Do or do not. There is no try."* Damn Matthew. Yet again, he must have figured out my password and changed my ringtone set-tings, a joke he finds endlessly funny. I'm still mortified about the time Sir Mix-a-Lot's "I Like Big Butts" filled the crowded waiting room as I waited for a dentist appointment. Even in the charged atmosphere, the classic quote gives Frank a smile as he flips through the call sheet and pages of sides—xeroxed copies of the pages from the script that we were scheduled to shoot today.

I read the text, which ironically is from the practical joker himself.

> Matthew: Fantastic weekend sis. Glad you made it. But if you don't come home again soon, I'm coming to LA to find out all about your secret double life.

Before I can reply, another text comes in.

> Matthew: PS: like your new alerts?
> Me: Ha freakin' ha. Jerk!
> Me: I'm def coming home for Tgiving. Just a few weeks, really.

I can't resist quickly adding a picture to my text. It's a perfect candid moment from Saturday afternoon, with my brothers hovering next to the grill with my dad. They're all laughing at a joke someone just told, and my dad looks so happy and young. I cringe again, thinking of my parents leaving Wolf. I know there has to be a solution. But first we need to resolve today's crisis. I glance up to see McCourt storming back toward us, coffee now in hand.

"Any developments?"

What could possibly have developed since he walked away? Aliens landed and handed us Adam Devin's doppelganger? I love that he thinks Frank and I somehow solved this problem in the ten minutes he was gone. We're good, but we're not that good.

"Maybe he'll sleep it off if we give him a couple hours?" I suggest unconvincingly.

"Maddy, he doesn't even look human. I told you to go see for yourself. I just ordered a car service to take him home. He shouldn't even be driving."

Something makes me think of Matthew's favorite movie, *Spaceballs*. He's made me watch it with him a hundred times. There's this scene where they capture the stunt doubles in the chase sequence by mistake—something that would never happen on my watch, but inspiration strikes.

"McCourt, I have kind of a crazy idea. I know we're scrambling here, so you tell me if this might work for you." This is my first time working with McCourt, and each director has a different, distinct interpretation of the script supervisor's role. Some directors see me as a necessary evil and minimize my involvement as much as possible. They never even want me to speak to the actors. Others see me as their right hand, and I end up doing everything from discussing the script with actors to being consulted on the sequence and specifics of the shots. (Obviously, the latter is more fun for me, but so far no one's asked my preference.) Since I don't know where McCourt fits in this spectrum, I try to be as diplomatic as possible.

"Maddy, if you can get us through this with Hogan Chenny still willing to hire me again, I'm in." McCourt clearly realizes he's on thin ice, cutting it so close with another gig back-to-back. McCourt needs to make this work as much as we do.

"What if you stage the scenes slightly differently so that the wide shots and sequences happen from Ahmed's perspective? Or at least from his angle. We can get casting to send us a body double to shoot from behind, and then I can keep screen grabs and we can shoot his close-ups later."

The silence is deafening. McCourt stares at me—through me, actually. Then he chugs the rest of his coffee in one swallow and crushes the cup.

"I love it. You haven't done anything like this yet, have you? I could talk to Hogan about editing the whole episode to be almost in the first person...Ahmed's take on how it unfolds. The script is already along those lines, since the reveal at the end of the previous episode is that Ahmed is really an undercover American Marine. I think Hogan will love this take." McCourt continues on animatedly, and even though Frank and I remain standing there, we both know he's in his own mind now, completely tuning us out. "Maybe we never see Adam in the episode; maybe he is completely in voice-over later? That would be amazing. I can see the handheld shots working everywhere...except..." McCourt grabs his script and starts flipping through pages.

"Maddy!" I turn to see Billy making his way to us. "What are we going to do? I just talked to Adam. He's barely coherent now. Even I would have called in. I can't believe he's here." I fight hard not to roll my eyes. Really? Billy is so impressed by Adam's martyrdom? You'd think no one's ever shown up at work sick before. "Do we cancel today? Try to shoot the stuff with Lucas and Naveen?"

Before I can answer, McCourt jumps in. "Billy, this has actually given me a fantastic concept for this episode. I have to pitch it to Hogan first." McCourt turns to me. "Can you get him on the phone?" Without hesitating, he turns back to Billy while I dial. "You're going to love this. It's sort of similar to that movie you did—" But before he can get into details, I hand him my phone.

"Hogan's assistant is getting Hogan on the line for you." McCourt steps away to pitch Hogan in private.

Billy looks at me for details. I hold up my hands in the international sign for "don't ask me," which earns me a disbelieving snort in return.

"Billy, you know I can't say anything." As annoyed as I am, and as satisfying as it would be to vent to the star of the show about the unfairness of Hollywood, I know taking the high road is the right call. So I don't say, "Well, Billy, it's funny you ask, but the wildly successful Rian McCourt just took credit for my idea and is now pitching it to our executive producer as his own." Instead I say, "I'm sure McCourt wants to sell you this idea himself."

But nothing gets past Billy Fox. "And when you rule the world...?"

"I'll take good ideas from anyone." I smile, pleased that Billy gets it. "I've got to start making some notes," I say, grabbing my script and notebook.

Frank squeezes my shoulder as a sign of solidarity. He knows, even if no one else ever will, that it was my idea, but he's also signaling me that I did the right thing by not making a thing of pointing that out. Frank turns to Billy. "I have a car taking Adam home, Billy. I'm going to have a PA drive Adam's car back to his place. Should I call his agent? Or his manager? Does he have a girlfriend or someone we can call?"

The two of them start walking off, so I don't hear Billy's reply. They really are making it sound like Adam is on his deathbed, but it seems like they are taking good care of him, so I focus on my list of notes for the change in plans:

1. Have casting find body double for Adam
2. Confirm with writers' office assistant what scenes need entire rewrites
3. Specialty cameras needed? All week or just Mon/Tues?
4. When will we get pink pages?
5. Does this change Thurs/Fri schedules too?
6. What am I missing??

My phone starts roaring. Apparently, the T-Rex from *Jurassic Park* is my new ring tone. Nice. A blocked call could be anyone, and during work hours, that means I have to be brave and answer.

"This is Maddy."

"Hey, babe. What's going on down there? Is Adam going to make it?"

"Craig. Hi." I glance over to McCourt, who is still deep in conversation with Hogan. "McCourt is pitching Hogan an alternate way to shoot the episode. I'm evaluating the script right now. I think we can take him out of most of the scenes today and tomorrow, but we'd still need him for Thursday and Friday."

"God, do we know what's wrong with him?"

"Frank says it's just a really bad case of the flu. We should probably have a doctor take a look at him anyway."

"I'll get someone over there tonight. I'll call his agent."

"Sounds good." With work out of the way, I hang on the line, wondering if the conversation will shift to personal.

"Did you have a good trip home?" Craig asks.

"Yeah, thanks. It was amazing."

"Good. Good. But I'm sure you're glad to be back."

"Yes, of course," I say, which is half a lie.

"Well, I can't wait to hear all about it. I hope you took a lot of photos. I would love to see where you grew up."

"I did. Are you coming by the set this week?"

There's silence as I wait for Craig to reply. I hear typing.

"Sorry, about that. Hogan just messaged me about McCourt's idea for the week."

I grit my teeth at the reference to "McCourt's" idea.

"He wants to meet up tonight and go over it with him."

I hear more typing in the background. I can tell Craig is distracted, which makes sense. He and Hogan must be going back and forth about how to make this episode fly, and what it means financially. I sign off with him quickly and head back to the production trailer to do some paperwork while the crew essentially starts the day over. A quick glance at my watch shows it's 11:12 a.m. and we're already three hours late. This does not bode well for the week.

Scene 010
Int. *Wrong Doctor* set--afternoon

When we see the first takes of the afternoon's scenes, I am blown away by Rian McCourt's unique and artistic interpretation of my basic idea of shooting from Adam's character's perspective. McCourt is clearly a gifted director, and the whole cast and crew is excited by how the shoot has evolved the last couple of days. The creativity, imagination and execution he employs definitely have the whole crew whispering "Emmy" by the end of the day. He may be a diva, like a lot of these creative types, but he's a genius at what he does.

The Steadicam operator has probably lost five pounds in water weight alone, sweating through these action sequences. The Steadicam is attached to Jimmy, the operator, with a harness, so he can walk around with it. Its fancy technology makes it smooth, not jerky, and it can go places and move in a way that stationary cameras can't. Rian has been using Jimmy's skills and several innovative camera angles to shoot everything from Ahmed's perspective. It's so creepy and intimate watching the other actors react to the camera lens as if it is Adam. It feels like they are looking right at me. I know it is going to be so unsettling for the audience, in a good way. Our audience will go nuts for this, and knowing that is fueling us through these grueling fourteen-hour days.

In addition to being time-consuming, this high-concept, more complicated shoot is costing the company hundreds of thousands of dollars, which is why an anxious Craig has been on set with us three evenings in a row now. When he's not on set, he's been calling and texting me practically every hour. Always the same question: "How's progress?" So it's no surprise to me when a PA brings up an extra director's chair and slides it next to McCourt's spot in video village. Soon Craig plops down, frantically pounding on his BlackBerry. It's 7:30 p.m. and we just started the next-to-last scene of the day. Based on Frank's initial call sheet, we should be on the last setup of the day and then wrap at 9:00 p.m. Now it's looking more like 11:00, if we're lucky.

Even as our eyes stay trained on the sequence on our screens, I imagine myself as Craig sees me right now. In my left hand, I am holding my notebook with all my notes scrawled everywhere. There was no time for my usual neat handwriting, so it looks like something a serial killer would have written. My script is spread out on my lap, a timer in my right hand, a pencil in my teeth, and a red pen sticking out of my ponytail. There was no time for makeup this morning, as I raced back to the set after grabbing five hours of sleep. I should have at least done something about the circles under my eyes.

There's nothing I can do about my slightly insane appearance, so I focus on my script, darting my eyes away from the screen to check the line and then back again. One of the actors playing a terrorist inverted his lines of dialogue, but it still makes sense in context. It's not worth stopping the take, especially given the snail's pace we are moving at today. It is something Hogan can decide to fix in the edit and replace with a different approved take, or accept, as the meaning is essentially the same.

The same actor screams out the last line of dialogue in the script, signaling the dramatic end of the scene where the army of jihadists charges into a meticulously constructed Red Cross tent. The handheld camera acting as Adam's character runs into the room and McCourt yells, "Cut. Print." He signs off using the classic old-fashioned term. We haven't exactly caught up with the digital age—we use the technology, but even I will admit "stop" just doesn't have the same ring as "cut."

Finally I can look away from my notes to say hi to Craig, but he is already standing with his arm around McCourt in a serious conversation. Victor gets off his camera stool and walks over to Frank. Their huddle looks equally intense.

While it's fresh in my mind, and since no one has called me over or announced what we're doing next, I make more notes about the scene and then review what's coming up. I glance at my watch and start adding up how much more we have to shoot tonight before we can call it quits.

Frank returns announcing that the second meal is ready. We don't normally have to break for another meal, but obviously, this is going to be one of many in a week of late nights. Frank protects his crew; that's why they love him. But he always does a fair and balanced job of looking out for the show, and the producer's pocketbooks as well, which is why he gets hired all the time. We both know the scene is at a critical point in filming. All the actors have to try and remember exactly how they moved and delivered their lines in that main version, so when we go back for close-ups and other tight shots, it will match. Therefore, now isn't the best place to stop.

Frank and I are both trying not to appear as if we are watching Craig and McCourt, but we are. The outcome of their conversation is pretty critical to all of us. When Craig smacks the director on the shoulder in the friendly but firm way that guys do when they're making a point, Frank and I slide a glance at each other and wait for McCourt to tell us the verdict.

Craig meets my eyes over McCourt's shoulder, winks at me, then disappears around the false rock walls that comprise the terrorists' hideout.

McCourt starts in as soon as Craig walks away. "This is why I hate TV. We're making a one-hour movie on a shoestring budget, but they expect it to look like the latest Spielberg blockbuster. You can't have it both ways."

Frank and I both nod in weary agreement. I'm pretty sure McCourt doesn't expect a reply. McCourt looks at the monitors that show the actors all still in position on set, and I can see his eyes refocus on the present.

"Maddy, was that last take clean? Did we get a good one?"

Sometimes you never get one perfect take, so you go into post-production knowing there's going to be a lot of editing and fixing to do. But every director would prefer to go in knowing there's something to fall back on. If you have one clean version of the scene, you know you can build from there. It's a safety net.

"Yeah, that last time was clean. I think the close-ups are going to get you better performances, and I know Victor wants to relight for Billy's angle, but we've got the shot." He's trying to be subtle, but I catch McCourt doing a fist pump. After all the extra time and work that went into getting that special angle, he needed it to work. I'm happy for him, but there's no time to celebrate. "So should we go in and get some of the close-ups you wanted?"

"Catering has the second meal set up for the crew. It's ready now." Frank's voice is low so the crew doesn't hear the announcement, or we might have a mutiny on our hands. He isn't telling the director what to do, but it's close.

"Some of that action is going to be hard to repeat as it is. We should try to get some of the close-up work done while it's still fresh in everyone's minds," I argue. Frank and I work well together, but sometimes our goals vary. He wants a happy crew; I want my shots to match.

"When do we go into meal penalty?" McCourt asks Frank.

Frank looks at the clock on his phone. "We could go another

eighteen minutes. We have to break them at eight." Lunchtime is no laughing matter; there are very specific union regulations about when the crew gets their meal breaks and stiff penalties that producers take very seriously before violating. It's not a lot of time, but I can think of two setups we can get done that will be critical. I glance at McCourt for the final decision, only to find him looking at me.

"What do you think, Maddy?"

I don't have time to feel flattered that at last he's asking my opinion. Before he even finishes his thought, I start talking. Eighteen minutes isn't much.

"Let's reset the cameras to their second position. I think we can get these two close-ups done if we go right now." I circle my script to show him what I'm thinking.

"Let's do it. Frank. Get people onto their marks for the second half of the scene. From Billy's line, 'We have to go now!' we'll take it to the end of the scene."

McCourt disappears after Frank to go over the plan with Victor and the camera team. I get my red pen out of my hair and start marking up my script with notes about the additional takes. Craig comes back to video village and takes a seat in his chair, sipping coffee. Still looking at the screen, he asks if we're breaking for dinner soon.

"Yeah," I say, not looking up. The audio guy is still at his station slightly behind my chair. "We'll break right at eight."

McCourt comes bounding around two set pieces and slides into his chair. Frank calls out, "We're rolling! Quiet on the set." And then McCourt bellows, "Camera!" prompting the cameras to start moving. A beat later, "Action!" I start my timer as Billy and the others come charging through the shot, and we're back in business. Seventeen minutes later, we have two of the pickup shots McCourt wanted, and Frank loudly dismisses everyone for the meal.

All of a sudden I'm starved. Maybe Craig and I can have some time to catch up over dinner. We've been so busy all week, let alone tonight, that we've barely had two seconds to talk. Those plans are quickly dashed as Craig tells me he is going to eat with McCourt since they have some "things to chat about." I feel for McCourt. Somehow I doubt an ass-chewing about cost overruns will complement his dinner.

"What time do you think crew call will be tomorrow?" Craig asks me. The crew always starts at least ten hours after they wrap (more union rules), so if we wrap at midnight, production can't start the next day until 10:00 at the earliest.

"We'll probably start at ten. I'm hoping."

"Do you want to grab breakfast with me? There's this place that looks good right by my club."

"Sure." Aside from the rare exception this morning, I'm not really a sleeping-in type anyway. "What time?"

"Let's say eight-thirty. I'll text you the address. But you know where Soho House is, right? It's right near there."

Soho House is a super-exclusive club on Sunset Boulevard. Lots of people in the entertainment industry are members. On any given night you can expect to see Leo DiCaprio there, Matt Damon, supermodels, and music legends. I've never been inside, but I've heard it's beautiful.

"Of course," I say as if I have been there a thousand times. "On Sunset, right?"

"Yep. I'll see you in the morning." We've gotten to the edge of the elephant doors that open wide enough to accommodate huge set pieces. Outside, catering is set up and all 200 crew members are gathered. In the shadow of the oversized doors, Craig leans down and kisses me briefly on the lips. It's nice and his lips are firm on mine, but the whole thing is over before I can process it.

"Oh hey," he calls back as he walks away. "Will you do me

a big favor? Will you check on Adam and see what we can do to make sure he's back by tomorrow? I don't want him feeling like we sent a PA and then ignored him. Make him feel HCP cares how he's doing, okay? We can't have any more delays."

This falls outside my job description, but I get why Craig asked.

I reluctantly grab my phone to text Adam. I don't even have to call the production office since his number is already conveniently in my phone. My pulse leaps as I reread his last text, which I didn't reply to but probably should have deleted altogether.

> Me: How are you feeling? Will you be back on set soon? Craig asked me to check in.

Seconds later my phone buzzes.

> AD: You're worried about me, huh? That's touching. Doc gave me a B-12 shot and I've been resting up. I'll be back tomorrow.

I sigh with relief. And then another text:

> AD: PS: If you made me some chicken soup, I know I would feel even better.

Well, if he's flirting, that's a good sign; he's going to be just fine. Several witty comebacks cross my mind, but I force myself to delete them all and go with the most innocuous thing I can.

> Me: Get lots of rest. See you soon.

Scene 011
Ext. Sidewalk café--day

___

I'm lucky enough to find a parking spot right in front of the café where I am meeting Craig, and I consider that a good omen for the day. We're in a fancy section of Sunset, lined with high-end boutiques where you can buy sunglasses for $800 and clothes by designers whose names I can't even pronounce. I didn't get much sleep again last night, but I did manage to put on lip gloss and an Anthropologie dress that I loved in the store window. I'm still not comfortable in a dress, but I figure it's like immersion therapy; maybe I'll become immune to it after a while.

A hostess ushers me to one of the prominent tables for two on the sidewalk with a perfect people-watching view. Craig is already sitting, looking at the menu, which turns out to be a perfect reflection of LA ideals—something for everyone, from Irish oatmeal, the sporty breakfast, to decadent-looking French toast (served with agave, so you can give the appropriate appearance of being health-conscious), to a wide variety of egg-white omelets and spelt toast for people who take their healthy eating very seriously. I order the egg sandwich because I'm in the none-of-the-above category.

While Craig orders his Greek yogurt with fresh cut (organic) fruit and granola (on the side), I check out his casual sweats and brand-new trendy sneakers, the type that will never actually see the inside of his gym. He's wearing a T-shirt Hogan gave to the crew as a wrap gift on his last big hit show, *The Warriors*.

The server heads off to place our orders as Craig puts his phone on silent and sets it screen side down on the table. "So, are you exhausted from last night?"

"It was definitely draining. That special camera operator we brought in to do the handheld work got quite a workout. I felt bad seeing him drenched in sweat the whole night."

"They're sending dailies to us today. Hogan and I are going to take a look later this morning. I can't wait to see what it looks like. McCourt seemed really excited."

I think about their chat during dinner last night. Whatever Craig said to McCourt really worked. We got through the last two scenes much faster than we had been moving all day.

"I talked to Adam last night and he's coming back today."

"Thanks, Maddy. That's a relief. We need to get back on track." Craig looks visibly relieved, as no doubt he and Hogan have calculated what Adam's missing any more time will do to the bottom line.

"He's got two really slammed days. Frank had to move all Adam's scenes to today and tomorrow." I wonder if Craig knows about McCourt's next gig, and how that affected us, but I decide not to say anything.

"Well, the upside is, we were forced to think out of the box and have something even better than we might have otherwise. I think we should keep exploring other angles like this for the season."

"I agree. It looked very cool. And I think the audience will respond to how we keep pushing the envelope, exploring new things." I feel a tug of pride that I was the original source of inspiration for the idea.

The waiter comes over with an individual French press for each of us. I try to remember how these things work so I don't look like a complete idiot.

When we're alone again, Craig asks about my trip home. "Was

your family thrilled to see you? How was the party?" He seems genuinely intrigued. I have to confess, I am flattered that he is taking such an interest in my hometown, my family.

"My mom had such a good party. Essentially the whole town was there."

I dig in my purse for my phone to show him a picture of me holding up my glass with about ten other people crowded in close. "Here's me giving my toast."

"Oh wow—who's that guy? That beard is something else." Craig zooms in on one of my parents' close friends.

"I think I mentioned him to you before. That's our neighbor, Walt Gordon. The one who stuffs the animals he hunts. Yeah, he takes the mountain man look very seriously."

Craig laughs. "Right. That story about your brothers sneaking up on you with one of the stuffed bears? That guy sounds like such a character." And he is. In the picture he's holding up his beer mug, so you can see his gut appearing out from underneath his shirt, which says, "GOT MEAT?"

"Next to him is Blaine. He runs the fish and game store on Main. He can literally talk about fishing and the right tackle and bait for hours. All day. One time, Matthew lost a bet to me and Mike, and his penalty was he had to ask Blaine questions about different kinds of bait and lures and listen until Blaine was done talking. The rule was that Matthew couldn't walk away; Blaine had to be the one to end the conversation. Matthew was in that shop from about three p.m. until it closed. It was brutal. What he didn't know was that my older brother Mike hung out in the parking lot all afternoon, keeping any other customers from going in to distract Blaine."

I can't help but laugh, remembering Matthew's misery. Craig laughs with me, still looking at the picture.

"I think there are more pictures; you can scroll forward."

Craig flicks through and settles on one I took at the campfire.

"This looks like something out of an L.L.Bean catalogue. Is that for real?"

I had used an app on my phone to make the photo seem vintage. That picture is everything I love about Wolf County.

"Yep, it was such a great night." I sigh, remembering. Was that only two days ago?

Craig hands me back my phone and tells me about his weekend, the speakers' tour he attended at the Directors Guild, the networking lunch he had at the Polo Lounge, and what celebrities were there.

When the waiter arrives with the check, Craig announces sort of abruptly, "There's something I want to talk to you about, Maddy."

Why do those words always sound ominous? Within seconds, I have mentally scanned through a list of work things that could be an issue (the cost overruns on the set design, the fact that we haven't secured a location for the finale shoot). Then just as quickly, I go through a list of personal reasons (he's seeing someone else, he's breaking up with me). God, it's schizophrenic dating your boss. While I wait with anticipation, the waiter comes over to pick up the check and starts chatting with Craig, who is clearly a regular. Needing something to do while I wait for this talk, I rummage through my purse to pull out my wallet, knowing very well Craig would never let me pay.

"Don't be silly," Craig says, handing the waiter his corporate American Express card. "In fact, HCP is paying for our breakfast this morning."

"Really?" Well, then whatever he wants to discuss is work-related. For a split second, I have a complete visual of Craig offering me a raise or a promotion. Or both...

"It's legitimate...I can see you already planning to call the IRS on me." Craig laughs and then pauses and takes a deep breath. "I have an idea, Maddy. A good one."

I wait, intrigued by his enthusiasm, as the busboy takes our plates away.

Craig leans in. "As you know, things are a little dicey at HCP right now, with the staffing changes. I really want to help Hogan see the company to the next level...to expand our footprint."

I have no idea where this is going.

"I think HCP should get into reality TV."

I stare at him. That was not what I expected.

"Just think about it. What people want to see is reality, right now. I think it would make HCP a mint."

As much as I am flattered if confused by why Craig is confiding in me, it occurs to me right away that I don't think Hogan will go for it.

"Have you talked to Hogan about this? I mean, HCP doesn't do any reality." Since Craig still doesn't know about my relationship with Hogan, I leave out the part where Hogan called the Kardashians the *Kartrashians* over dinner last month and gave me a hard time for watching *Housewives of OC*. I think he may have even referred to reality TV as "evil" and an "assault to the medium."

"Leave Hogan to me. I just want to know you're on my side," Craig says as we make our way around the tables to the parking lot in the back. "Let's talk about it this weekend. Okay? There's a lot of upside to this." He kisses me quickly on the lips when we get to the street and jogs to his car.

"Think about it, Maddy," he says as he slides into the driver seat. How can I not? It's all I'm thinking about as I walk back to my car. But not just reality TV in general—a very specific show. The stories I told Craig today barely scratch the surface of the uniqueness that is Wolf County, California. The town has what all the best reality shows offer: drama, great characters, a stunning backdrop, all wrapped up in one. I don't know what Craig had in mind, but this seems like it would be a perfect project if HCP decides to explore reality. I don't start the engine right away. I sit staring straight through the busy Sunset traffic, seeing only what a little publicity and business could do for my parents, for everyone in Wolf. This won't be an easy sell to them either. The people in Wolf aren't exactly the types to crave their fifteen seconds of fame, or whatever. I try to imagine pitching my brothers and Brian the idea.

> BRIAN
> (always ready to be helpful)
> I bet some people would really get excited about
> the idea, Mad...Lily & I will do it.

> MIKE
> (a definite pragmatist)
> It would be a great source of income; not just the
> fees, but the crew in town while we shoot would
> totally boost the local economy. What would Dad say?

> DAD
> (can always argue both sides)
> It would put your town on the map, wouldn't it,
> just. But I'd be like a kitten in a room full of
> rocking chairs, that's for damn sure.

> ME
> It would mean tons of attention and PR...and
> tourism, Daddy. That's a big plus, right?

Given my parents' situation, the economic argument is very persuasive and the timing uncanny. Could this be the saving grace Wolf needs? But I don't want to get my hopes up, or my parents', because a reality show about Wolf seems like a long shot for so many reasons. Or as my dad would say, "About as likely as finding a penguin in a pickle patch."

Act Two

Scene 001
Int. studio set--day

"Anybody seen Scripty?" My ears perk up. Great, now I'm actually responding to Adam's new nickname for me. It's not really annoying yet, but he changes his lines too much for it to be endearing. I look up from my list of pickup shots we're going to need to make the complicated chase scene we're working on today. It's a challenge since it's very windy, making my hair and notebook pages fly around. The location managers found us this fantastic stretch of highway out near Lancaster that is doubling as our Middle East desert road. The CHP officers have shut down traffic while we are filming, but given the number of vehicles and camera angles and speed, it's tricky to get everything right—which is why I am making note after note to track the shots we need:

1. cut-away of Lucas's hands grabbing the gun (use Billy? Or hand double?)
2. wheels skidding (burning rubber) close-up
3. close-up of legs running, turning corners
4. pedestrian/bystander reactions and POV shots

"Over here, Adam." I wave from my director's chair in the makeshift outdoor tent we have set up.

Adam's face is smeared with dirt and fake blood from our last scene. He's still adjusting the fake AK-47 he has strapped over his shoulder as he comes over.

"Maddy. Good. I need your help."

"Are you going to shoot me if I don't?" Did I really just make that lame joke?

He looks confused for a second and then looks down at his gun. "Ha-ha, well, I might take you prisoner."

Okay, I set myself up for that one. Time to get back to business.

"Okay, really, what's up?" I ask with not a little dread in my voice.

"When we started the fight scene with Billy yesterday morning, I was wearing this jacket and it was unbuttoned. But in all the sequences we're shooting this morning they're saying they want it buttoned. I told Molly it's not going to match, but they had a set photo that showed it was buttoned. I know I remember it being unbuttoned. I was hoping you could check your notes from yesterday so that we match it properly today."

I glance over at Molly, the head of wardrobe, who is paging through a huge notebook, which I recognize as the Costumes continuity folder. It has a ton of pictures and pages of notes keeping track of every character's outfit in each scene. Because we shoot out of order so much, the only way to keep track of the details is to be extremely meticulous about it. So far, this wardrobe department has been pretty accurate.

"Okay, let me take a look," I say with an internal groan, and get out my own notebook, which gives Molly's a run in terms of size.

"What was that look?"

I should've known Adam is too quick to let me get away with that.

"Nothing," I say dismissively.

"That was an eye-roll. I saw it." He doesn't seem offended. In fact, he seems slightly gleeful for having caught me out. "You don't believe me, huh?"

Well, really, it's the look I have on my face when actors start confidently spouting off about stuff they should really butt out of. But, of course, I choose not to tell him that and instead I flip through my notes from yesterday and start examining all the pictures I took of each scene. Adam steps up next to me and leans over my shoulder to look too.

"See there," he says right at my ear, and points to a picture of himself standing next to Billy talking to the director about the stunts they were about to do. His jacket is unbuttoned.

"Yeah, your jacket was definitely unbuttoned when we were rehearsing. But look here..." I flip the page to the photos I took of the monitors as they were actually shooting the scene. In every frame, Adam's jacket is most definitely buttoned.

I look up at him and he is still hovering so close that I can pick up the distinct scent of his aftershave. It's definitely aftershave, not cologne. It's kind of musky and clean-smelling. It distracts me for a second from confronting the next awkward moment— telling Adam he's wrong. Sometimes actors don't take that very well. Is this that moment when I'm going to have to massage his ego? Or worse, even in the face of evidence proving he's wrong, will he continue to insist he is right? (That happens more than you'd think.) But when I look into Adam's face, his eyes immediately connect with mine with a chagrined smirk.

"Oops. I must still have a muddled brain from that flu. My bad. Thanks for keeping such good notes, Scripty." He squeezes my shoulder, and I can't even try to pretend to be annoyed or offended. Why am I such a girl around him? My stage direction should read:

Cut to: close-up on Maddy, twirling her suddenly bleached blond hair while popping bubble gum.

"That's what I'm here for, Ahmed." Calling him by his character's name as he walks back to the trailers is a tiny retaliation, but his laugh as he disappears around the corner says he appreciates the effort, which makes me smile.

As soon as Adam walks off, Frank comes over and announces we're going to break for lunch early so that the lighting team can get set up. We want to start the afternoon earlier in order to have more time to take advantage of the bright afternoon sun. I grab my usual from the catering truck and sit at the tables set up under a tent alongside the road. My phone makes no noise when it lights up, signaling an incoming call. I see that it's Craig and answer as I swallow a big leafy bite. Multitasking at its finest.

"Hey, Craig. What's going on?" I scoop up another forkful of salad, trying to chew silently so he can't hear me eating while we talk. I know it's so rude and I would love to say that I don't normally do this, but I do. It's always so busy, I have to seize this break to get a good meal. Otherwise I'm a wreck the rest of the day.

"Are you on set?"

"No, we just broke for lunch."

"Oh, great. How'd the morning go?" he asks, all business.

"Good. I was just saying to Frank, I think this chase sequence is going to cut together well. It's really intense, even just the pieces we're doing. I think it's going to look awesome."

"Great. So I have some news for you," Craig says coyly.

"Oh, really? Does it have anything to do with your meeting with Hogan this morning? Spill."

"Well, I'll give you a hint now if you promise to come over for dinner tonight so I can tell you the whole thing. Deal?"

"Deal. Let's hear it."

"Let's just say it involves travel north."

"That's a clue? What does that even mean? Wait—is it about Wolf?"

After giving it some more thought and talking about it with Brian, I had decided to pitch Craig a reality show about Wolf. I e-mailed him a summary of my idea last night. I still don't think Hogan will ever go for it, but if Craig wants to do a reality TV show, why not Wolf? Could Craig have already gone to Hogan with the idea?

"You'll see. Gotta run. See you tonight!"

As intrigued as I am, I have no time to focus on reality TV, when the reality of the afternoon's shoot is kicking my ass.

The lighting team is falling behind schedule, so our thirty-minute lunch break has stretched to an hour and a half. As I pace uselessly, I watch another piece of lighting equipment get shoved into the "bad guys'" truck. I have no skills in light design and nothing but hero worship for what Victor can create with lights and shadows, but we are really falling behind schedule. We have to get going here.

"Maddy." Billy appears from behind a false backdrop. "Frank told me it's going to be at least another thirty. I'm sending a runner for some coffee. You want?" He grabs his phone, sunglasses, and sides from the pocket of his chair.

"I think I'm going to need it," I say, resigning myself to the long hours ahead. "A double-shot cappuccino, please."

"You got it." Billy disappears.

My spiral notebook is calling my name as I sit down. I've finished all the bookkeeping I can do on the scenes we shot this morning. And I can't really do anything until the director tells me we're back on track. So I don't really feel guilty as I flip to the pages where I've written my notes on the Wolf County reality show idea.

I figure I might as well be prepared if we're going to discuss it tonight. Ever since I drafted up the official pitch, I've even been mulling over the details, who and what story lines could be good.

The Gordons, who live next door to my parents, would be perfect with their kooky taxidermy-in-the-garage thing. It's TV gold. My brother's team of blasters and ski instructors are perfect for the young/hot/single guys and girls aspect. And, of course, there's how everyone is being affected by the economy. So that's three different story lines to focus on. It's balanced, compelling, and something for everyone. I start imagining how the pilot episode might shape up.

Act 1: Introduce my parents, show the mountain, the skiers having fun, the glamorous side of a ski resort town. Then, the camera zooms past the glitz and happy kids in a ski class all the way to the back office where my dad is slaving away on his computer trying to balance the budget. He discusses the finances with my mom and brother, admitting the make-or-break season we are facing. This winter has to work.

Act 2: Follow my brother back outside to the ski school. Listen in on a lunchtime meeting with the instructors. Perhaps the introduction of a few new employees gives the audience a fresh perspective/viewpoint on what life in Wolf County is like? Mike ends the meeting with the quick announcement that no snow is expected tonight (groans from crew).

Act 3: Introduce the Gordons. Perhaps show Mom and Dad going there for dinner? Social time in Wolf County? Cut between their adult dinner and the kids out on the town drinking at the Pub & Pizza? Show the dynamic between locals and the townies who come up for vacation...

"Maddy!" I jump about a foot out of my chair and look up from my notes to see Adam with a Starbucks cup in each hand. "I've been calling your name. You were a million miles away. PA's

back with coffee. It's not a fruity cocktail, but it'll have to do. "
He hands me one of the cups and sits down in the director's chair
next to mine.

"Oh, I..." I think about explaining that I'm actually not a
fruity-cocktail-type girl, but I don't know...I think I'm starting
to like the girl Adam seems to think I am. "Sorry, I didn't hear
you. I was just working on a...project."

"Something top secret? I promise not to tell anyone."

"It's not top secret. It's just...well, I don't know. I haven't
really talked about it yet."

"Okay," Adam says agreeably. He takes a sip of his coffee, making no move to leave. "Oh, I forgot." He stands and pulls a variety of
sweeteners out of his pocket. "I wasn't sure which you preferred,
so I grabbed them all." He's not kidding. Splenda, Equal, sugar, raw
sugar, and a packet of honey are all displayed on his palm.

"Thanks," I murmur, self-conscious all of a sudden for some
reason. I take a packet of raw sugar and begin fixing my drink.
He seems perfectly comfortable sitting in the silence next to me,
but I have to fill it.

"Was that your girlfriend on set yesterday? She seemed nice."
Truthfully, she didn't really talk to anyone on the crew. I offered
her a headset so she could listen to the dialogue in the scene as
she watched the monitors, but she just sat there watching impas-
sively. She didn't seem interested in interacting with any of us.

"Did she really seem nice? She's not." From his position in the
chair next to me, I can see a half-grin on his face.

"If you don't think she's nice, why are you dating her?"

"I didn't say I was *dating* her." There is a slight emphasis on
the word "dating."

"Okay, whatever." Playing word games with Adam Devin does
not seem like a wise idea. Better to nip this in the bud now. But
as usual, Adam reads my reserve the way a bull sees a red flag.

"I'm just teasing you, Scripty. She's my agent's daughter. She just graduated from NYU and was here to check out what Hollywood is all about. I was just playing host."

"Ahh," I reply as politely careless as possible.

"Did she ask you anything about production? I told her not to hesitate if she had questions."

"Nope, but I would have been happy to tell her everything she ever wanted to know about the glamorous role of a script supervisor." I smile. "Actually, I didn't see her talk to anyone."

"Yeah, that's what I figured." Adam takes a sip of his latte. I can't help but look at the side of the cup to see if there are complicated markings indicating his picky drink choice. But there's just his name and a smiley face. Guess the barista was a fan.

"What do you mean?" I ask, genuinely curious.

"Well, I try not to make snap judgments about people, but I got the vibe pretty quickly that she's not up to the task of actual work. Even TV work." That makes me laugh. Most of us who work in TV forget how lucky we are to get to call what we do "work."

"You call that a 'snap judgment.' I call it a 'first impression.' And I find they're usually right on."

"Yeah, I guess. So what was your first impression of me, then?" He grins from ear to ear.

Is he fishing for compliments? *Keep it professional, Maddy.*

"Well, truthfully, I was impressed that you arrived right on time. Punctuality and professionalism are big in my book."

"So, not my abs, then?" He laughs and I surprise myself by joining him.

"I could stand for you to be more accurate with your dialogue." Hey, if he's really looking for honesty . . .

"I always know my lines, Maddy. Come on, you know that. What's the big deal, a word here or there?"

"I'm not saying you're not prepared. I know you are; it's just...it's supposed to be exact, you know. I'm sure the writers would appreciate it if it were word for word."

"It's not like I'm rewriting the script. Sometimes in the moment, things happen. Don't you think it's important to go with the flow sometimes too?"

I wouldn't describe myself as a "go with the flow" type of person, so I really don't know how to answer that. "I guess I see what you mean," I say vaguely.

"I don't know, so far you seem a very by-the-numbers type of person, Scripty. But I like you anyway."

His voice is teasing, but I still have no idea how to respond to that. Panic sets in at the awkward silence. Adam seems totally comfortable, though. I am about to reach for my phone or notebook to fake a distraction when he turns toward me.

"Did you always know you wanted to work in the industry?" He makes exaggerated air quotes. A little thrown by the direct question, I shift in my chair to look at him more fully and I see that he has already done the same. His steady gaze seems sincere, prompting me to answer honestly. I tell him a very abridged version of how I ended up here, glossing over the connection to Hogan. He seems genuinely interested, asking questions, so I end up telling some of my favorite war stories.

"What about you? Was *Days* your first role?" Turning the tables gets me out of the hot seat, and I'm actually curious to hear Adam's backstory.

"Nah, I sort of fell into this career. My parents were pretty disappointed when I told them I wanted to try acting. I was on this fast track to becoming a lawyer, joining my dad's law firm in New York. He still thinks someday I'm going to wake up and get a 'real job.'" Adam laughs, but this time there's a definite edge.

"I don't know how long I would've hung in trying, and I guess I'll never know. I got a couple commercials right out of the gate and then booked *Days*," Adam says modestly.

"And the rest is history."

"Exactly. Well, it's the present anyway. And that's how I like it."

"Living in the present?" I think about how much time I spend mentally making lists of all the things I need to do and remember to do in the future, whether it's five minutes from now, next week, or next month. *I should try living in the moment,* I think. And then can't help but laugh at the thought.

"What's funny?"

"Oh just the thought of me 'being in the moment.' I wouldn't last five minutes without trying to plan something," I confess.

"Well, Maddy. Like with the ad-libbing, I guess we'll have to work on that." Adam looks directly into my eyes again. This guy is not shy about eye contact. "This moment may be all we have. All we'll ever have. I don't know about you, but I don't want to spend the rest of my life wondering 'what if?'"

It takes me several seconds to pull myself together. Is he for real?

"Wow...you're good." I give a little chuckle. "All that training in daytime TV. Do your girlfriends expect you to be like that in real life? Endlessly sweeping them off their feet with perfect lines and romantic moments?"

Adam laughs. "Well, some have, I guess. Maybe that's why I'm single." More heart-fluttering eye contact. "I'm more your laid-back romantic, I guess. I think sincere, thoughtful gestures can be better than expensive flashy ones."

"Unless 'laid-back' is just code for classic guy laziness."

"Could be. To me, a romance is about knowing her so well that you know that she'd rather find a handwritten note tied to the tree she always rests on during her morning hike than some meaningless expensive jewelry bought last minute because Facebook reminded him it's her birthday."

Even though his tone is casual, I have to get up to shake off the absurd fantasies now running around my imagination. My excuse is taking my empty coffee cup to the industrial trash can behind the audio equipment.

"Do you mind if I steal that idea for the guy I'm seeing?" I chuckle, but even to my ears it sounds a little forced. Again, I wish I had a writer helping me with this conversation. I've waited too long to bring up that I'm seeing someone. I wonder if Billy has spilled the beans even though I told him that, for now, Craig and I are still trying to be as discreet as possible on set.

"I didn't know you have a boyfriend."

"Oh, well...he's not officially my 'boyfriend.'" What am I, fifteen? "It's actually new...very new, and still casual...but you know, it's fun." I force myself to stop stammering as Adam looks at me for what feels like a full minute before he speaks.

"Hmmm. You don't seem like someone swept away in a brandnew relationship." Adam gets up, too, and tosses his with mine.

"What is that supposed to mean?" I can't decide if I'm more defensive or curious about this observation.

"Nothing at all. Never mind. I didn't mean to offend you."

"You didn't." But in fact, what he says stings a little.

"Good. I'm happy I've gotten to know you a little better, Maddy. I'd better go get touched up." His hand is warm on my shoulder as he gives a squeeze and heads toward the makeup trailer. Now that he's gone, I notice that everyone on the set seems to be moving more quickly. Frank hollers, "Picture's up!" and it's time to get back to work.

Scene 002
Ext. Craig's front door--evening

It's after 9:00 p.m. when I knock on Craig's door. I haven't even
had time to change from my work clothes. When he'd invited me
for dinner, I had imagined having the chance to put on a dress
and maybe even some makeup, but after that lighting debacle, we
ended up jamming through the rest of the material. So now I'm
starving and ready for a home-cooked meal.

Craig gallantly, or wisely (or both), has a glass of wine for me
when he opens the door.

"What a day! I heard about the issues on set. You must be
exhausted."

"Thanks so much." I take a sip of the chilled white wine. "This
is delicious."

"Glad you like it. It's from my favorite vineyard up in Napa.
They have the most gorgeous tasting room. We shot on location
there once, and of course I needed to visit the set, for some very
important reason," Craig teases as he ushers me into the dining
room.

"Wow, this looks beautiful." The table has been set like we're
having a four-course meal. It looks very formal and like it took a
long time to set up. My worn Chuck Taylors look even more out of
place. Would it have killed me to throw on some lip gloss? "I'm so
sorry you did all this and I'm so late. I didn't mean for you to go
to so much trouble."

"It's no trouble at all. I wanted to do it. You know I love to cook.

And I had my housekeeper stay and set the table. She wanted it to be very special for us. I told her we're celebrating."

I pause before taking another sip of wine. "We are? What are we celebrating?"

"I was going to wait to tell you, but I just can't... You and I are going to develop a full pitch and sizzle reel for Wolf County! Isn't that fantastic?!" He holds up his wineglass and clinks it with mine.

"Really? How did you manage to get the go-ahead that fast? I really didn't think Hogan would go for it."

"The thing is, Hogan can't keep his head in the sand forever. He has to stay current, up with the times. And he knows it. That's why he hired me to run HCP, not just the day-to-day stuff. He wants me thinking big picture."

"I just thought he wanted to focus on his writing. Hasn't HCP traditionally stuck to just one show at a time? I've never really even heard him talk about watching reality TV." Again, I don't mention that when it comes to reality TV, Hogan has used the words "Never. Nope. No way." But I suppose it's completely possible that he's changed his mind.

"You sound like you wanted him to turn us down."

"No, I don't mean it like that at all. When I pitched you the idea, I guess I didn't realize it would happen so fast. I mean, I haven't even really talked to my parents, or anyone else in town about it yet."

"Oh, don't worry about that. It's probably better that you haven't done that yet. We can tell them together." It doesn't even register right away how quickly Craig has latched on to this idea, but every time I think about how it could help my parents, and the town, I'm more excited about it. I decide to let the "we" and "us" stuff go, for now. "In fact, I was making a breakdown today of what the pilot episode could be about," I say.

"I'm so glad you're excited about it. Keep in mind it'll have to be down and dirty. We won't have a big budget for this," Craig warns me.

"Well, it isn't about high production value. It's about the people, and how hard they're working to keep the town alive. But we're going to need some budget to get going. I mean, we'd have to stay competitive against the other shows that look glossy. What kind of numbers did you give Hogan?"

"No specific number. It's a little preliminary for that. I'm just warning you that we'll have to be conservative as we map out our concept."

"To be honest, Craig, as exciting as this is, the whole idea does make me a little nervous." I put down my fork. "This is my hometown, and it's really important to me that you take that seriously. Invest in doing it right, committing to it." I continue before he can say anything else. "I understand that the show has to make money; it's a business. I get it, *but* it also has to be real, and true to what Wolf County is all about. That's all. I don't want it to turn into some reality train wreck. These people are my family, my home. They matter to me."

Craig puts his hand on top of mine and meets my eyes. "I totally understand how important this is to you, Maddy. And that's what's going to make the show so successful. I know you have a vision for it, and you are the heart of the pitch. It's exactly this passion and enthusiasm that's going to get it sold. And for what it's worth, I agree. We don't need to manufacture drama; it's all right there. Good, hardworking people dealing with the realities of this difficult economy, just like everyone else in this country. It's going to be amazing." He is smiling so hard, he can barely eat the delicious coq au vin he made.

"Is it too soon to ask if I'd get a screen credit?" His enthusiasm is contagious. I picture my parents' reaction to EXECUTIVE PRODUCER——MADELYN CARSON rolling across their screens. They would flip out.

"Nice one, Maddy." Craig's knowing glance somehow rubs me the wrong way. "I'm sure we can get you a 'created by' or something in the tail credits. But first, we've got to find the perfect person to be executive producer. Don't worry, it'll be in good hands. And in the meantime, you and I can do a great job putting together a pitch that will knock everyone's socks off."

As we start hashing out details, my wariness fades to the background. This could be really fun, and Hogan would be so proud that he gave me a chance way back when. Speaking of Hogan, this is a good opportunity to finally mention our connection to Craig. I am about to do so when he abruptly jumps up from the table, announcing he'll be right back. He returns two minutes later with a printout of our reservations for a trip to Wolf County. In three days.

"Craig, this is crazy. We can't go to Wolf in three days."

"There's no time like the present. We have to get up there and get everything sorted out. I'm going to bring my Canon 7D to take some great sample footage for the sizzle reel to show Hogan by next week. I've told you how crazy things have been at HCP. The only way to ensure job security is to have a new show green-lit this development season. Wolf County is it—I can feel it. Hogan and I are meeting next Tuesday morning, and I want to have something to show him to get excited."

"But, Craig, I don't see how that's even possible!"

"We can do this, Maddy. And besides, I can't wait to see where you come from and meet your family. Won't they be excited to meet me too?"

"Um, yes, of course." I'm sure that the universe will forgive me for this little white lie. I'm sure that if my family actually knew he existed, they would be excited. So now I have to introduce my family to the guy I am dating, who is also my boss, sell them on a reality show, and put together a sizzle reel that's going to impress Craig... and save Wolf County.

No problem.

Scene 003
Int. Maddy's car--morning

Well, here goes nothing.

If Craig and I are going to head to Wolf County this weekend, I have to tell my parents. I don't know why I'm so anxious about this. Oh wait, yes I do: one, they have no idea that I am dating my boss; two, I haven't brought a guy home since, well...Brian; and three, we're going to try to sell them on the idea of cameras following their friends and family everywhere for national TV. Oh God.

They are going to be full of questions. Which is why I'm calling now, fifteen minutes before I arrive at the set, so I'll have to hop off the phone. Not the best evasion strategy in the world, but it's all I've got right now.

The phone rings and I hear my dad's booming voice. "Maddy? Is that you?"

Who else would be calling from my number? But Dad doesn't trust the caller ID.

Seconds later my mom picks up a different line. "Hi, Maddy!"

"Hi, Mom. Oh good, both of you are there. Guess what?"

"What, dear?" they say in unison, which makes me smile.

"I'm headed back up to Wolf this weekend!"

"You are? That's great, but you were just here. What's going on?"

"Well, actually I am bringing...a coworker...a friend. It's sort of a business trip...."

Pull it together, Maddy.

"Oh, okay," Mom says.

I can just see their confused glances across the living room.

"Look, we're going to explain everything when we get there. It's actually very exciting. But I want Craig to explain."

"Craig is your...friend?"

"Well, yeah...actually we've been seeing each other."

"Madelyn Rose Carson! We had no idea you had a boyfriend. How long has this been going on? Why on earth haven't you mentioned him?" I can hear the hurt in her voice.

That's a very good question. Why haven't I mentioned Craig?

"Whoa, Mom. He's not my boyfriend. It's really new actually. And this is more of a work trip anyway. There's a project we're working on...about Wolf. We want to talk to you about it in person, and Craig wants to tour the town."

"Wait, you and Craig work together? You're dating someone in the company? You know that's about as smart as bringing strawberries into a bear cage, right?"

Yup, my dad loves skipping right to the bottom line.

Luckily, by this point I've pulled into the studio lot, but something tells me I'm not going to be able to hop off the phone. I stop the engine and take a deep breath.

"Well, it sort of just happened, guys. I didn't plan on it. He's not an actor or anything. You'll like him. He works with Hogan directly. One of the suits."

I assume this will allay her concerns, but again, she doesn't miss a thing.

"He works directly with Hogan? Madelyn Rose. Does that mean you are dating your boss?!"

Suddenly, I jump a mile high as someone knocks very loudly on my car window. I look up and see Adam's beaming smile through the glass. How does this guy seem to pop up out of nowhere all the time? I point to my earpiece to let him know I'm on the phone, but he does provide a perfect excuse.

"Look, Mom, it's all good. Please don't be weird about this when we get there. I'll explain everything. I'm so excited to see you again, but I gotta go. I just pulled into the office and one of my coworkers needs me." Adam is now leaning against my car. The top of his well-defined backside is right at my eye level through the window.

There's a pause as if neither of them is quite ready to let this go. Dad finally says, "Okay, we'll see you this weekend." And Mom adds, "We'll make up the guest room for Craig." A not-so-subtle hint that we will not be sharing a room. I can't help but laugh as I get out of the car.

"Your boyfriend say something funny?" Adam asks.

"Not that it's any of your business, but I was talking to my parents." I grab my notebook, my bag, and my coffee cup and take off with a purposeful stride. Adam's long legs allow him to catch up to me without even exerting himself.

"You in a hurry?"

"Well, I'm late, actually." Meaning, of course, that I am only three minutes early. "I have to get a lot done since I'm going out of town." I am not sure why I feel the need to share this and invite the inevitable follow-up question.

"Oh really, big weekend plans?"

I hesitate for a second. "Just going to visit my family."

"Ahhh." Adam makes a knowing, sympathetic sound.

"No, it's fine. I love my family. They're awesome. But it was a little last-minute and I'm sure they'll have a million things planned for . . . me." I almost slipped and said "us." I know Adam won't be shy about asking more about "us," and I don't want to invite any more questions about my love life.

"So how about next week we go get that drink you owe me,

and you can tell me all about them." I look up at Adam, wondering if his persistence is impressive or annoying, and I completely forget to look where I'm going. Which is why I trip over the big yellow speed bump that has always been there, that I have seen and treaded over carefully with no problems for years. But today, in front of Adam Devin, I trip right over it. My JanSport backpack wasn't fully zipped and it flies out of my hands, papers skidding everywhere. I would have gone sprawling after them if not for Adam's quick reflexes. He catches me by the waist and pulls me in to him, steadying me against his chest.

"Are you okay?"

"Yeah, I'm fine. Thanks." The less said on my end, the better. I can feel the redness of embarrassment heating my neck and flushing my cheeks. There is no way I'm looking up at him from this proximity. I'm no geometry expert, but that angle would lead to nothing but trouble. Not that my nose pressed into his chest inhaling his clean soap scent is necessarily better for my equilibrium.

Adam gives me a slight squeeze and then sets me loose. "You're sure you're okay?"

I'm standing there like those kids in ski school who are slightly dazed after their first high-speed run down the mountain.

"Oh, yeah...you know, thought you'd wanna see a demonstration of gravity," I mutter to give myself a second to recover from the head rush. I watch him picking up my papers, stuffing them back into the bag.

"Ha! I know that movie..." He thinks for a second. "*Real Genius*, right? Val Kilmer?" He grabs my spiral notebook and that snaps me out of it.

"That's the one." I'm so busy collecting my stuff from him, starting with that notebook, that I don't really appreciate his movie trivia skills as much as I should. The last thing I need is for him to see any of my lists. "Thanks, I got this."

"No problem." He smiles, handing me my stuff. "So, next week? We can go near here if you want. I'd love to get you down to Venice. There's this awesome café that looks out over the water. But that's too much of a drive after work."

I think it's his assumption that I will say yes, even though I've been clear that I am not available, and that helps me find my backbone. This is a man who clearly isn't used to taking no for an answer. "Well, first, we don't know that you actually won the bet, so I don't owe you a drink. And anyway, Adam, I'm not sure it's a good idea for us to get a drink together. I wouldn't want anyone to misunderstand, thinking that it was a date or something."

"Why can't it be a date?" Adam says with that same confident smirk on his face that I have seen so many times in close-up shots during filming.

"Because (A) I don't date actors; (B) I'm definitely not breaking rule A for you; and (C) I already told you, I'm seeing someone." That came out a little bitchier than I had intended, but his arrogant assumption that women everywhere will fall all over themselves for him gets under my skin. You're barking up the wrong tree here, buddy.

"Interesting rules you've got there." Adam's smirk stays in place as he looks me up and down. "A and B have got to go. C... well, that's fair, but you did say it was casual, right?"

Did I? I don't even remember. I guess it's not a total lie. Then again, Craig is meeting my entire family in twenty-four hours. But since I haven't come up with a witty reply, I wait for Adam to fill the silence.

"This isn't just some game to me, Maddy," he says, as if reading my mind. He seems more serious, and I can hear the New

Yorker twang in his voice. "I dig you. I respect that you're seeing someone. Lucky guy. But I know you won't regret giving me a chance."

He grabs my hand and squeezes it before he strolls off toward his trailer. It was totally innocent, but I still frantically look around to see who may have been looking. It would have been exactly like a scene from a soap opera, except that he's serious. I let out the breath I didn't know I was holding. He raises his hand in a backward wave but keeps walking. Which tells me two things: one, I'm still watching him walk away, and two, he knows I'm still watching. *Damn it.*

As if things couldn't get more complicated, I am barely through the door to the studio when my phone buzzes with an e-mail from Hogan's assistant, Hudson, wanting to schedule a dinner with Hogan in two weeks. I don't see how I can go for an entire meal without fessing up to Hogan that I've been dating Craig. But first, I'll have to tell Craig about Hogan. And even before that, I have to get through this insanely busy day and a weekend in Wolf with Craig. I take a big deep breath and e-mail him back confirming that, yes, Thursday the 13th works for me. Then I take another breath and head to set.

Scene 004
Int. Maddy's living room--morning

Craig's text sets off "La Cucaracha" (I have got to figure out how to change these alerts!) to let me know he's outside at 5:30 the next morning. Having been packed and ready to go for thirty minutes, I was sitting on the couch taking deep breaths to calm my anxieties about the weekend. Matthew's 3:00 a.m. text didn't help:

> Matthew: I can't believe you're bringing your booooooyfriend up the one weekend I'm out of commission. Was that on purpose? I gotta meet this guy. DO NOT leave town before I see him. In the meantime Mike knows what to do.

I feel like a bad sister that I totally forgot that Matthew is doing a twenty-four-hour relay mountain bike ride for charity this weekend. But part of me is relieved that it won't be two on one with my brothers and Craig all weekend.

> Me: Don't worry, bro. I'll be at the finish line ... with Craig. Go easy!

I really don't know what my brothers are going to make of Craig, and vice versa. All I keep picturing when I see Craig in Wolf is something akin to Billy Crystal in *City Slickers*. Or that John Candy traipsing terrified through the woods in *The Great Outdoors*. My first clue was how fascinated he was about our garbage rules, which I happened to mention last night when he called to ask if he should pack his summer blazer for dinner. Answer: no.

Start close-up on Craig's hand nervously tugging at the Armani tie, cut wide to show him pacing back and forth across the same strip of carpet in his office.

CRAIG

What do you mean they don't collect your garbage at your house?

MADDY

Well, we can't leave our trash out on the street like you can in LA. The bears will come scavenge it.

CRAIG

Bears????

MADDY:

(patiently)

Yes, Craig. Bears. They don't really hurt people unless they feel threatened, but you don't want to encourage them to hang around the neighborhood.

CRAIG

Will I see a bear? Should I go buy bear spray?

MADDY

Usually they stay away from people.

CRAIG

(covering his disappointment)

Oh. Okay.

Seriously, if a bear doesn't try to maul him, he'll be heartbroken. Of course, in Craig's head it's just a stunt. I can imagine he thinks if things get too scary, he could just yell, "Cut!" or perhaps e-mail someone in the stunt department, and the bear will immediately take five.

As I gather my bags and head to the car, I laugh out loud, imagining the visual of Craig raising up one finger to a big mama bear because he's got an incoming call. Sure enough, even though it's not even 6:00 a.m., he's talking animatedly into his Bluetooth as I get in the car. As he leans over to kiss me, I also get an earful about the promotions campaign surrounding the new season of *The Wrong Doctor*. National billboards and media buys in local markets. I've seen the pictures of Billy and Adam that will appear on those billboards, and let's just say, I think it will be an effective campaign.

Craig arranged for us to catch a commuter flight up to Fresno, and then we're renting a car for the forty-five-minute drive up the mountain. As much as I'm starting to get into seeing Craig, and I like talking to him—especially when we find topics outside of Hogan and the company to talk about—I don't know if I could handle a five-plus-hour driving trip with him. Or anyone, for that matter. I love the drive when I'm by myself, listening to music with the scenery whizzing by. Besides, I would rather not stew for five hours anticipating my parents' reactions. A quick flight will be so much better.

We get to the Burbank airport for the 8:15 flight and, thank you, Southwest, we're taking off right on time. It's a no-muss, no-fuss airline with no first class, and I can tell this is not Craig's favorite way to fly. He is seated in the middle seat, having politely insisted that I take the window, and now is holding himself perfectly still so he doesn't touch shoulders with the bigger guy sitting on the aisle.

"Nervous flyer?" I ask, mostly to make conversation. I know that's not what he's reacting to.

"Not at all. I fly all the time." It works. He relaxes a little into his seat to prove what he's saying. "You?"

"I don't love flying, but I'm not going to freak out on you or anything. I like to understand how things work, and I'm always surprised these things get off the ground."

"You should take flying lessons." Craig looks really enthusiastic about this idea. "Seriously. I bet it would really help you love to fly. We could take lessons together."

As I settle in to look out the window at the thin clouds around us, I actually fantasize about Craig and me taking flying lessons together. Being trapped in a small plane, our lives in each other's hands. I'm trying to picture things we might do together in the future, meeting the family, flight lessons, maybe a vacation—I can't remember the last time I've had a proper vacation—spending the night together. It's been five dates now and we haven't even slept together yet. Janine thinks that's crazy, but I don't know what to think. A part of me, truthfully, is relieved. I don't know how I feel about Craig yet, and I'm comfortable and grateful to take things slowly. But at the same time, I wonder maybe if he were more assertive, I would respond. Of course, I'm not nearly as open about stuff like this as Janine, who flat-out asked me yesterday, if this was "the weekend." I explained that the separate-rooms situation at my parents' house would make that difficult and that besides, we're taking it slow. This was met with a big eye-roll.

"Slow, Maddy? We're not in eighth grade. It's time to check out the goods. Oh God, I can't believe I am saying that about our boss. Gross." Then she added all sorts of melodramatic gagging noises. But the truth is, she has a point. Maybe it is time to "check out the goods." I don't realize I'm laughing out loud at that absurd expression, until Craig turns to look at me. "What's so funny?"

Rather than answer, I spontaneously lean over and kiss him.

"Wow, Maddy." I'm not sure what I expected, him to stick his tongue down my throat in this cattle car in the sky? It's not exactly a romantic setting, I get that, but it's still hard not to be offended by how shocked Craig looks. "What was that about?"

"Maybe it's the altitude." I try to laugh it off. "I was just thinking, our first sleepover ever is going to be at my parents' house. That's sort of weird."

"Well, I'm assuming I'll be in the guest room, right?"

"Yes. My parents' house, their rules." Maybe I just need to be the one to make the first move… "But when we get back to LA, there are no rules, right?" I raise my eyebrow as suggestively as I can. "We could pick up Chinese food and compare notes from the trip…"

It's Craig's turn to lean over and kiss me. "I like the sound of that."

My stomach does that weird dropping thing, and I don't think it's just because we've started our descent.

Scene 005
Ext. Henry's gas station--morning

We've been in Wolf County for less than ten minutes before we manage to have our first awkward situation. When we stopped at Henry's Gas and Grill to fill up, Craig went inside and, unbeknownst to me, tried to order an "extra dry cappuccino." I learn of this when Henry comes trailing after a sheepish Craig, laughing heartily and saying, "You weren't kidding. You really were going to buy Maddy Carson a cappuccino." I'm mortified as Henry comes around and gives me a warm embrace with a stage-whispered, "Where'd you get this guy?" Mercifully, there's the loud click marking the full tank and we can make our escape, but not before Henry calls after us, "And how the heck can a drink be dry, anyway?"

The second cringe-worthy moment happens at the red light not three minutes farther down the road. Harriet Burns, my mom's beautician (and the woman responsible for giving me my first terrible perm), pulls up next to us at one of only a handful of stoplights in the whole town.

"Maddy! Oh, you're here! And is this him?! Oh, it must be! Hi! We can't wait to meet you later!! Bye, sweetheart." Of course, town gossip Harriet would have heard about Craig's visit and has no doubt spread the news to anyone sitting in her chair for a roller set.

The best part of that whole interaction was that Harriet didn't stop talking the entire time, so there was no room to get a word in edgewise. Not that I would have had much to say if she'd paused for air. I haven't really worked out yet how to introduce Craig around. Yes, we're dating, but he's definitely not at "boy-friend" status. And yet, here he is with me in our hometown. And we do want to tell a few people about the idea of a reality show. I mean, we're not here to secretly put them on tape without their knowing, but that isn't exactly the kind of thing you blurt out at a traffic light. Luckily I don't have to cross that hurdle quite yet, as the light turns green and Harriet jets off. I look at Craig and he's grinning at me. "I don't know who that is, but she's got to be on the show. I can already tell Wolf County is going to deliver."

I regale him with more stories about Harriet, like the time she chased her son, Eric, across the entire neighborhood because he tried to ditch out on detention. In her pajamas. I get to the part where he's hanging on to the streetlamp as she and the local aging sheriff take both his feet and pull as hard as they can when someone grabbed a picture and sent it to the town paper. We're both still laughing when we finally get to the mountain. Since it's off-season and things are slow, my dad only checks in a few times a week, but Mike will be there. There's no snow yet this early in the season, but it's still beautiful. As we pull up in the parking lot and Craig looks around in appreciative awe, I can tell that he agrees.

"See those trails coming down from the top of the run? We rent mountain bikes and operate the trails for biking in the sum-mer. It's closed down for the season now, but we get a lot of adven-ture seekers in the summer months too."

Dad left the side door unlocked for us, so I take him past the ski rental window and the lift ticket booths.

"Have you guys upgraded to the card system? They have that in Colorado. It's amazing."

Awkward moment number three begins right now, I think, as

my brother appears just in time to hear Craig unknowingly bring up a touchy subject. My dad and brother almost ruined Christmas last year fighting over whether or not they should invest the money to do the upgrade this summer. Obviously my dad won, and it didn't happen. And Mike is still pissed about it.

"Mike, this is Craig." I know I'm doing that overly upbeat voice to try to cover the tense moment, but I just can't help it. My not-so-subtle squeezing of Mike's upper arm is a silent warning: *Be nice.*

Mike doesn't even glance at me as he reaches out his hand. "Hey, Craig. Gotta be honest, Maddy sort of sprung this on us last week. So we're all just trying to get warmed up to the idea."

Mike is not exactly giving off warm vibes.

"Oh, well, that's all right." Craig looks over at me. "I thought we were going to tell everyone together anyway. But I guess she decided to get a head start. Sounds like Maddy, right?" He forces a laugh.

Even though I am annoyed that Craig is talking about me like I'm not standing right there, I am more than a little relieved that he misunderstood Mike's comment. Clearly, Craig thinks I talked to my family about the idea of a reality show, which I haven't. Mike is referring to me announcing to my family a few days ago that I'm bringing a guy I'm dating up here. He's doing the intimidating-big-brother thing, which is, fortunately, going right over Craig's head.

"Mike, I was going to give Craig a tour of the lodge and then head over to Mom and Dad's." I start walking down the extra-wide front hallway, meant to accommodate skiers and snowboarders and their equipment. My voice echoes like crazy in the empty space. "See you there?"

"Yep, I'll be there for dinner. See you later, Maddy. Craig."

Mike disappears back inside his office. I smile apologetically as I lead Craig toward the main area of the lodge.

"Sorry about that. My brother has always been really over-protective of me."

"Of course he is." Craig smiles, but his eyes are already scanning the central gathering area for the lodge. He pulls his fancy Canon out of its leather case and starts taking pictures of the Claw Café, its cute seating areas clustered around a gorgeous stone fireplace.

"This place is always busy in season. Skiers warming up during the day, all the way through après drinks after the lifts close."

"The younger set? Like romantic hookups or like families?" I can tell Craig is setting the stage, trying to picture the "scene." I collapse into one of the cozy oversized leather love seats.

"A little of everything. During the day, a lot of families come through here, but they don't stay long. The kids usually gravitate toward the few video games we have in the other main dining area. And I think families prefer to eat at the tables we have set up in front of the big windows looking at the mountain." I point in the general direction of the dining area. "Since the main bar is here, there are a lot of adults, couples, singles, who come through. You're right, the ski bunnies stake out these comfy sofas, and there are always love connections." I smile, thinking of the time when I caught—

"It would be a great b-story for the show. Don't you think?" Craig says. He presses his phone to activate Siri. "Start a list: party games and socializing at Claw Café."

Instinctively, I reach for my notebook, only to realize I left it back in the car. I feel a wave of separation anxiety.

Craig turns to me, oblivious to my anxiety. "This is great.

Who's your bartender? Or maybe we can cast someone great, you know? Plan bar games for the nights we're shooting here, get the locals involved. We can generate some great story from that."

"We have a couple of terrific bartenders who work for us in the winter. I'm not sure who's committed to stay for this next season, but I'm sure they'd love to do it."

It's been so strange referring to the people in my life, my hometown, as I would with *The Wrong Doctor*, as a series of story lines and characters. I wonder if I'll ever get used to it.

"Exactly. And you said that your parents and the older set hang out at"—Craig scrolls down on his phone—"Pete's Tavern?" He looks up at me for confirmation.

"Yeah, where we had my mom's birthday. That's kinda the old-school watering hole for their generation."

"Yes, yes, love it." Craig is making notes again, this time typing into the phone instead of speaking to Siri. "Let's keep going."

He grabs my hand and pulls me up from the deep couch, the same one I used to nap on when I was a kid. We walk past the clothing store, locked behind sliding glass doors. Ironically called "Left Behind," the store has all the basic necessities of skiing, everything from socks to lip balm for desperate skiers who show up only to realize they forgot some piece of equipment crucial to surviving the elements. Craig pauses to snap a picture of me underneath the sign.

"My mom used to work here. She ran this shop when I was a kid."

"What about you? Did you work here after school?"

"Me? No way. I wanted to be out on the mountain. I started teaching ski school when I was thirteen."

We spend the next two hours hanging out at the lodge and batting around ideas. I have to say, Craig's enthusiasm, which is growing by the minute, is infectious. I'm glad we did some reconnaissance before sitting down to pitch to my parents. I know I'll do a much better job selling this idea to my family if I truly think it could work. After this tour, I am a lot more convinced.

"You think your parents will be a hard sell?" Craig asks as we get in the car and head over to dinner.

I fasten my seat belt. "I guess we're about to find out."

Scene 006
Ext. Carson family home--evening

"Well, knock me down and steal my teeth!" My dad comes bounding out of the front door and sweeps me into a bear hug. He bellows back toward the house, "Maddy's home!" He lets me go and turns to Craig, who's awkwardly watching this embrace. "So, Maddy, are you going to introduce us?"

"Yes, Dad. This is Craig. Craig, I want you to meet my father, Jack Carson."

"Pleased to meet you, Jack." Craig steps in and shakes his hand. One of my dad's favorite ways to judge a guy is by his handshake. He loves to tell the story about how he knew not to trust some banker in Sacramento who was later splashed all over the local papers caught in a fraud scheme. "His handshake was weaker than a chipmunk in the winter," Dad would chortle every time he retold the story. I can't read his face so I'm not sure whether Craig passed or not. I can't read my dad's face before we're all heading into the living room to join my mom, who's still wiping her hands on a dish towel as she comes out of the kitchen with Mike.

"Craig, we've heard so much about you," my mom lies by way of hello. She brushes a quick kiss on my cheek, but it doesn't even slow her down on her way over to Craig. This is beyond embarrassing. I realize now I should've been bringing random guys up here every weekend for the last ten years to immunize my parents to this. Instead, since Craig is the first, he's getting this full-on alien treatment.

Craig makes small talk with my parents while Mike stays mostly silent. My mom finally gets us on track for the evening. "Dear, why don't you and Maddy make drinks for everyone? We can continue this conversation out back."

"Are you going to be making a round of Waxy Sours?" Craig laughs. "Maddy told me about them. I was hoping to try one."

"Waxy Sours. Coming right up." My dad is thrilled. Mike groans and my mom chuckles, leading the way outside.

As my brother slides the screen door shut behind him, he looks at me and mouths the words "suck-up." I stick out my tongue at him. Sometimes that's the only way to handle a brother. Craig is clearly good at this meeting-the-parents thing. It's nice watching him listen so intently to my dad, who is showing him how to make the drink. And when he raises his glass and smiles, toasting me before taking his first sip, my cheeks get pink. I've forgotten how nice it feels to have a guy in your life. I could get used to this.

We get settled with our drinks around the red wooden picnic table with requisite wobbly benches. The charcoal is preheating, making the whole backyard smell delicious.

"So how are you liking Wolf County, Craig?" my mom asks. "Not what you're used to in LA, I'm sure."

My mom is the queen of easy social chitchat. She is utterly incapable of feeling awkward. It's a gift I wish I inherited.

"It's beautiful here. Maddy took me to see the mountain. I'm sure it's amazing with snow."

"Well, we think it's amazing all year." Mike obviously did not get his conversational skills from our mom. I kick him under the table.

"Of course we do, dear," Mom steps in smoothly and covers. "The snow is what the tourists know and, we rely on it for their business. But the locals are a bit sensitive. We like to think it's just as nice in the summer as the winter."

Craig takes my mom's olive branch and runs with it. "I didn't mean it like that...it's incredible now too." He shoots me a *help me* look.

"We only had time to check out the lodge and look around. We're going to maybe go for a hike tomorrow and go into town. And I'm hoping Brian will organize a trip to the hot springs or something." I say this casually, as if I don't have a specific list of exactly what we're doing minute by minute all weekend. It's been tough narrowing it down. We only have two days, so the list in my notebook looks something like:

Must Do
Ski lodge
Hot springs
Pete's Tavern

Maybe
Gordon's taxidermy
Hike the mountain
See the lake

If There's Time
Go to art walk (all the local vendors showcase their wares in
    the town square)

"Sounds like you have a busy schedule planned. No time to relax and actually enjoy it," Dad says.

"Dear, I'm sure Maddy just wants to make sure Craig gets all the best Wolf County has to offer." Mom turns to Craig. "And that's just it. In the winter, there is amazing skiing, but in the summer, there are so many things to do. And it sounds like Maddy is getting it all in on this weekend."

"Yeah, a regular Wally World trip," Mike pipes in, knowing the Chevy Chase reference will egg me on. Normally any mention of the movie *Vacation* sends me into an extended movie-quoting frenzy.

"It's going to be great." Loftily, I ignore Mike's dig. "It's like you said, Mom, I just want to make sure I hit all the high points for Craig." I take a breath...this is sort of the opportunity I've been waiting for.

"Because actually, Craig and I aren't just here for fun." I reflexively take Craig's hand. "We wanted to talk to you about something. Something...big." I pause and look at Craig, hoping he'll jump in. When he doesn't, I continue nervously. "Well, Craig keeps telling me how much he loves my..."

"OH!" my mom gasps, and puts both hands over her mouth as I stop mid-thought to stare at her, wondering what happened.

"Well now, who would've thought...this...it's so sudden, honey." My dad sort of gruffly puts his arm around my mom. I look at them. What the hell are they talking about? Mike is just staring at me blankly. Craig looks like a deer in the headlights and slides his hand out from mine. Then it all clicks. I turn bright red in a nanosecond.

"Mrs. Carson, um, we're not...That's not what Maddy was going to say," Craig says gently. "I mean, not that I wouldn't, it's just that I, we...that is..."

"MOM! Oh my GOD! This is so embarrassing. Craig and I are just dating!" Awkwardly, I get up from the bench. Since I'm squeezed between Craig and Mike, I have to twist my knees to slip out. Suddenly I'm suffocating.

"I meant that we're here for work. GOD." I run my hands through my hair and cover my face as I pace. "We are working on an idea for HCP. My idea, actually. That's why we're here. But Craig thinks it's a really good one...to see if maybe Wolf County would be a good location for a reality show."

So maybe I shouldn't have just blurted it out like that. I certainly had planned to ease into the subject and softball it to them. But under duress, it just all came pouring out. Craig steps into the awkward silence. As he charmingly describes the concept of the Wolf County reality show to my parents, I see why Craig is so good at what he does. He is definitely in his comfort zone, painting a picture of the best-case scenario, of how amazing this show could be, bringing the pitch alive.

"That sounds so interesting, Craig. Really." My mom responds with genuine enthusiasm. "But do you really think people in this town are going to want to be on TV? I mean, no one here is like the Kardinians."

"Kardashians, Mom." I correct her because Craig is clearly too taken aback by her naïveté to explain. Mike covers his laugh with a cough.

"Well, the idea is a bit different than shows like *The Kardashians*," Craig says. "But it is in the docudrama category. From the way Maddy has described it, there are so many fascinating people here who would make very compelling TV. Just the folks I met today...Harriet? Henry? They are so great. And I imagine, like other tourist towns, the economic downturn has been hard on Wolf. I think audiences could really get behind a town banding together to get through these tough times. There's lots of precedent to prove that being a part of a show like this could really help the community by driving tourism."

I see Dad catch Mom's eye and know this particular angle is really resonating. Craig continues. "That's the best part! As we go around pitching this idea to people, we have real evidence to back it up. Shows like this have helped make the people on them very successful."

No question my parents and even my brother were stopped in their tracks by Craig's persuasive case. The truth is, even if my parents were reluctant, they really don't have much of a choice but to give this a try, given what it could mean financially. As my dad grills burgers and we tuck into dinner, the conversation turns to specifics. Even Mike can't help himself and jumps in, asking questions and suggesting ideas. It's not a slam-dunk, but it seems the Carsons are on board with the show. Although the jury is still out in terms of what they think of Craig as boyfriend material. I'm a little relieved that they are so focused on the reality show and Craig as TV producer, not as a future son-in-law.

"I'll tell you what," my dad says suddenly, taking a bite of potato salad. "It means a lot to me that Hogan is behind you on this. He's smarter than a pocket on a shirt, and he cares about Wolf."

My stomach drops. Of course my parents would bring up Hogan! *Shit, shit, shit.* This is not how I wanted Craig to find out. Then my mom pipes in, "I agree, honey. I can't wait to ask him about it. If this show has a chance, it'll be because Hogan is a part of it and the people here respect him."

Craig has stopped eating and has a confused smile on his face.

"Yeah, so, Craig, my parents actually know Hogan," I begin casually, hoping he won't make a big thing out of this in front of my family.

"He's been coming up to Wolf since Maddy was a kid. He never mentioned it?" my mom asks. Actually, it is surprising that Hogan didn't say anything when Craig explained our idea for a show in Wolf.

"Oh, well, I am surprised *you* didn't mention it, Maddy," Craig says.

I detect a note of hurt in his voice. My parents look perplexed. *Damage control, Maddy.*

"Well, it's not a secret exactly. I don't like to mention our connection since I don't want people to assume that it helps my career at all...because it doesn't."

"That's true, our Maddy earned her success fair and square by being so talented," my dad pipes in, literally patting me on the back.

I'm still trying to decipher Craig's expression when suddenly he breaks into a wide grin.

"I totally understand why you didn't say anything, Maddy. But this is good, this is very good." He turns to my parents. "It's good to know how much people around here respect Hogan. I can't wait to tell him all about the great material we found this weekend. Would you mind not saying anything about this to him in the meantime? We don't want to give him any spoilers until we have our reel ready to go. Pitching is all about the 'wow' factor."

Later that night, after Craig helps my mom with the dishes and we strategize about who we should talk to about being on the show, I'm lying on the same single bunk bed I slept in when I was eight and breathing several deep sighs of relief. Craig is sleeping on the pullout sofa bed in the living room snuggled under an afghan with reindeer on it. All in all, I feel like the night went pretty well.

Then I get up and go to the bathroom. I hear a hushed snatch of conversation through my parents' bedroom door. "I don't know, Jack. He's nice enough I guess, but he just doesn't seem right for Maddy. He's a little...slick, don't you think?"

Abruptly, I turn around and pad as silently as possible back to my room with my mom's words reeling in my head. I don't need to hear any more. I guess the jury is in, and the verdict isn't good.

Scene 007
Int. Crazy Eights Café--morning

It was Craig's idea to have breakfast at Crazy Eights Café. Clearly he knows without my having to say that this first impression is key. We have only one crack at getting the town excited about this show, so we'd better do it right. And starting the day at Crazy Eights is a good way to begin mixing in with the locals. It's a small town, and my parents own the ski resort that for the most part sustains the community, so everyone will be talking about what I'm doing, and with whom, by lunch. By the time we make our way to the art walk this afternoon, everyone will have turned out, eager to talk to us and hear more about the show since no doubt word is already out. Having grown up with the small-town rumor mill, I'm used to it and it doesn't really bother me. And for all Craig's LA attitude and clothes, he grew up in a small town, too, so he gets it. Even if he did cut his chicken off the bone with a knife and fork last night, as Mike looked on, horrified.

I can't help but keep replaying my mom's words from last night in my head. *"He's a little slick."* Ugh. I totally trust my parents' opinion—maybe too much—and the fact that this was my mom's first impression isn't good. That said, we have twenty-four more hours to win her over.

I smile brightly at Craig, who is gamely scraping off the cheese he asked to be held from his bacon and egg plate. "I can't wait for you to check out the Gordons' attic. They make Norman Bates's hobby look normal."

"I love the quirkiness. We could show what goes into making it and how much they sell stuff for. The negotiation part. A little *Pawn Stars* meets *Duck Dynasty*. Networks love that."

"Well, who knows how much of it they're selling these days, with the tourism down. My mom mentioned that they move some of it on eBay too."

"That's not a big deal. We can get some people in there, produce some 'customers.'" He's scanning his e-mails as we talk. I'm taking notes about our plan for the day.

"Maddy." Craig looks up all of a sudden, a serious look on his face. "I still can't believe you didn't tell me you're family friends with Hogan. Why didn't you say anything?"

"It's not really the kind of thing you just casually toss into a conversation, you know? I mean, I thought about telling you when we started dating." I hasten to correct myself. "I wanted to tell you. It just always seemed weird to bring it into the conversation. Hogan and I try to keep our personal and work worlds separate, and he knows better than to try and interfere in my career. I want to earn it, including this show. I hope he isn't giving it the go-ahead as some sort of favor to me or my parents. They wouldn't want that."

"I'm sure that's not it at all, Maddy. I'm telling you straight up, it's a good idea. No doubt about it. And when the network falls all over themselves to buy eight episodes up front, you'll see what I mean." I nod in agreement as I chew. God, I missed these waffles.

"Hey." A weird look crosses Craig's face just as I am swallowing a huge bite of buttery goodness. "Have you mentioned to him that we're seeing each other?"

"Oh, no." Flustered, I put my fork down. "I would have told you if I had. I mean, at some point it will come up, right? But no, I haven't mentioned it. In fact, what should we say? I guess we should come up with a game plan."

"Yeah, we should. Can I think about it?" Craig wipes his mouth and drops his napkin on his cleaned plate. "That was delicious. What time do we need to be at the Gordons'?"

Okay. That seemed like a weird subject shift, but I decide to go with it. I'm sure Craig's as worried about awkward office politics as I am. We'll figure it out. I put it from my mind on the way to the Gordons'.

"Darling girl! Come in, come in!" Merry probably hasn't bought new clothes since 1978. Her Hawaiian-print housecoat fits in perfectly with the avocado-green-trimmed furniture.

Craig walks in, wide-eyed. It's clear he doesn't know where to look first. I glance around the place, seeing it from his perspective. It really is appalling. And since my last visit, it's starting to look a bit like one of those houses in *Hoarders*. There are stacks and stacks of magazines, books, and things I can't even identify all over what used to serve as a dining room.

"Your parents filled me in on your young man here. Greg, is it?"

"Craig, ma'am. Maddy's told me all about your incredible collection of taxidermy. Since we were in town, I begged to come have a look for myself." Craig's charm has Mrs. Gordon blushing as she oohs and aahs us to the garage.

"It all started as another one of Walt's crazy hobbies," she explains as we navigate our way through the cluttered kitchen and pantry. "He's done it all, I swear. At one point I felt we were in the navy what with all the model boats everywhere. And then he started fixing up old cars. He never could get them running, though."

We are now walking along the outside of the house, my parents' house visible just through the trees, headed to the garage. Merry is still talking. "He's always loved hunting; he worships those animals, you know. So the taxidermy has his heart, not just his head." She is now speaking in a stage whisper, so we both lean in. Given our true reasons for being here, we don't want to miss a word of this backstory.

"Here it is!" With that Ed McMahon—worthy introduction, she presses the remote control and with a mechanical groan the door starts its slow but steady ascent.

Since I know what the door is going to reveal, I watch Craig for his first-timer's reaction. Even prepped with how gory this stuff is, I watch the sight transform his features, and then witness him struggling to replace his genuine reaction with a more socially acceptable smile. I can't help but giggle as each new creature he fixates on causes his polite mask to slip.

"Walt, Maddy's brought her beau here. They want the tour!" Merry trills.

"Well, you came to the right place. Maddy, girl." Walt squeezes me quickly, reeking of the chemicals used for curing, and moves on to shake Craig's hand. "Nice to meet you, I'm Walt Gordon."

"Craig Williams, sir. Pleasure to meet you. I'm not sure how much the Carsons explained to you about our visit."

"Very little, really. It was actually quite confusing." Walt wipes his hands on an oily cloth and turns his full attention to Craig. "Something about a new show?"

Merry pipes up, grabbing my arm. "Honey, are you leaving your job? You know we are hooked on *The Wrong Doctor* now. You can't just leave! Billy Fox needs you! I still have those signed DVDs you gave us. Right, Walt?"

I laugh at her theatrics, as she intended me to. Merry and I both know she would continue to watch Billy Fox no matter what I did with the rest of my life.

"Don't worry, guys, I'm not leaving."

"Oh, what a relief." Merry sighs.

"But Craig and I are working on a new show idea for Hogan."

They may not be as close to Hogan as my parents are, but the Gordons have met him several times over the years. Everyone in Wolf is very proud of their connection to Hogan Chenny.

"Your mother mentioned something like that," Walt says as he puts a calming hand on Merry's shoulder. "Let her explain, dear."

"Actually, Craig should explain." I don't mean to pass the baton, but at this point Craig is way more experienced at this kind of thing. And he's better at salesmanship than I could ever hope to be.

Merry and Walt turn expectant looks toward Craig, and like any good performer in front of an audience, Craig lights up.

"Well, actually, Maddy deserves the credit for this idea. She's done nothing but rave about Wolf County. As I found myself asking a million questions, becoming more and more interested in life here, we quickly realized it would be a great location. That you all would be perfect people to star in a show." It isn't the first time Craig's told this revised story of how the show idea came about, and it's starting to make me uncomfortable. I make a mental note to bring it up to him when we're alone.

"Who? What people?"

"You! The people of Wolf County!" Craig enthuses. "Maddy's been showing me around, and there are so many great people, but honestly, I feel like you, your business…you would be a major selling point. Please tell me you'd be willing to participate. I really think it would make such a huge difference."

Merry and Walt exchange dumbfounded looks. Their reaction is exactly what would make them so perfect for the show. I look at Craig with an "I told you so" smile. They are exactly what the show needs.

"Look, Mr. and Mrs. Gordon," Craig continues. "I don't need an answer now. Please take your time and think it over. But if you wouldn't mind, I would love a tour of your...your..." Craig hesitates for the first time.

"Shop?" Walt jumps in. "Of course. The missus and I don't jump into a mud puddle without discussing first, so you'll have to give us some breathing room on that one. But I'd sure love to show you my beauties since you're here." Walt begins walking Craig through the wildlife in various stages of embalming. Craig unobtrusively uses his Canon camera to video Walt's explanations, and perhaps it says it all that Walt doesn't even hesitate when the camera comes out. He keeps talking as confidently as ever. This is going to work.

After we say our good-byes to the Gordons with promises to meet for pie later, Craig and I are back in the car, driving to Echo Peak Park, which marks the finish line of Matthew's twenty-four-hour mountain bike race.

"Matthew and his buddy George do this race every year. They're both insane," I explain to Craig.

"Literally twenty-four hours without stopping?"

"Well, that's why you do it in teams, up to four guys, so one guy is always racing. But if you need to stop to pee, or rest or whatever, you can. It's just going to cut into your lap total."

"You're right. It sounds nuts." Craig wryly shakes his head. As we pull up to the parking area, I think that now would be a good time to talk to Craig about how the idea for Wolf was really mine. I have had to turn the other cheek too many times to do it again now. This isn't a set, where I have to concede to the director or the producer. This is my baby, and I am discovering that there is a fire in my belly to protect not only my idea, but also the people I'm asking to be a part of it. Not to mention, common sense tells me that when it comes to pitching the town, I think everyone will feel better knowing that this all came from one of their own. But I don't know how to bring it up without it being awkward. Not for the first time, I wish I had my mom's grace when it comes to these things. I'm trying to figure out how to say it as I pull into the dirt parking area. There are cars everywhere. "This many people participate in this?" he asks as we begin trolling the lanes looking for a place to park.

"Well, probably there are a lot of people here like us, to support a friend who's doing the race." Almost every car we pass is a 4x4, all coated in several layers of dirt. Our shiny rental car looks so out of place in the spot we found, half on the road, half on a dirt embankment. It's squished between a mud-splattered pickup truck and a beat-up SUV with a bike rack loaded down with all sorts of bikes.

Craig locks the car as we start to walk away. The double chirp from the car makes me smile. "You've been in LA too long."

Completely unaware, Craig looks at me. "What do you mean?"

"We don't lock our cars here. I guess I just figured it was like that where you grew up too."

"You're saying I'm completely citified? Is that it?" Craig gets into the spirit of my teasing easily. As we approach the festivities, he takes my hand and squeezes it, which is nice. I squeeze back as we follow the crowds of onlookers to the finish line. It's slow going as we keep bumping into people I know. Well, this is what we came here for, I concede as we engage in another long conversation with old friends of my parents who have done nothing but tell stories from Woodstock for as long as I can remember.

"Maddy." I hear a deep voice and before I can even start to disengage myself from the Wentlys' musical debate, we are cast in the literal and proverbial shadow of Moses. At six foot seven, his shoulders and chest leave one with the solid impression of a bull. He literally towers over us, though perhaps as a way to balance out his size, his voice is little above a murmur. Although the Tongan native is incredibly gentle as I wrap my arms partially around him in greeting, my feet leave the ground in a bear hug that would probably intimidate the bear. His low rumbling chuckle as he sets me down sounds like the beginning of an earthquake.

"Craig, this is Moses. Moses Finau, meet my—Craig." I can excuse my almost-slip as I am still catching my breath. Craig has either truly learned the art of the poker face by working in Hollywood, or he deserves major nerves-of-steel credit for reaching out his hand and keeping his unassuming smile in place.

"Nice to meet you, Moses."

"Likewise," Moses responds politely. It's weird, but all of a sudden, I am seeing people so familiar to me, people I've known my whole life, with all-new eyes. I can't help but size everyone up, trying to objectively judge their perspective as characters to include in the show. And with that framework, Moses may as well glow like he's been dipped in TV gold.

Craig is chatting him up casually, as if there weren't two hundred pounds of muscle between them. But it's Craig doing the talking, dissecting the racecourse as well as a color analyst on ESPN.

"You must've done some sports growing up? Football?" Craig has a crick in his neck looking up at Moses.

"A little football. Mostly some wrestling," Moses replies modestly. Yeah, "some wrestling." In fact, Moses was an incredibly popular wrestler in his day. His character generated lots of ticket sales and even his own merchandise.

"I would've taken you by his bakery in town, but the line is always out the door."

"Really?" Craig is clearly intrigued, and since I haven't seen him eat a carb yet, I don't think it's because of the sweets. "You run a successful bakery now?" I can practically see his wheels turning.

"You're welcome in my shop anytime. I would be in the dog-house for a week if LeAnn heard that you were in town, Maddy, and I didn't drag you over there to say hi."

"My brother buys all our bread for the mountain café from Moses. I used to do the pickups first thing in the morning. Nothing smells better than their kitchen at four a.m."

"I always thought you offered to do the pickup for the choco-late croissant you would sweet-talk MJ into giving you." Moses laughs as I blush.

"He was such a cute kid. I would love to hear how you all are doing these days. In fact, there's something I would like to talk to you and LeAnn about, if you'll be in the shop later."

"Oh, I'm headed back there now. I promised the missus some of Denny's Cajun-style peel-and-eat shrimp." He holds up the to-go bag. "Gotta get it back while it's still hot. Promise you'll come by?"

"I wouldn't miss it." I reach up on my tiptoes, but he has to lean down more than a foot for me to plant a kiss on his cheek.

"So? What's his backstory? I can tell he's a treasure trove," Craig comments.

"Wait till you meet his wife. Moses is six foot seven...LeAnn is barely five feet tall. She's this tiny, delicate little red-haired firecracker. She definitely wears the pants in that family. They would be great for the show. Seriously. And Moses doesn't just bake cookies and stuff. You should see what he can do. He makes the most beautiful French macarons; he bakes his own crois-sants; they do teatime at the bakery, and he makes these gorgeous delicate tea cakes and scones." I am starting to salivate—not at the description of the delicacies Moses can create, but at how brilliant he will be for the TV audience. Every time we bump into someone, I get a hundred new ideas for the show. I can make this show great; I know it. I know this town, the people, better than anyone else ever could. Is it crazy to think I could be executive producer?

"Craig, listen, this may seem out of left field, but I've been thinking..."

But the closer we get to the finish line, the more people are smushed in the narrow clearing where the race ends. Craig can barely hear me over all the shouts and cheering.

"Did you say something, babe?" He doesn't wait for an answer, just turns back to keep pushing through the crowd. He finds us a spot at the ropes, but it's clear this isn't the right moment to bring up something that important. "We have to go secure things with Moses and his wife. Right? Who else should be on the A list?" he asks. I'm craning my neck but can't see the pack of riders yet.

"Um, let me think about it." Is now the right time to convince him I should be the person in charge, running the show on a day-to-day basis? If I'm going to prove to him I can be the show-runner, I need to learn to assess these people as objectively as he does. I ignore the knot in my stomach when a group of cute twentysomething girls near us start shrieking, "HERE THEY COME!" They must have bat radar because only after they've started cheering wildly do I see the tips of a few helmets coming toward us around the last dirt hill. I start shouting, too, and behind me Craig claps and yells.

The first group of guys comes pedaling around the last bend, a tight pack covered in mud. I can't tell if Matthew is with them, so I just scream and shout until every last rider crosses the finish line. I grab hold of Craig and start pushing my way through the crowd toward where the riders have stopped and are pulling off their gear. Each rider has a pit crew, usually made up of their girlfriends who are pouring water down their shirts or handing them towels. I see a brunette in Daisy Duke shorts help pull off a rider's protective vest and helmet. Then I see Matthew's dirt-streaked, smiling face. I tug on Craig and race toward him and his friends.

"Hi, you guys! Congratulations!" I scream at Matthew as he gets off his bike and takes a water bottle from Jen, his on-again, off-again girlfriend. He throws himself on the grass, still gulping in huge breaths.

"Matt! That was insane!" Jen hugs him giddily. Anyone can see how much she adores him. "I can't believe you did that! How do you feel?" He raises his hand to give us the "okay" sign before letting it fall back to the ground. I can't help but laugh.

"We'll give you guys a minute to recover. You're getting old, Matthew. You used to talk nonstop when you got off the bike. Meet us over by the food," I say. He raises his hand again to flip me the bird as Craig and I head toward the main food and drink tents. Coming back up from the riders' area has put us on the rise slightly above the park area and now we have perspective on the event, which causes Craig to stop short.

"Wow! This is quite a setup. Hold on a second." Craig takes off the camera's lens cap and records some panoramic video of the festivities.

"I know we were going to focus on the winter season, but the fall and summer are just as fun, really."

It's weird, looking at something I've seen a million times, and yet seeing it again for the first time. "Wolf does events like this practically every weekend. There's always something going on and in terms of the show, there's usually a lot of the same people. In fact, there's a committee in the city council that focuses on arranging these events."

"Yeah, you said it was a thing, but I didn't really expect all this at a mountain bike race."

"Any excuse to get people together. We have a triathlon, a biathlon, a river dash, canoe races, mud runs..."

"Shrimp toast, shrimp kabobs, shrimp soup..." The *Forrest Gump* quote is my only warning before my brother attacks me in a bear hug from behind—the show of affection offered only to cover me in mud from head to toe. Nothing new there.

"Ahhh!" I can't help but shriek at the dirt and grime. "Matthew!"

Everyone is laughing as we engage in a full-on sibling tussle that I win. Admittedly, Matthew is probably a tad undernourished and weakened from the last twenty-four hours of exertion, but a sister knows when to press her advantage, and I jump up, victorious.

"Never mind the town, Maddy. I could make a show just about you and your crazy family." Craig laughs as I brush my hair with my fingers. He kisses me on the lips as I am pulling my hair back into a ponytail. He lingers for a second, but pulls away before I get my fingers untangled from the hair tie.

Matt takes it all in with a smile. "All right, you two lovebirds, let's go get something to eat so I can grill you properly, Craig."

We sit at a picnic table with Matthew and a dozen or so of his friends, many of whom work at the ski lodge with Mike and our dad. We each have plates of food from several different restaurants around town; it's the Wolf County version of tapas. I'm having the same peel-and-eat shrimp LeAnn Finau had been craving, while Craig had settled on short ribs. Between us are some pot stickers we share as we bring the group up to speed on our plan for the reality show. Matthew is predictably very excited about the show (and no doubt the starring role he is imagining for himself) and has been peppering Craig with suggestions, which has gotten a lot of others on board too. Pete the Third, aka Petey of Pete's Tavern fame, is quiet the whole time, until he finally says with not a little attitude, "How do we know you're not going to make us look bad? I know how you can make it seem like a fight happened, when it wasn't like that at all. How do I know you won't make my dad's bar seem all sleazy just to get people to watch the show?"

"Because I would never let that happen. Come on, Petey." I'm aware that everyone has stopped talking to listen to this. "It's me. Wolf County is my home. I would never do anything to hurt this town. I hope you know that."

"Of course not. Petey didn't mean that, did you?" Matthew can't help but jump in. "Maddy is doing this to help the town."

"That's right. This show is going to get people excited to come up here again. And I promise, Pete, if your family lets us film in the Tavern, Craig and I will protect you."

"Well, we're not going to sugarcoat stuff either, though, right, Maddy? Let's be clear," Craig interjects. "If there is a fight, and the two people agreed to be on the show, we won't hide from that. We'd also love for some of the business owners to talk about how tough times are financially. I think America will really relate to that. And I love the idea of showing all these amazing events, things you as a community are doing to pull together."

"Amen," says Matthew, giving Craig a spontaneous fist bump. Even if Craig looked a little awkward doing a fist bump, the bonding moment makes me smile.

"Do we get paid for being on camera? How does it work?" my brother's friend George asks.

"Yes, the main people involved with the show will get a nominal fee. But you won't see real money from the show. It doesn't work like that. The real money will come from the added tourism in town, and if the show is successful, advertising and maybe even merchandising, stuff like that."

"I have another idea." Matt jumps in again. It's like he's aiming for a producer's credit. "You should film the snowboarding competition we hold. We usually get a couple celebrities here for it anyway—you could make it a charity thing and get a lot of big names."

"I love that idea, Matthew!"

Without hesitation, Matthew leaps into a detailed description of what an intense weekend it is, the stress on the restaurants and small B&Bs, everywhere filled to max capacity, the party atmosphere created by the guests at the big events, the superstar snowboarders, the celebrity fans in attendance—it's a pretty big deal. Jen and George throw in a few ideas, and Craig and I walk away with our pockets full of business cards and my notebook overflowing with names of people and businesses that may want to participate.

Craig has his camera out again, shooting locals barbequing ribs, kids playing badminton under some trees. He gets down on the ground to get a good angle of a fisherman showing his kid how to clean his catch. He gets up and tries to brush off some of the dirt, but now he looks a lot less polished than I'm used to seeing, and I like it. "Wow—anything for the shot, huh?" I tease.

"I know it's just in-house footage. We'll have to come back with a crew for the real pitch reel, but it's fun, you know? Like film school all over again."

"I didn't know you went to film school."

Craig smirks. "Well, I wasn't born an executive at HCP, Maddy. As you know, probably better than I do, Hogan doesn't suffer fools. I had to prove myself before I got to where I am." He's flipping through the video files he has on his phone, but I can tell he's waiting for my reply.

Yikes, Craig seems a little touchy about this. "I didn't mean anything by it. I know you're good at what you do. I'm just used to seeing you on the business side. You know, suit, tie, crunching numbers. Not getting dirty, literally, for a camera angle. I guess I didn't see you having such an... artistic side."

"Yes, I'm a regular Quentin Tarantino," he jokes. He untucks his shirt and cleans the screen of his phone with the underside of his polo. It hits me that this more casual version of Craig has been so much fun to be with this weekend. In fact, I like his untucked, laid-back side more than the by-the-numbers executive I thought was so perfect for me.

"Anyway, there's a lot you don't know about me, and I'm sure vice versa," Craig says, linking his arm through mine.

Scene 008
Airplane cabin--morning

With all of the good-byes and last-minute visitors and promises to keep everyone posted on the show, we're almost late for our flight back to LA. I let Craig have the window seat as we board the plane and luckily no one comes to sit next to me, so we actually have the row to ourselves. I slide to the aisle seat and put our magazines and my notebook on the empty seat between us. Craig, no surprise, is on a call, using his earpiece. Since he's looking out the window and there's so much noise around us, I can't really figure out if it's work or something else.

I'm glad he's distracted, because frankly so am I. I get out my notebook and pen to make notes about the show, but instead I can't help replaying the conversation I had with my mom last night. She came in my room as I was falling asleep and got into bed with me just as she did when I was a girl.

"Oh, Maddy," she said, wrapping her arms around me. "We just love having you here. I know you flew the nest a while back, but I still miss my little birdie."

No matter how grown up I feel 99.9 percent of the time, it's moments like these that transport me back to being a little girl. I snuggled in deeper, inhaling my mom's vanilla scent.

"And we're so excited for this show. Your dad and I were talking last night. This might be just the thing the town needs. We're so proud, but hardly surprised, that our little Maddy could save the day."

"I don't want you and Dad to have to leave Wolf. Your whole life is here. This is home. You'll see; the show is going to be a hit."

"Well, that would be terrific, but the best part of it is that we would get to see you more, right? You would come up all the time?"

"Mom, I think they're gonna want someone with more experience to run the show."

Concern clouds her features. "Honey, you've been working in Hollywood for more than ten years. If that's not experience, I don't know what is."

"I know, but..."

"Honey, is this like when you were coming out of high school? Even with those test scores, you didn't even want to leave the valley for college. You are stronger than you think."

"Mom..."

"You need to believe in yourself or no one else ever will."

"Okay. I hear you. I believe, I swear I do."

"So then you'll be coming back to see us, a lot. Right?" She shifts gear at lightning speed back to her immediate goal.

"Yes, I'm sure I could finagle some trips, and Craig too." I take a deep breath and ask the question I wanted to all weekend. "Speaking of Craig, what do you think of him?"

She was silent for a minute, stroking my hair. Finally she said, "He seems very driven, Maddy, just like you." Another pause. "What matters is, do you like him?"

Classic redirect, which told me everything I need to know. I know I'm an adult, but it really matters to me that my parents embrace Craig. And it really matters to me why they aren't. I tried to keep the defensive tone out of my voice when I told her that yes, I liked Craig and was excited to see where this would go. I told her that I hoped once they got to know him, they, too, would see his charms.

"I'm sure we will, dear. I'm sure we will," she said as she tucked me in and headed to bed.

The flight attendant breaks into my thoughts, advising us that it's time to turn off our devices. I dash off one last text to Mom and Dad, thanking them for having us, and then dutifully tuck my phone into my carry-on. Five minutes later Craig is still on his call. The flight attendant sounds really annoyed as she says again that all cell phones and electronics must be off—an announcement clearly directed at Craig. I look at her and she is glaring at us.

"Craig!" I tap his arm. He holds up one finger. I look back at the flight attendant and she rolls her eyes at me. Embarrassed now that she saw him brush me off, I tap Craig harder on the arm.

"Craig, come on. The whole plane is waiting for you."

He looks at me and looks around. "Okay, okay," he says, and then back to the phone. "Sorry, we'll finish this tomorrow. I have to go."

He hangs up and then waves the now-black screen at the flight attendant, who disappears behind the curtain.

"That was a development executive I know," he says, without a thought to delaying the whole flight for his call.

"I was giving a bit of a sneak peek about Wolf," he continues. "Not too many details, don't worry." He pats my thigh. "But I can tell you right now, we're going to have lots of interest."

He leans in to look at the notes I was writing. I'm glad I was working on Wolf County and not one of my personal lists, like ranking my favorite contestants on *The Voice*. That would be embarrassing. I make a mental note to start a notebook for just Wolf County so he doesn't ever read something he shouldn't.

"This looks great, Maddy. Good idea. Get all the highlights on one page. Actually, it will be good to get a full season's worth of episode synopses written up. I can help you do that. It'll be even easier to convince Hogan to give us a budget for the pitch if we've thought through every angle."

"I thought Hogan was already excited about this idea."

"I mean he is, but you know Hogan, even if it's his favorite place in the world, he's going to be objective about the show. We have to win him over."

"True. That sounds like Hogan." He can be a tough boss, for sure. "And again, Craig, I'm sorry that I never said anything to you about my family knowing Hogan. I wasn't trying to keep secrets. And I would never go behind your back to him. I hope you know that."

"I do know that. Frankly, it may come in handy that you and Hogan are close. Maybe he'll listen to you more than he will me about this whole reality thing, and see the opportunity."

"Well, obviously he's already changed his mind about reality TV. Even just letting us do this initial recon for a show is a huge step for him. I think he'll respond really well to everything we've got marked up. What are you going to do with the footage you shot?"

Now that we're at altitude, Craig activates his phone. It irks me a bit that he just put it on sleep mode and didn't actually turn it all the way off the way you're supposed to. I'm not going to say something, though. I know he'll just tease me for being such a rule-follower.

"I'm going to take the best shots and videos and work it into a presentation to show Hogan. Hey, you know what? You should come to the meeting on Tuesday too!"

"Really?" I say, a little annoyed that Craig is only thinking to invite me at the last minute.

"Well, given your connection to Hogan and Hogan's to Wolf, I think he would love hearing from you."

Craig is looking at me with this gleeful, expectant look on his face, and I agree to join him on Tuesday morning.

"Fabulous! Maddy, this is going to be great. There's no way Hogan can't share our excitement now. This is going to be my ticket—our ticket—to the next level. We just have to have everything ready for Reality Buzz next month."

"What's that?"

"It's one of the most important reality TV conventions held in the world. All the important network executives, show runners, and producers, meet up to exchange ideas, listen to pitches, and acquire the rights to new shows for their networks."

The flight attendant comes over and serves our drinks with such a stink eye that if I hadn't seen her pour my soda from the can myself, I would question whether it was safe. Wow, way to hold a grudge. I look to Craig to judge his reaction, but he seems totally oblivious. For a moment I truly wish I didn't care what other people think of me.

"Sorry about earlier. He really didn't hear you," I say to her quietly as she passes me my drink.

"Honey, I'm just glad he's not my problem," she replies at full volume. He definitely heard that. She moves on and I sneak a look at Craig, but he has his nose back in his tablet. Thank God for Wi-Fi. I pick up a copy of *People* magazine that I bought in the terminal. I start flipping through it, happy to have a break from nonstop Wolf County conversation. An article about Blake Shelton grabs my attention. Okay, it may have been the picture of Blake Shelton that did that, but the article is interesting too. It's talking about how he's made country music popular with the mainstream. Interesting. Then I turn the page and there staring back at me is Adam Devin sitting on a rocky shoreline looking back at the camera, his hair all mussed in the wind, looking brooding and gorgeous. After a one-way staring contest that lasts longer than I'd like to admit, I finally start reading the story about how Adam, too, is leaving his comfort zone, having broken out of daytime and landed a lead role on *The Wrong Doctor* (*season two coming this spring*). The writer goes on and on about Adam's down-to-earth personality, adding that he's avoided the bad-boy reputation of his costar Billy Fox by not turning up at every red carpet with a different bombshell on his arm. In the article Adam acknowledges that he's single but explains that he wants to focus on his new character on *The Wrong Doctor* right now. He adds, "I'm always open for what comes next."

I tap Craig since he has his headphones in and show him the article, in case he hadn't seen it. It's great promotion for the show.

"Wow, he's at it already. Huh," Craig says after he skims the article, a bit louder than necessary since he hasn't taken his earbuds out.

"What do you mean?"

"Obviously, he's hired that publicist to raise his profile. I heard him talking to Billy about her. Sophie Atwater? But this is quick, even for her." Rapidly he flips back through the magazine. "I'm surprised he's going for that angle, though."

"Angle?" I ask quietly enough that he has to take his right earbud out of his ear. I repeat the question.

"You know, the Goody Two-shoes, hardworking thing. I think that Billy going to events with all of those supermodels gets him great PR, not to mention all those leading man offers. It makes women want him even more. You know you guys all love the bad boys." He nudges me with his elbow. "Well, at least it makes the show look good."

I'm surprised at how quickly Craig dismisses the good PR, not to mention his new hire, Adam Devin. And for the first time I actually find myself wanting to defend him.

"I don't know... I think it's sincere. From what I've heard, he isn't dating anyone, and I've heard him talking to some of the cast about this acting class he's in. I think he genuinely does want to focus on his career."

Craig just shrugs. "Hey, whatever works." And then he goes back to his music. I read *People* for the rest of the flight.

When we land, it's almost 10:00 p.m., and there's a chill in the air in LA, so I'm still dressed perfectly for the weather in my favorite gray hoodie and fleece sweats.

As exhausted as I am, it was such a productive trip, and I do feel really optimistic that Wolf County is going to make a great reality show. And I'm more than a little proud to be part of reality TV that isn't all about negativity. I say that aloud to Craig. I want to end our weekend on an upbeat note.

"Me too. And so will Hogan. I'll meet you at the offices at eight on Tuesday morning. Thanks again for coming."

"No problem. I'm excited. It will be fun to see things from another angle."

"And thanks for showing me such a good time this weekend," he says as he pulls me into an embrace and kisses my forehead. I tilt my face up and he takes the cue to kiss me sweetly on the lips, and then again with more passion. When the cab pulls up, I put out of my mind that I have a 7:00 crew call in the morning, that I have laundry (clean, at least) strewn all over my bed, and that I haven't shaved my legs in two days. I turn to Craig. "Come home with me?"

Craig, of course, knows what a 10:00 p.m. invite means. He picks up his duffel bag and smiles. "Well, I already have my toothbrush. Let's go."

Scene 009
Int. HCP reception--morning

I'm annoyed at myself for being so nervous right now. I've sat on this couch a thousand times; the print hanging above the desk is a gift from my parents, for God's sake. And yet it is taking everything in me to not pace back and forth, pick imaginary lint off my dress, bite my fingernails, or all three. Then a part of me realizes that I kind of like the butterflies in my stomach. I like that it means I really care about how this turns out. As much as I like working as a script supervisor, this is new and exciting... a challenge. And when I think of what it could mean for Wolf, the stakes feel so high. Thinking about those stakes sends me right back into another tailspin of anxiety. I don't need this pressure, and creative stuff like this has never been my strong suit. I don't have a freaking artistic bone in my body, and now I want to create a TV show? Who am I kidding? And what if the show doesn't work?

"He's going to love it." Craig's voice jolts me out of my spiral of self-doubt. I almost forgot he was sitting next to me.

"Yeah, I think you're right," I say with false confidence. Yesterday, we went over and over all the elements of the show via e-mail. We worked through several different possible formats, but we have a good, well-thought-out concept. Objectively, I know it's good, but that didn't stop me from lying awake last night, playing out the million reasons why this won't work. For someone who's never considered herself creative, I was pretty impressed by the extremely imaginative ways I pictured this meeting bombing. Everything from Hogan kicking me out for offending his ears (unlikely) to an earthquake knocking the whole building down (it could happen).

"I watched the video at least ten times yesterday. For a quick rough cut, it's good. If I do say so myself." Craig repeatedly taps his laptop. Though he's been giving a good show, his fidgety behavior makes me realize that he is nervous too. All of a sudden I have compassion for his situation. The stakes are high for him too.

"Great. I made a copy of the video on DVD so we can leave it with him. Oh, and I also made extra copies of the write-up," I say, digging the crisp folder out of my bag.

"If he takes his time to think about it, we're golden." Craig has worked with Hogan for years; he knows him as well as I do. "Hogan never makes snap decisions, so the best thing we can expect is for him to think it over. It would be better not to push him for an answer right away. Just let him mull it over."

"Okay..."

"We don't want him to feel pressured into giving an answer right away. And I think it's better to talk just broad strokes. We want him excited about the overall idea before we start talking about the details of budgets and below-the-line details. Okay?" As Craig keeps talking, he seems more in control.

"Well, I'm sure he's already thought through the basics, right? Based on your initial talk with him? This should just confirm that we have the right direction for the show, and then we can figure out the budget from here." I did some quick and dirty number crunching last night, so I have a rough idea of what we'd need. I also hashed out a very rough shooting schedule, so we have all our ducks in a row.

"Right. Maddy, here's the thing..." He trails off. I can tell

Craig is gearing up for some sort of practiced speech. He has that even tone that I've come to know as his "Hollywood" voice.

I wait for him to continue.

"We really have something special here." Craig looks at me with such conviction. What does that mean? He isn't saying it lightly; I can see he really means it. And all of a sudden I wonder if he means us...our relationship? Or are we still talking about the show? I start to stutter a response when Hogan throws open the door.

"Maddy! Craig! I had to get that call done so we could have some time to talk. I can't wait to hear what this is all about." And then he disappears back inside. Wait. *What?!* I am now frozen in my seat. Craig gets up and takes two steps toward Hogan's inner office before he turns back to see the shock followed by horror on my face.

"God, Maddy...I know...you thought...okay, listen." He squats down in front of me so we are eye level. In a low voice he quickly explains, "So Hogan didn't really come right out and say he was interested in reality TV. And we don't exactly have the green light here."

I stare at him, mouth agape.

"But this is a good idea. He's going to love it. You know Hogan..." Craig's voice switches to wheedling. "Sometimes he can have his head in the sand about moving forward. I wanted to have everything a little more buttoned up before I came to him. Now he's going to see how perfect it is."

Finally my brain starts functioning again. "How dare you?" I spit out at him in a whisper. "I'm not going in there. I'm not selling Hogan anything he doesn't want to do. That's insane!"

"Maddy! Craig! Come on, I don't have all day," Hogan bellows from the interior of his office.

"You've come this far. Wolf needs this. You said so yourself.

Give Hogan a chance to change his mind. I know you can get him to see what a good idea this is." Craig knows better than to touch me, so he rises and starts to walk toward the office doors. He looks back at me. "This isn't even about me, really. You can hate me right now if you want, but you know your family needs this."

And the worst thing is, he's right. I can't let Craig's political games stop me from at least trying to make a go of this show. It would actually help my family, my community.

"You are unbelievable." As far as witty comebacks go, I know it's not the best, but it's true. I hold my head high and sail past him into Hogan's office holding the DVD we slaved over and the write-up of the show.

Hogan envelops me in a big hug, and I tightly embrace him back. I have no idea how this conversation is going to go, and I hate that. One thing I do know: I'm furious with Craig.

Act Three

Scene 001
Int. Fifteenth-floor elevator bank--day

I walk out of Hogan's office in a daze, while Craig lingers to talk about some *Wrong Doctor* business. I know I participated in the rest of the conversation, but it's all blurry to me now as I walk back to the elevators and wait for the ding. He lied to me. I still can't wrap my head around it. People tease me about my first impression thing, but I have always trusted my gut. And for the most part I've been right, so I feel completely blindsided by what Craig has done. And I really don't know how to handle it.

I hear the heavy footfalls of a man rushing down the hallway as I board the elevator. Oddly, I don't care whether or not Craig makes it. I don't press the hold button for him, but it doesn't occur to me to hurry to shut the doors either. At the last second his hand slides between the closing doors and triggers the motion sensor to reopen them, but I still don't react. It's just the two of us in this extremely confined space. And I know he's talking to me. I can hear his words, and a distant part of my brain is cataloguing what he's saying, but I just can't react to it right now. I don't look at him. I stare at the doors, waiting for them to open. He steps in front of them. His face comes into sight. He seems genuinely upset, but right now I don't care about his excuses or explanations.

By the time I get to my car, he's not following me anymore. As I start the engine, I realize that I'm angrier at myself for not seeing through Craig's lies than I am at Craig for lying.

*   *   *

I flash back to Hogan's ill-disguised shock at the purpose for our meeting. The look on his face was like a slow-motion sequence.

"HCP doesn't do reality TV. I told you that when you suggested this a few weeks ago, Craig. Why are you guys pitching me this?"

"It's a good idea, Hogan. I thought if you could just see the great footage we got, you might be persuaded. And think about what it could do for Wolf County." Craig didn't hesitate to use his newfound knowledge of Hogan's connection with my hometown to make his case.

Different moments in the conversation keep flashing past me as I put the car in drive and head home on autopilot. To Hogan's credit, he agreed to watch the video we created and read the pitch materials and keep an open mind. Finally he turned to me. "Are you in, Maddy? You know my concerns, but you also know Wolf. And if you think this a good idea, I am happy to be proved wrong. But you'd better get it right."

I could feel just how livid Hogan was at Craig for going behind his back and pushing this idea. I was livid, too, but I decided in that instant that I was more embarrassed for Hogan to know how fooled I had been by Craig. I couldn't stand losing Hogan's respect on top of it, so I decided to weather the storm.

"Hogan, it's a good idea. Avoiding the world of reality TV isn't going to make it go away. It's the future. You may hate how Craig went behind your back, and you can be mad at me for being a part of this. But all of that doesn't change the fact that it is a good idea and there's a way to do this right. I do think you should give us a chance."

Craig had the nerve to pat my leg as I said this, and it was all I could do not to smack his hand. I couldn't bear to look over at his beaming face. Just because this is working, doesn't change the fact that he duped me…and Hogan. I'm sure he thinks I am doing this for him, but I'm doing this for me. For my family and my home. In the end, Hogan gave us the green light and I'm going to run with it. But not before I give Craig a piece of my mind.

Upon arriving home, I hunt down my MacBook, which after I tore my living room apart, is sitting on my bed. The bed Craig and I slept in two nights ago. A fresh wave of rage inspires me to unleash the e-mail I've been composing in my head for the last twenty minutes. It appears Craig has beaten me to it, since the first thing I see in my inbox is an e-mail from him with the subject line: *See? We Did It!! Forgive me?!*

Is he serious? I change the subject line and my fingers start flying over the keyboard.

To: CJordan@HCProd.com
Subject: spineless moves

I really don't even know what to say to you. I am so angry that you would put me in that position with Hogan. He is my boss. You took advantage of my relationship with him. You took advantage of me.

It makes me sick to think I went up to my hometown and asked all my friends and family to trust me (you!) with their futures. And the whole time you were gambling, just pulling your standard Hollywood crap.

And then you shove me in Hogan's face, counting on me to save you. That is seriously spineless. You didn't tell me your plan because you knew I would never go along with it. I told you it was important to me to keep my personal relationships separate from work. I trusted you with my reputation and you trashed it.

And don't think I didn't see your face as we walked out. You could hardly contain your glee. I trusted you, Craig, and I feel very betrayed.

The truth is, I don't know how I am ever going to trust Craig again. This is exactly what I get for mixing work and my personal life. All I wanted was to keep things simple, and now they are more complicated than ever. But I know that firing off an angry e-mail probably won't help matters. This is a conversation we should have face-to-face, when I am calmer. So, after staring at the screen for a while, I delete the e-mail and then restlessly wander into the kitchen. I am so relieved that we have a day off today; there is no way I could face being on set. I can deal with Craig and *The Wrong Doctor* tomorrow. Today, I decide, I am going to treat myself to a rare afternoon of lounging on the couch and regrouping.

It's 1:15 by the time I grab some carrots, slather them in extra crunchy peanut butter, and collapse onto my shabby chic sofa. I'm hoping the History Channel has some gruesome show about World War II that will distract me from my problems. The TV is still on NBC from when I was watching last night's *Tonight Show* interview with Billy Fox. Before I can wipe the peanut butter off my hands to grab the remote, the commercial ends and Hope Brady is on the screen, flashing a badge and grabbing some grubby-looking dude in a twist hold, keeping the pressure on until he collapses to his knees at her feet. I am immediately transported back to my college dorm, where my girls and I would gather around the TV in the lounge and watch *Days of Our Lives* every single day.

I watch the scene with relish, wishing I could do something like that to Craig right about now. I stuff another carrot into my mouth as the scene changes and there's Adam Devin right there on the screen. I'm surprised to see him since he's been working with us for almost two months. How could he still be airing on *Days*? Their shooting schedule must be incredibly far ahead. The mechanics of production schedules momentarily distract me from the scene unfolding, where Adam's character, Grayson, is talking to a clean-cut, cop-looking guy in an outdoor balcony set. I haven't caught an episode of *Days* in years, but I immediately work out that Adam's character has hurt a lot of people in Salem, especially Sabrina.

My phone rings from the kitchen counter and I let it go to voice mail. A few seconds later it rings again and then again. Finally, I go to check it, worried that it could be an emergency on set, but nope, it's just Craig calling. Seven times to be exact. I ignore all of the voice mails. I still don't want to hear his lame excuses. Without thinking too much about it, I put Craig out of my mind and start writing a text:

Me: Watching Days right now—you're really good.

My thumb hovers over the SEND button. It's definitely the first time I've initiated anything with Adam that couldn't be defined as "professional courtesy," but what the hell? So I hit SEND and toss my phone down on the coffee table just as *Days* returns from commercial break. Soon Adam/Grayson reappears, entering a lovely restaurant where there seems to be a wedding reception taking place. I recognize Megan Keef, who used to play Annabelle on *Black Mountain Valley* and is now apparently playing Sabrina. Grayson hesitates for a moment and then starts cutting through the crowd toward her. The dramatic music tells me something big is about to happen. Given what a disaster my own love life is right now, I'm all too happy to get lost in this soap drama. Sabrina sees Grayson approaching, and before he can even speak, she leaps to her feet, clearly ready to tear into him about something. He tries to take her hand, but she jerks away and shoves his chest. She goes to slap him and he grabs her wrist just in time. All of a sudden, the chemistry and tension between them is through the roof. Then the music changes and there is the familiar downbeat of a tango. Sabrina narrows her eyes at Grayson and he smiles and releases her arm. He pulls a rose from the convenient bouquet nearby and offers it to her. She stares at the flower as if it might bite. Grayson bows gracefully and extends the rose again. "Dance with me," he says, which also clearly means "I love you" and "I'm sorry" and "I don't care who watches me make a scene over you" . . . it says everything.

Sabrina takes his hand and stops in the middle of the dance floor, where they perform a spectacular tango together. Adam pulls it off flawlessly. It's sexy and romantic, and I am more entranced than I like to admit when my phone beeps at me, signaling an incoming text. It's from Adam:

> AD: Thanks for the compliment. Glad you're enjoying the show. Did you see the tango? You have no idea how many rehearsals that took! I've got two left feet.

I'm smiling as I write him back:

> Me: I figured it was a body double. JK. It's beautiful. Gotta love the great "romantic gesture."

I don't even have time to put my phone down before it beeps again:

> AD: You'd better keep watching.

I wonder what that means. Looking at the clock, there can be only one more act in today's show. Right out of the commercial, we're back with Adam and he is down on one knee, pouring his heart out to Sabrina.

I can't help but wonder how much of that speech Adam ad-libbed, and if they have a script supervisor somewhere tearing their hair out trying to keep up with his changes. And even now, a part of my mind is still dwelling on my own drama. Perhaps Craig should ask one of our script writers to help him craft his apology to me since he so clearly sucks at it.

Sabrina is suitably moved, but right when she's about to speak, a loud brash yell intrudes on their moment and, wait,

Adam comes barreling into the room. He's playing twins! The two Adams get into a heated argument and...a gun is pulled... Grayson collapses to the ground. Okay, I did not see that coming. I immediately set my DVR to record tomorrow's episode, and then pick up my phone again to text Adam.

> Me: Holy crap! You played twins? I didn't know that.
> AD: Yeah, right at the end, they wanted to have me
> go out in classic soap style. I killed myself. And went
> to prison for life. ☺

It's not like I don't see Adam on set, acting every day, but for some reason, it's bittersweet that I caught his last episode on *Days*. I start writing a reply:

> Me: That's too bad. I was rooting for the blonde to find happiness,
> and you were so close to winning her heart.

Then I reread it and come to my senses. The last thing I should be doing is flirting with Adam right now. Flustered, I swipe my finger across the screen to delete it. I need to snap out of this momentary insanity and get back to business. After my little soap escape, the memories of the morning come flooding back. Hogan green-lit our sizzle reel, which means Craig and I have to deliver. At this point, the idea of working with Craig makes my stomach churn, but I'll cross that bridge when I come to it. Right now, I should be spending this afternoon doing research. I turn off my phone and get out my notebook.

Four hours later, I've watched eight different reality shows (how many *Housewives* franchises are there?!) and have polished off a takeout order of chicken tikka masala (aka, "the usual") from Gardens of India.

Inspired by my research marathon, I furiously make notes about the show:

1. Pick 5 main "characters" that really work, focus on their stories
2. Find a romance (Matthew and Jen?)
3. Interviews? (I like the format, but don't want it to seem overly produced or have them end up griping about each other all the time)
4. No catfights
5. What's the main cause of the show? (Save the mountain? Save the town? Revealing what life is like in a small country town?)

I get into the zone mapping out story lines and making lists of production opportunities and potential shooting schedules. Right now I don't want to think about the faceless person who will get to be in charge of running the show and have the final say for all these things. As I flip pages in my notebook, I wistfully fantasize about myself at the helm:

Fade in: gritty makeshift office

Camera starts on the beautiful snowfall through the window, pans to rugged cramped space that is ground zero for the production team. We hear off-camera dialogue as the camera sweeps the room to land on a beautiful, if clearly exhausted, dishwater blonde, midthirties.

MADDY

All right, everyone, let's stay focused here. What's on tap for today? Do we have everything we need for the overnight hike? How's it coming getting the camera equipment prepped?

PRODUCER #1

Maddy, a couple of camera crews volunteered to go on this shoot, because they have outdoor experi-

ence. But I'm just glad I'm not going--it's going
to be below zero every night. And getting all the
way to the ridge?

(*A couple of producers leaning against a wall snicker. Maddy
quells them with a look. The wall behind them is covered in notes,
pictures, and a big wall chart with the whole series broken down
by episode.*)

> PRODUCER #2
> (needing to jump in)
The Red Camera team used to work on *Ice Road
Truckers*. We should use them.

> MADDY
> (moving along quickly)
Okay, Red Camera leads the prep for the crew and
equipment.

> (she refers to her notebook)
And we've got Lewis slated to go as producer.

> (Maddy looks up at the group, in chairs, on the
> floor, leaning against the wall)
Where's Lewis?

> PRODUCER #1
He hasn't responded to any of my texts. We were supposed to meet for breakfast, but he was a no-show.

> MADDY
> (checks her phone and laptop)
How is this just coming up now?

MADDY (cont.)
(with a stern look)
We look out for each other, people. Who saw Lewis
last?

PRODUCER #3
(from her position on the floor, raises her hand)
We were out shooting footage at a couple of bars,
you know...schmoozing with the locals like you
wanted us to...

MADDY
(soothingly)
That's fine, Vanessa. I'm sure it was great. Just
tell me what happened. Did Lewis say anything?
Did you separate at all?

(They are interrupted by the phone ringing. Maddy quickly
grabs her phone.)

MADDY
This is Maddy Carson...yes, Lewis works for
me. Is he okay? We were starting to get really
worried...oh. Oh no.

(she gestures reassuringly to the worried
faces around the room)
No, of course. Yes, just let him know we'll be by
to visit him as soon as we can. Thanks so much.

MADDY
(hangs up the phone, turns to her worried staff)
Lewis is gonna be fine. He's at the hospital. But
he fractured his leg, slipping on some black ice

last night, so he's out. We can't push back the
hike or get behind in the schedule, so here what's
going to happen. I'll be the producer on the hike.

       (she silences the startled murmurs
          with a strong look)
I know it's dangerous, but I'll be fine. I know
these mountains like the back of my hand. You...

       (pointing at producer #1)
...are going to man the field interviews. You...

       (tossing her notebook at producer #2)
...will get these action shots done--we need
it for the opening credits and show intro. The
rest of you stick to your regular assignments.
Get back here for our calls. Stay on top of it,
people. We've got a show to produce.

       (she waits a beat)
And I've got to pack.

Energized by my extreme capability and calm (fantasy or
not), I decide to stay up as late as I need to get the concept fully
mapped out. I take out my trusty label maker so I can create a tab
for the Wolf-related section of my notebook. I don't know if it's the
coffee, or the curry, or the fact that I am in a zone with this idea,
but inspiration strikes and I know I have the perfect name for the
show. I eagerly punch the letters into the label maker, feeling a
little giddy. I hold the notebook away and look at my handiwork:
Never Cry Wolf. It's perfect.

Scene 002
Ext. Highway location shoot--day

It's a new day and I am back in the trenches, knee-deep in problems. I'm sort of regretting staying up until 2:00 a.m. working on *Never Cry Wolf* (I can't stop saying the name) since Murphy's Law is in full effect on the set of *The Wrong Doctor* this morning. The actors' hair/makeup trailer went to the wrong location, so the head makeup artist is throwing something of a tizzy on the travel coordinator and me (guilty by association). Either way, Stella made herself heard that she does NOT work under these conditions. How can she be expected to put on the stunt makeup, the bruises and the scars and the tattoos, when the heat of the day—it's only 8:00 and already about 85 degrees—will make it sweat right back off?

There is more to her tirade, but I offer to go get Frank and flee as fast as I can. I text him to let him know there is a fire to put out in the makeup trailer and head over to the set to see what the holdup was there. The director and Victor are moaning and groaning over a few set pieces that got blown over in an unexpected windstorm last night. It's going to take set design at least an hour to get things repaired enough to shoot. None of the close-ups can be shot until later in the day when they've had more time to get new pieces brought in from the building warehouse.

Fantastic. Well, at least the silver lining is that Stella doesn't have to panic so much about the makeup wagon. I text Frank to make sure he knows about the holdup and to see if perhaps the delay will help Stella chill out.

My phone immediately chirps with Frank's reply:

Frank: Nothing will do that. ☺ But thanks.

I laugh because it's true. Stella is definitely high-maintenance, but she's one of the most talented artists I've ever worked with. You'd think she really beats Billy up in the trailer before he comes to set, with those realistic black eyes and bruises.

A bit at loose ends since we have time to kill, I finally listen to Craig's messages from yesterday. They are all variations of "I'm sorry" and "Don't you see the bigger picture?" and "Please let's put this behind us and move forward with Wolf." I've got to say, it's nice that cool, calm Craig seems so out of sorts. I know I have to be an adult and have a mature conversation with him about how he hurt me and how I don't know if I can trust him, when what I really want to do is unfriend him and ask my friends in gym class never to speak to him again. I know, it's not high school, and that's why I am taking time before I make the call. I have to find my big-girl pants first.

I dare to wander back toward the trailers to make sure things have settled down with Stella, and I see her dragging a shirtless Adam Devin out of his trailer. I hear a string of Spanish curse words as she grabs a nearby apple box, turns it on its side, and shoves an acquiescent Adam into a sitting position.

"I don't know how they expect me to see in that cave you call a trailer. Frank thinks I can work miracles? *Ya vamos a ser!* I can't just slap a tattoo on you in the dark and think no one will notice. The fans, they notice." Adam's character has a tattoo high on his right shoulder, near the base of his neck. The tattoo is a critical element of the show's plotting for this episode. Lucas sees it by accident, recognizes that it's a military tattoo, and realizes that Ahmed is actually working undercover.

"Ah. Maddy, you're back. I need your continuity pictures. Mine are in that *chingado* trailer, and who knows when we'll see it again." Stella keeps track of her own continuity, but she and I always compare notes. I love that she's as meticulous as I am, and she appreciates my backup, especially on days like this.

"Did Frank let you know that set is running behind today too? You're fine on time." I focus on keeping my eyes locked on Stella. They do not roam even a little toward half-naked Adam, other than to nod hello.

"*No manches*. Bring me the pictures." And she returns her focus to prepping Adam's shoulder. Duly chastised, I go and fetch my book. I'm back within minutes and they are both right as I left them. Adam patiently sitting still, Stella doing her prep work, still bitching.

"They don't just give out Emmys for nothing, you know," Stella complains. As far as I can tell, Adam has said very little, but he keeps nodding and biting back a grin. I have my photo book open to the close-ups I'd taken of the eagle tattoo.

"Hold still, *mijo*." Adam does as directed, holding unnaturally still as I approach. Stella lays the premade tattoo on Adam's shoulder, and we compare it to the photos, getting the placement exactly right.

"It looks a little high on this side. I think it should be here." I run my finger along his spine, so focused on my obsession with getting the continuity perfect, it sneaks up on me that I am actually touching Adam's sun-warmed back. I try to cover my instinctive flinch as I pull away, but nothing gets by Stella. "He's not going to bite, you know."

Adam risks Stella's wrath to look over his shoulder at me. "Yeah, Maddy, I'm not going to bite."

"Turn around," Stella commands, and she adjusts the tattoo as his shoulders settle into stillness.

I am feeling a little useless and am about to walk away, when Adam says, "So you thought the tango was enough to win Sabrina's heart, huh?"

"Those moves were impressive. Did the show send you for weekly lessons?"

"Are you kidding? No. They brought in a choreographer for a couple hours the day before. Megan and I only had two days to learn the dance."

"Seriously? You did a dance like that with what... four hours of rehearsal? How many takes did you have to do?"

"Takes? Plural?" Adam gives a bark of laughter that apparently moves his shoulder and earns him a smack from Stella. "I wish. We do everything in one take there. No time."

"Wow! Now I am really impressed. You were really good," I say.

Adam turns his head slightly to look at me without moving his upper body at all. "Thanks," he says seriously. "That means a lot coming from you."

"You're welcome." I feel slightly awkward about the compliment. "So, what was the backstory? If you hadn't died, you would have gotten the girl? Soaps are dangerous that way. It gives people the idea that men sweep you off your feet like that in real life."

Stella snorts and then starts muttering under her breath in Spanish.

"What do you mean, Maddy? Real men don't tango or sweep women off their feet? I would beg to differ. Right, Stella? Tell her."

"Oh yes," says Stella. "I used to tear it up on the dance floor—salsa, tango, merengue, you name it... real men definitely know how to dance." She lets out a slow whistle.

"See?" Adam says to me, and then looks up at Stella. "And what do you mean 'used to,' Stella? You've still got moves."

"*Claro que si.* I could teach you about life and love in one dance, *mijo.*"

"Promises, promises. One day you're going to tease the wrong man and he'll take you up on your big talk."

"Well, then, he would be the *right* man, now, wouldn't he..." Stella laughs knowingly and Adam joins in.

I have to shake my head to get the somewhat disturbing image of Adam and Stella tearing up the dance floor out of my mind. "All I meant is that scenarios like that are unrealistic; they are the fantasy. In real life, you can't just ask the girl to dance in front of the whole town and have it solve all your problems."

"No one said it solved their problems. It was just Grayson's way of making a statement to Sabrina. A statement bigger than words. Anyone can say 'I love you.' In fact, that was the thing with these two characters. They'd both been through the wringer and had no reason to trust their words anymore."

"Yeah, I can't tell you how many times I've had to stop guys from sweeping me off my feet into sexy dances."

"Maybe you go to the wrong places," Adam replies.

"Or no places. You work all the time," Stella interjects, to which I maturely respond with an eye-roll.

"Or with the wrong guys," Adam adds.

I know when to take cover and change the subject. Besides, the least of my problems with Craig is that he doesn't dance. "Well, anyway, it was a rare treat to get to catch *Days.* I used to love that show so much. And it was fun to see you."

"Yeah, what did you do for the dark day? I imagine you, everywhere you go, unable to resist taking notes on everything around you. Sitting at a Coffee Bean, noting which hand the customers use to open the door, what shoulder her purse rests on, how many cups are stacked next to the register...," Adam teases.

"Ha-ha. No, I just had a meeting with Hogan...and Craig in the morning. It ran later than I thought, so I just worked from home in the afternoon." It feels weird to even mention Craig's name.

"Ah, with the big cheeses, huh? Are you already plotting who's coming back next season? I hope you put in a good word for me." Adam laughs.

"No, if you must know, we're pitching a new show." I find myself telling Adam and Stella all about the idea for *Never Cry Wolf*, leaving out Craig's treachery. They both seem really into it.

"Don't tell me you're going to leave *The Wrong Doctor*, though?" Adam asks.

"Oh no, no, this is just something on the side. I'm not even sure it's really going to happen. This is still my job." I want to squash any gossip that I may be leaving before it travels through the set faster than it would through Harriet's beauty parlor.

"Well, I think the show sounds amazing, but I'm glad to hear you're not leaving. We need you around here. Right, Stella?" Adam risks Stella's wrath to shift as he looks up at me.

"Oh, *dios mio*, I need you to stop moving," Stella mutters. "I think I've got the picture down now. Maybe you should leave so this one can concentrate on being still. You're distracting him."

"Yeah, no problem. Frank's texting me anyway. I'll see you on set."

The truth is, I'm the one who's distracted.

Scene 003
Int. HCP reception--day

Walking into the HCP offices, my stomach is tied in knots. It's been two days since the debacle in Hogan's office. I'm pretty sure I made my point with Craig. After all his texts and voice mails, I called his office yesterday to schedule an appointment to meet with him here this morning. I don't even have a chance to sit on the sofa in the lobby before Craig's assistant appears around the corner.

"Craig will see you now." She smiles at me and I follow her to his office. Obviously, she and I both know that I know where I'm going, but for some reason we both play out the formal ritual. His door is open and I hesitate. For all my righteous indignation, I am really not good at confrontations.

"Maddy. Come in." Craig stands up from behind his desk. He goes to take a step around it, but then changes his mind and just gestures to the open seating on the other side. "Please sit."

I choose one of the armchairs facing his desk instead of the sofa seating area so that the desk stays between us. Craig smoothes his tie and sits back down behind his desk.

"Craig, listen..." Now that I'm here, there are so many things I want to say, but I still don't know where to begin.

"Maddy, please, would it be all right if I start?"

"Fine." I take a deep breath to steady myself.

"First of all, I owe you a huge apology. I'm so sorry I put you in that position. It was never my intention to blindside you like that."

"Really? Because that's exactly what happened. That whole time in Wolf County..."

"When we were in Wolf, I honestly wasn't thinking about Hogan. I had such a great time. All I was thinking about was how there's such potential there, and how we can make it such a great show."

"It didn't cross your mind when we were sitting there with my family that Hogan hates reality TV? My mom told you they felt comfortable with the idea because Hogan was on board, and yet you knew he wasn't. You got everyone's hopes up on a HUGE gamble that Hogan would change his mind."

"But you see, it worked! I took a calculated risk. You have to do that sometimes to get ahead."

"Yes, it worked, but you didn't think about the fallout at all. That people, like yours truly, wouldn't take well to being lied to. You led me to believe Hogan was into the idea. I would never go into his office and tell him how to run his company or spend his money! He *is* Hogan Chenny Productions. If he doesn't want to get into the reality business, that's his prerogative."

"Listen to me, Maddy. I didn't make this up out of thin air. Everyone knows reality TV is here to stay. You know Hogan doesn't want to just retire to Palm Beach and sip mai tais after *The Wrong Doctor* wraps. And having his toe in reality is a good way to secure the future of HCP. It'll give him a good financial base and a solid platform from which—"

"Craig. Stop it. I'm not here to argue with you over whether it's a good idea or not. I like reality TV. It is a good idea for HCP. But that's not relevant. I'm angry and hurt because you intentionally lied to me about Hogan's approval of this project. I hate that you put me in a position of having to use my family's relationship with Hogan."

"You should know by now that this town is all about relationships. You put your relationship with Hogan behind safety glass? 'Break only in emergency'? That's not how Hollywood works."

"Exactly!"

"You are misunderstanding me. Hogan didn't listen to you in that room because he owed you a favor or because he knows your family. He listened to you because you have proven yourself to him over the years, and he knows a good idea when he hears one."

And he's right. I know that I deserve this job, and I deserve this chance—and Hogan knows it too. I'd never realized how much it bothered me, thinking that if people found out about my background, they would believe I didn't deserve this job. It feels like a weight has been lifted from my shoulders. A part of me is still pissed, and aware that Craig has neatly shifted the conversation away from his manipulation. I also hate that Craig put me in that room under those circumstances. But at the same time I feel good, knowing that I've earned Hogan's respect, and yes, even the right to disagree with him and be heard.

I can tell Craig realizes he's won this round and that my anger has softened. He doesn't make a thing out of it, though; he's smarter than that.

"Look, Maddy, we're really both on the same page. We love this idea. Hogan is on board now. We can put the past behind us and move on. I've spent the last few days pulling together our notes. I put a team together with the money Hogan granted us." He holds out the folder. "I'd like you to go up to Wolf during the hiatus next week and produce the footage. I have two great shooters to go with you. Get as much footage as you can. Then we can spend all next week editing for Reality Buzz, which is next weekend in Manhattan Beach." He pauses. "And I know I have a lot to make up to you. Don't give up on me, okay?"

I just sit there in silence. It was hard enough for me to address the work issues with Craig, but I know he's talking about our relationship now. I just don't have the stomach for it.

Undeterred, he starts again. "This was just a misunderstanding. I'm really sorry. I feel like we have something special. When you're back from Wolf, let me take you to dinner. Actually, let's go on that hike you suggested...Please? Maddy?"

I make him sweat it out a little more before I finally speak. "We'll see, Craig. There's so much to do for the show. Let's see when I get back."

Not the response he was anticipating, but it's the best I can do right now.

Scene 004
Int. Dark edit bay--night

Even though Janine is here with me in the HCP edit bay, it feels very empty as I clear away about a hundred empty Coffee Bean to-go cups. The caffeine has long since worn off. I don't even want to look at my watch. I've pulled all-nighters before. Certainly working in Hollywood means you have to be ready for unusual working hours. But this is by far the most intense thing I've ever done.

After shooting for two days straight in Wolf, we slammed the gear in the truck and headed back to LA. I slept the whole way. And now it's Sunday, and Janine and I have been holed up in the edit bay all weekend. I'm so lucky she was free this weekend and willing to help me work on the sizzle.

Tomorrow I go back to work at *The Wrong Doctor*, and I know Craig will want to make changes and finesse our presentation, so Janine and I are trying to get as much done as we can before Monday. Janine has been amazing. As much as I've learned about the different specialties in Hollywood, and what it takes to make TV, editing is a bit like the Wizard of Oz...they are the magicians behind the curtain that take all this raw footage and turn it into a polished, beautiful finished product. As I watch her work the Avid equipment, it's clear to me how far outside my skill set I am.

"Janine, it's been at least ten minutes. I have to thank you again for helping me with this. I don't know what I would've done without you."

"I shudder to think." She laughs. "Maddy, stop it. You're picking this up really quickly. I think you'll be a really good producer.
Look at this footage you got. You have good instincts."

"I don't know about that. I basically followed Craig's
instructions."

"I don't have time to give you a lecture on not selling yourself
short." Janine sighs. "I'll save it for next week. Right now, we
have work to do."

Again we focus on reviewing the hours of raw footage the
crew and I shot. We got some great images of a lot of the town,
views of the different locations we think would play prominently
on the show, lots of b-roll. Then we interviewed all the people
who'd agreed to be a part of the show. We set them up in different scenic locations and talked to them for hours about the town
and their lives. I was the interviewer, which I have no experience
with. But I got the hang of it by the end.

Watching Mrs. Gordon's interview when she tears up talking about how proud she is of her husband, Janine gives me a
thumbs-up. There are some truly great moments like this one,
and it gives me a rush of excitement and pride.

Screening all the footage takes forever. I keep reminding
Janine that I have notes on everything, that we don't have to
watch it all again, but she absolutely insists. She was right. We've
discovered lots of little interesting scenes, like the eclectic crowd
gathered to watch the band in the town square. Funny things
that happened, like Merry Gordon trying to sell Walt's taxidermy
to some hapless tourists. There were even a few awkward or tense
moments: the volunteers working so hard on the wine-tasting
event, only to realize that once again funds ran short this year,
and the crowd gathered wasn't as big as last year.

But now, late on Sunday night, I have to call it quits.

"Janine, thank you for helping me get such a head start on

this. And helping me understand it. This has been incredible. But honestly, we both have to work tomorrow—you know, our regular jobs. I can't ask you to pull an all-nighter for this. I have all next week to finish with Craig."

"I won't argue. And you're welcome. But seriously, you have good instincts for this. You're going in the right direction. I'm glad we had the chance to go over this just between the two of us first. So when you're in that edit bay with those guys, don't let them walk all over you, okay? Stick to your vision."

She grabs me by the shoulders as she finishes her pep talk and gives a little shake to emphasize her words. She's deceptively strong for being so lean. I am listening to what she says, but I can't help also wondering if she does that super-intense Pilates or something.

"I'm proud of you." She smacks me with a kiss on the lips, and then lets go. That's Janine for you; always expect the unexpected.

She hands me the box with all the discs of Wolf County, carefully labeled with the show's name.

"What do you think? Do you like it for a title?" I hold up the box.

"Are you kidding? It's perfect. And you don't think you're creative? You're crazy."

Those positive thoughts echo in my mind as I drive home and collapse onto my bed, still dressed and on top of the covers. I barely rally to set my alarm before letting my eyes close.

Scene 005
Int. Studio set--day

I check my phone again, for the tenth time in as many minutes. I sent Craig the draft of the sizzle reel as soon as I got home last night, and he has yet to respond. Just as I decide to give him five more minutes and then call, he texts. I pause before reading it, realizing how anxious I am waiting for his feedback.

> Craig: Definitely a great place to start. I have some ideas. I'll work on it today and we can meet up later tonight and take another look. I'll text you.

Hmmm, not exactly the strongest of praise, but I guess that's how these things go. It is only the first draft. Still, I am a little disappointed.

"Quiet on set!" Frank bellows, bringing me back to the present. I drop my phone and get my timer ready, pull my red pen out of my ponytail, and get my focus on the scene. The day drags, though. Usually when I'm on set, I feel like there's never enough time. Every minute flies by while we're trying to get as much done as we can. But all I can think about today is heading to the edit bay as soon as we wrap and working on the sizzle reel. I'm eager to see what Craig and his team have done with the footage.

It's 4:52 p.m. when we're about to wrap, but I haven't heard from Craig. Of course, I don't want to nag him, since he's working too. It's just harder than I thought it would be, not knowing what they're doing up there. Working with Janine all weekend may have given me the bug. I'm ready to get back in the booth, but somehow I feel like I have to be summoned by Craig, which is annoying.

I check my phone five minutes later and feel ridiculous. Not so ridiculous that I don't check it again five minutes after that, and finally there is a text from Craig.

Craig: Hey! It's really coming along. You have great stuff. Would you grab me a plate from catering when you come up? I haven't eaten all day.
Me: Yeah, sure. We're on the martini now. I'll be up in 30?

Every crew I've been on refers to the last shot of the day as the "martini shot." It's been around forever; it's a universal truth that everyone is ready for martinis after a long day of shooting.

Craig: Awesome. We're making good progress. Are you serious about the name? Never Cry Wolf?
Me: Yeah, what do you think?

I'm used to feeling so much more confident in my own opinions and ideas than I do about this show. You could fill a Costco with what I don't know about selling and making reality TV. But after the intense editing session with Janine, I feel like I'm getting the hang of it. I may not trust Craig dating-wise right now, but he certainly knows far more about how to sell this show than I do.

Craig: I love it. Seriously. Really clever. I think it'll sell. Good job.

His text puts a huge smile on my face. I can't help it. This is starting to feel so real. So possible.

"Wow. I wish I'd put that smile on your face." Adam stops in front of me. His grin lets me know he meant the come-on, but he also wants an answer to the unasked question.

"The Wolf project, the one I was telling you and Stella about. It's going well, that's all." I can't resist bragging a little.

"That's all? That's great! I'm happy for you." And again, he isn't prying exactly. He isn't asking for details, but he doesn't walk away. So I fill the silence.

"Yeah, I got some really great footage this weekend, up in Wolf. Now we're...Craig and I are getting it edited for some pitch conference this weekend."

"Oh, you're going down to Reality Buzz in Manhattan Beach?"

"You know about it?"

"Sure. One of my friends is a successful independent reality producer. He's going to be speaking on one of the panels. It sounds like a pretty important event."

"Yeah, Craig says it's the best place to sell the show. So, you know, we're busting it to get it ready by then."

"Well, I'm excited for you, Maddy. Good luck." He brushes my cheek with a kiss as he heads back to the trailers.

What is it with this drive-by kissing lately? I breathe out, 97 percent sure that I am hallucinating that I still smell his aftershave as I make my way to Crafty and grab two plates of food.

I find Craig and one of the HCP editors, Paul, in one of the edit bays. It looks much the same as it did when Janine and I were camped out this weekend—empty coffee cups and protein bar wrappers everywhere. When I walk in, they are scanning through Mrs. Gordon's sit-down interview. They must be looking for something specific because they are blazing through on fast-forward and her voice sounds like a chipmunk at this speed. I smile when I catch that emotional moment when she talks about Mr. Gordon. It's one of my favorite scenes in the whole reel.

"How's it going?" I set down the food on a nearby table. It's a small room, with huge computer monitors taking up most of one wall. Paul stays focused on whatever it is that he's looking for as Craig looks up at me.

"Hi, Maddy. Glad you're here. It's going great. You took perfect notes. I mean, of course you did." He thinks he's flattering me, complimenting me on my note-taking. And it's a new feeling for me, realizing that I don't want good notes to be my only contribution here. I know I did a lot more than that.

"What did you think watching the raw footage, though? We got such great stuff we didn't even expect."

"Oh, we don't have time to screen every minute. We just went off your notes. I already worked on an outline for us to go on. Paul and I have pretty much had no problem finding the right beats to fill in the blanks."

Fill in the blanks, I think. After the lecture I got from Janine about how important it is to review the footage from scratch, I'm surprised to hear that Paul and Craig just went off my original notes, which I know left out such good material. *Never Cry Wolf* is more than just a paint-by-numbers concept; it's about these people, and he needs to see their whole interviews to know that. But I haven't even seen what they put together, so maybe it's premature to worry. I still am such a rookie in this field, so I bite my tongue.

"Well, can I see what you have so far?"

"Sure. Paul, cue it up." Paul grunts something unintelligible and drags the Mrs. Gordon interview off his main viewing screen. He uses his mouse to pull up another window that has a red graphic on it. He presses PLAY and the graphic contorts into the shape of a wolf and then slowly reshapes itself to read *Never Cry Wolf.* It's a really cool effect, and I whisper that quickly before any talking starts. Craig smiles at my compliment but keeps his eyes on the screen. There are these quick flashes of the different views we shot. The beautiful scenic shots fill the screen, piling on top of each other.

"I'm not sure what kind of music will work best here. We're kind of thinking a rock song. You know, like how *Deadliest Catch* has that Bon Jovi song? Something classic rock, like that." Watching the rhythm of the different images on the screen, I can imagine what he's talking about.

Then the scene cuts to Mike meeting with the blasters. It's not winter yet, obviously, so I had them mock up what their early morning meetings are like, when the snow is fresh and they have to get up there by five or six o'clock and make sure the mountain is safe for skiers. They talk about setting off the charges in certain areas, safety, and so on. It made me uncomfortable to ask them to "act" for the camera, but the guys got into it quickly and they did a pretty good job. Besides, I reasoned, it's only for the sample reel. We will get the real footage when we shoot over the winter.

Obviously Craig had pulled avalanche footage from public domain because he'd added that to the footage, really hammering home the dangerous element of their jobs. It's effective.

Next up is Pete's Tavern. Paul clearly added a lot of cuts to the footage, making it seem like the crowd's been there a long time. Again, they added shots from somewhere else of drinks being passed around, close-ups of people drinking. And then they cut to the guys I interviewed, Matthew's friends, talking about life in town during the season. Just when I'm about to object that we're not trying to make a winter version of *Bachelor Pad*, the video cuts off. Paul hits PAUSE and they both turn to me.

"That's as far as we've gotten. What do you think so far?"

"It seems like it's coming together," I say honestly. "I'm glad you found some footage to add of snow and avalanches because the visual really does enhance how dangerous their jobs are. It makes it look really cool. I wonder if you're going a little too far, though, selling the nightlife in Wolf? It's not *Girls Gone Wild* in the Snow."

Craig barks laughter between bites of the food I brought up. "It is hardly *Girls Gone Wild*, Maddy. Don't be such a prude. You've got to make it a little sexy, right?" Paul chortles a bit, too, which is annoying to me. I don't even know this guy.

"No, I get what you're going for. And we talked about playing up the singles scene. But it's still... I don't know... Are you thinking this is a ten p.m. show? I saw *Never Cry Wolf*"—I love saying it aloud—"as a show you could watch with your parents."

"We need to keep our options open. We're not creating a sizzle reel for a specific network, so it's a good idea to show what we're capable of. If a family network is the highest bidder, they can reel us in. If Nat Geo buys it, they'll want to focus on the guy stuff—the blasting, the technology, the dangerous outdoors stuff. Who knows, Bravo might want to do a *Real Housewives of Wolf County*. We might want to have more of that angle ready to play up."

Listening to Craig rattle off all these different approaches, I again am reminded how out of my element I am.

"We've made great progress," Craig says, taking a sip of cold coffee. "Let's call it quits, huh? Pick up again tomorrow?"

"Sure, Craig." Paul starts saving the files on his computer. "I have a deadline tomorrow for Janine. We have to get the rough cut of episode one done. So I can't really get to this until after probably four."

"Sure. Great. We all do still have our day jobs to deal with. Right?" Craig laughs casually. As he gathers up his briefcase and iPad and starts making his way to the door, I catch on. I definitely do not want to be left to make small talk with Paul, so I grab my stuff and follow him out. The elevator doors ding open the second Craig presses the down button.

"Craig, we're going to be shooting till eight p.m. at the best tomorrow." I hate not being there for this part, but there's no way I can replace myself on *The Wrong Doctor* set. I wouldn't even ask. "I didn't want to say anything in front of Paul, but I'm really concerned about the direction of the presentation. I want to make sure that we represent ourselves accurately. Right?" I hesitate, unsure of how to say this. " I mean, I know this is your specialty, but what's the point of selling the show under false pretenses?"

"It's not a problem, Maddy. We're on the same track here."

"I don't know if we are." I take a deep breath. "Did you even look at the version I started with Janine? It wasn't polished or anything, but it was definitely on the right track..."

Craig looks at me for a second, saying nothing. He takes a deep breath and sighs. "Okay. I get it. You obviously have a vision for the reel. Go with it. Do you want to work with Paul?"

"I think Janine really understood the show. She was pulling it together exactly as I had pictured it."

The elevator dings and the doors slide open, and we both walk off together. "Then you set it up with Janine. We'll screen it together on Friday so we can make any final adjustments and have it ready to go on Saturday, okay? You've obviously got a strong feeling about this. I think you should go with it."

Craig leans in confidently, aiming for a gentle kiss on the lips. I should have been expecting it, but I jerk my head away. I take the time to gather my thoughts as I pull out my key card to unlock the door. With my hands full, I go to shove my shoulder into the door when Craig reaches past me and holds it open.

I mutter a "thanks" automatically as I go through, and he follows right behind me. I stop outside the building and turn back to face Craig with a deep breath. "Listen, Craig. I think we need to put any sort of personal relationship on hold for now. This project is already pretty intense, and I just don't think it's going to work for me to try to balance everything all at once." I'm pretty proud of that line actually. I nicely dodged all the bullshit he's pulled, knowing that I still have to work for him.

Craig looks away and sighs. "Maddy, I don't think we need to make any big decisions right now. We're both busy with work and doing this on the side; I understand that. But that's not going to last forever. In fact, once we sell the show, we can step back and let the show runner do all the work."

My spine straightens at his automatic assumption that I will allow myself to fade into the background, even if I don't get to be in charge. But Craig keeps going. "We're really good together. Let's put a—"

"No. No pins. I'm not comfortable leaving this up in the air. We are working together on a project that is very important to me. And I have to report to you at HCP, so the waters are already muddied enough. Let's please not make this more awkward than it already is. Okay?"

"I think you're making a big mistake." For a second, looking into his eyes, he seems really angry. This conversation could get ugly quick. But when he looks back at me, he has contained whatever that was. "Okay, but don't worry. I'll be waiting when you change your mind." And then he steps off the curb and into his car, parked right in front.

Keys in hand, I start heading toward my car several rows back. Maybe I was wrong about the anger I thought I saw in his eyes. He seemed pretty calm as he walked away. This really could all be fine now. I can't help feeling like I dodged a bullet.

As the engine roars to life, I have one mission to focus on—making the best sizzle reel ever, to prove I'm right about *Never Cry Wolf.* Things can still get dicey dealing with Craig on this, but at least the personal thing is resolved. Breaking up with your boss is not easy. I'm thinking I need a new rule #1: No bosses.

Scene 006
Ext. *The Wrong Doctor* set--morning

Friday morning I wake up from what could only be termed a long nap. Janine has been such an amazing friend and has burned the midnight oil by my side all week, unflinchingly going again and again over the footage, until finally we have at least five minutes of a perfected sizzle reel. I head to work with my iPad loaded with a final version that is fun, exciting, and dangerous—all of the elements we wanted. I mentioned to her the way the boys had pumped up the action/danger element of the blasters, and we added that into it. A good idea is a good idea. But we definitely kept to the heart of what I think *Never Cry Wolf* is really all about: the people and their stories.

Even though I haven't slept more than four hours at a time for the last three nights, I am revitalized. I'm not on set more than ten minutes before both Billy and Adam are teasing me about how giddy am I.

"Hmmmm, someone must have had a good night last night. Did you get lucky? Or were they playing *Can't Buy Me Love* on TBS again?" Billy teases.

"Ha-ha, Billy. If you must know, it's work related."

"You got the reel done for the conference tomorrow?" Adam asks, and I am touched he remembered.

"Yep! I finished it!" I guess it's redundant based on the look on my face, but I can't help but add, "I'm really happy with how it turned out." It takes everything in me to refrain from begging them to watch it. I am clutching my iPad like a proud parent. Luckily Adam beats me to the punch.

"Well, when are we watching?" Adam asks eagerly with Billy chiming in, "Let's do this."

I am suddenly consumed with excitement and nerves at my first real objective viewing.

"Yes! I would love for you to see it." *Deep breaths, Maddy. Be cool.* "Maybe during a break or lunch, but you have to be honest. Don't tell me it's awesome if it isn't, okay?"

"Of course, Maddy. I would never lie to you. Romeo over here, I can't vouch for him."

"Shut up, Fox." Adam hits his arm, which must really have hurt, because even though Billy doesn't flinch from the contact, he does reach up to rub the spot a minute later. "I'll definitely tell you what I really think. I can't wait."

We finally get a break in the action of *The Wrong Doctor* around noon. Billy said they'd be in his trailer, so I head over when I'm done reviewing the next setup with Frank and the director. I was trying not to rush them, but Frank finally looked at me funny and asked if I had to go to the bathroom or something. I sheepishly said no and simmered down until they wrapped things up.

Knocking on Billy's trailer door, the butterflies in my stomach are so strong I feel like I might explode. The door opens at the same time I hear Billy shout, "Come in!" Adam answers the door, holding it open for me from the inside, so I have to brush past him to climb into the Honey Wagon, the fancy RV actors get on location.

"Nice digs, huh?" Adam comments, seeing that it's clearly my first time inside Billy's trailer.

"Is that a stove?" I am momentarily distracted by the fact that there is an actual full-sized stove in Billy's trailer. When would that ever be necessary?

"Billy insists on warm milk before bed. And a microwave just won't cut it," Adam says. "I'm surprised he doesn't have a towel warmer too. Aren't you?"

I don't have time for their ribbing. "Do you guys want to see this or finish your pissing contest?" I don't wait for an answer. I sit down on the sofa and find the video file Janine saved last night, or was it this morning? I turn the volume all the way up as both guys sit, one on either side of me. Adam braces one hand on the sofa behind me and leans in over my shoulder as I hit PLAY. We watch the whole thing like that. I try to see it with a fresh perspective, imagining how they must be looking at it as objective viewers.

When it fades out at the end, I can't stand the silence. I jump up and turn around to look at them both. "I should've given you guys an introduction or something. Do I need to explain it at all?"

"Maddy. It's fantastic." Adam is the first one to speak. "Really. It's clear and compelling and tells the story of Wolf County. I think it really sells your show."

"The people are awesome," Billy adds. "That moment with Mrs. What's-Her-Name? The older woman."

"Gordon," I say, at the same time as Adam does. I look at him, surprised. He just taps his head above his ear and smiles. Ah yes, that soap star memory.

"Right, Mrs. Gordon is perfect. She's exactly the moment that sells the heart of your show. I really liked that part." Billy finishes his thought and they both mention a few other moments in the video that they really liked. I can't believe what I'm hearing. They both point out all the same things Janine and I did as their favorites.

"Thank you both. So much. Seriously. It means a lot to me that you liked it. I'm so excited." They take turns hugging me, and I know I am not imagining it when Adam's hug lingers a beat longer. As good as I felt this morning about what we had done, I am twice as excited and, maybe more importantly, confident sharing the reel with Craig. I know I'm going to have to sell it to him; this isn't exactly what he pictured. But after Billy and Adam both had such a positive response, I know I'm right. I know this is the show. I leave the trailer on cloud nine.

Scene 007
Ext. *Wrong Doctor* location--evening

It's been two hours, fourteen minutes, and eleven seconds (not that I am counting) since I sent the sizzle reel to Craig, and it's been complete radio silence.

We're supposed to meet after production wraps tonight to go over the plan for tomorrow. Reality Buzz starts at 10:00 a.m. We need to be in Manhattan Beach, with everything set up and our pitch ready to go by then. I have no idea what happens at these conferences and maybe that is fueling my stress, but it feels like we're really down to the wire here. That said, I have faith in Craig's experience in this. He knows how to sell shows; his résumé speaks for itself. Even if he hasn't sold a show since coming to Hogan's company, he obviously has the skill sets. Also, based on the way he convinced everyone in Wolf to go along with the program, he can be persuasive and passionate. So we just need to put some finishing touches on the plan, practice the presentation a few times, and everything should be fine. I repeat that in my mind and take a deep breath.

At least the afternoon flies by. Frank had been working with Tanya, the director this week, on a fancy camera setup for the romantic reunion between Dr. Lucas and Vivian, the woman who's been fighting to get him freed from the insurgents. The simplicity of their performances had even some of the toughest on the crew tearing up. After seeing it all laid out, Tanya decided to eliminate the big tricky camera angle, determining that the straightforward close-ups would be more intimate and thus more effective, which means, as I glance at my watch for the thousandth time in the last ten minutes, that I'm done a lot earlier than I thought I would be. I can barely concentrate on getting all my paperwork turned in to the production office before forcing myself to walk, not run, across the crew parking lot to my car. Still having not heard a peep from Craig, I'm on a mission.

The setting sun is blinding as I drive up the hill to Craig's home. It isn't until I've pulled up to his driveway that I start to ask myself if this is even a good idea, just dropping by unannounced. Maybe he has a perfectly logical explanation for not replying to my texts. Maybe he had to go to a meeting or something. Maybe it's something personal; he could even be sick.

Well, it's too late now; I'm here. I walk up to the front door, with those big bay windows looking into the living room, and just as I am about to knock, I realize the lights are dim, as in "mood lighting." Does he have a woman over?

With everything going on with *The Wrong Doctor* and the big Wolf deadline, I'm so glad I ended things with Craig. Being diplomatic about it because we have to work together on this project made me want to swallow my tongue, but I did it. I know I don't want to be with him, but I *really* don't want to walk in on Craig and another woman right now.

Lying snake. I mean, where are his priorities? We have work to do tonight. How can wining and dining some chick be more important than texting me back about Wolf County? I am really working myself into a frenzy standing on his porch, and then I look up and see his security camera and realize my little reverie has been caught on tape, or worse, is being watched by someone right now. Pure pride fuels me to knock on the door instead of skulking away.

"Coming!" Craig sounds annoyed. I'm determined to be adult

and mature about this, whatever awaits on the other side of the door. Either way, we still have work to do, and I can get through this. I have to, for the sake of Wolf County. There is too much at stake for me to wimp out now.

The door swings open.

"Hi, Craig. I've been trying to reach you all day." I notice immediately that he has moved to stand in front of the open door so I can't see into his house.

"Maddy. What are you doing here?" he asks, trying to sound casual.

"I've been trying to reach you since lunch." I step right up to him. Either he's going to let me in or embarrass himself coming up with some lame excuse for why he can't. He relents and steps aside slightly. "I sent you the final cut of the Wolf County sizzle reel," I continue in a cheerful voice. "I'm so excited about it. I was waiting for your reaction all day. I mean, I'm assuming you got it. The Dropbox file shows it had been downloaded."

"Um, yeah, Maddy. I got it," he starts, and then his eyes dart slightly over to the study door, partially ajar. I give up all pretense and march to the door, determined to catch him in the act. I barely beat him to the door, and I manage to swing it open, completely ignoring whatever nonsense he is uttering.

It takes me a minute to digest what I see. I guess I really had been expecting to catch some sort of intimate scene. My eyes travel over to the girl who is indeed hidden away in his house, but she's fully dressed in mismatched denim on denim, and not even paying attention to me standing over her shoulder. She probably hasn't even heard us, due to the headphones she has on. Her eyes are glued to the three huge computer screens on Craig's desk. On all three monitors are different scenes from the footage of Wolf County. She's replaying the same section of dialogue between my brother and one of the blasters in that mock meeting I'd staged just for the sizzle. But as I watch, feeling Craig over my shoulder, now not even trying to get me out of there, this woman literally puts words in my brother's mouth. Or rather takes words out. She deftly types out a few commands, drags the mouse, and presto, my brother's innocuous instruction comes across like an accusation. She rewinds it, and with this new edit, and whatever else she's done before I got there, I don't even recognize the conversation playing on the monitor. It now seems as though Mike and this guy Sam are exchanging confrontational verbal jabs. If I hadn't filmed this interaction myself, I would never have believed it happened completely differently.

POP! The twentysomething editor loudly snaps her gum, pulling me out of my stupor. I turn to Craig with every accusation in my mind clearly spelled out on my face.

"Maddy." He has the nerve to heave a huge sigh. But I stay silent, waiting. "You have to know that your reel won't sell. It's too...happy. Simple." I force myself to breathe evenly. "There wasn't any conflict. We need drama to sell this thing." I stare into Craig's face, searching for some sign of remorse.

"So, let's see your version." I want to see what he's done, but I also am giving myself time to figure out what to say, how to handle this. I am in shock that he is sitting here editing a new reel behind my back. When was he going to tell me about this?

"Look at it this way...People argue, right? Are you telling me that Mike has never gotten into it with one of his crew?" I don't respond. I'm thinking that, yes, of course they disagree from time to time, and Mike had agreed to allow a certain amount of that kind of conflict on the show, but manufacturing it like this is over the line.

"We don't have the time or money to shoot everyone until we see their real interactions, what we'll really get for the show, so we're just enhancing the footage we got. Showing the potential."

He's so persuasive, which is exactly why he's good at selling shows. He's a salesman, I remind myself. He went around Wolf telling everyone he'd helped me come up with the idea...and he was so convincing that even I was starting to fall for it.

"Show it to me," I say quietly.

At this point the girl sitting at the computer has pulled her headphones off. She's watching us intently as if we were on a fourth monitor, another scene playing out for her to edit.

"Go ahead, Pam. Play it."

She turns around and hits a few buttons on the keyboard. The opening logo pops up on the big screen on the right. She's still popping her gum as she says, "It's not finished. We haven't gotten to the last sequence, and I haven't sweetened it yet." She hits ENTER. "But here ya go."

I take a calming breath, preparing myself to be open-minded. I see that they've used the intro I put together with Janine, which makes me think maybe I've overreacted. Maybe Craig has a point, and he just made some small adjustments. But then the montage ends and it lands on a scene at Pete's Tavern. Somehow, from even what I saw that first afternoon in Paul's edit bay, they've gone even further and turned it into a raging club scene. They added flashes and neon lighting, and the whole impression is now more Vegas nightclub than casual bar hangout. It feels wrong to me, and my discomfort builds as they cut from that to the intimate hot springs footage, that I thought was plenty edgy already. But now they've turned it into *Temptation Island*. I know Craig will just say I am being naïve, so I silently keep watching.

Similar changes keep stacking up until we get to the Gordons' garage. I don't know how they did it, but they took one awkward moment between the loving couple and turned it into a serious marital confrontation. The magic of editing. A part of me marvels at this sloppy-looking editor's meticulous skill. Obviously

Craig went to someone with a talent for exactly this type of manipulation. I stare in fascinated horror at Merry rolling her eyes at a comment from Walt. Both moments are totally taken out of context and streamed together to create tension and animosity. Another exchange, again completely misrepresented, shows Walt making a belittling comment about Merry, which was said to me as an inside joke but was edited to seem deadly serious. I feel tears of rage spring unwillingly to my eyes. It just won't stop. If my parents saw this, if the Gordons ever saw this, they would be so hurt, so betrayed. By me. They put their trust in me. I was the one who allowed this to happen. They believed me when I said I would protect them and make it a show they could be proud of.

"Stop it! Turn it off. I've seen enough!" I look at the completely foreign and complicated keyboard. I don't have the first idea how to pause the video, never mind delete the damage they've done. I am shaking as I turn to Craig. "How dare you?!" From the look on his face, it's obvious that he knew this would be my reaction. And he did it anyway.

"Calm down, Maddy. This isn't that big a deal." He seems resigned, which only adds to my rage.

"Calm down? Not a big deal? Are you kidding me? This is a huge deal. This isn't who these people are. This isn't what Wolf was supposed to be about." Perhaps I should have a lucid argument, some sort of calm way to convince Craig to do it my way, but this is so far beyond that any chance of calm flies out the window. I can't be next to Craig for five more minutes, never mind work with him on this project.

"So what was your big plan, Craig? Show the networks this terrible video and then deal with the consequences later? As if Hogan would ever be okay with that!" I don't even bother to wait for his answer. It doesn't matter what his latest scheme was—in his mind, the end will always justify the means. "We are done. I mean, the show. Everything. I am absolutely not going to be a part of the hatchet job you are trying to do on my hometown." I am practically spitting the words at this point. I turn toward the door and walk out. It's not some grand exit line, but I'll take it. As I stride toward my car, I feel like I'm practically floating on my righteous indignation. Perhaps it's the anger distracting me, but I don't see the little edge on the driveway where it meets the sidewalk. I stub my toe so hard I know it's probably bleeding, but I refuse to look at it until I get inside my car, which thankfully is blocked from view by a large row of hedges. Tears burn under my eyelids as I slam my hand down on the steering wheel, again and again.

I want to scream it at the top of my lungs: *I was WRONG! I was WRONG!* I'm so mad at myself for believing that he could be different, especially after what he already did. Does he think that I'm that big a fool?

I take a deep breath and wipe at my tears. I don't have time for a pity party right now. Craig cannot show that tape, and I know just what I have to do to stop him, even if I dread making the call. I turn my car on and dial.

"Hogan Chenny's office," Hudson answers.

"It's Maddy. I need to speak to Hogan. It's urgent."

"One second. Let me put you through to his cell."

I practice my yoga breathing while I wait. I know I have to collect my thoughts and explain in a calm, coherent manner. I've never complained to Hogan about anything, really. I've always settled it myself or with my direct boss. I know I'm right to go straight to Hogan on this one, but I can't help but be nervous too.

"Maddy, honey. What's going on?"

"It's about the reality show. I'm sorry to bother you with this, but I felt really strongly that you need to know what's going on."

"I'm listening." Hogan goes from friendly concern to business in an instant.

"I know you picked up on the tension between me and Craig at the pitch meeting. I didn't want to get into it then; I thought we could work it out. But if you'll give me a second, I think you need to hear the whole story now. The bottom line is, Craig had completely misrepresented the situation to me about the show. He implied to me that you had not only allowed him to pursue developing a reality show, but also were encouraging it. When I came up with the concept, he made me think you were completely on board."

"I figured as much based on your reaction. You know how I feel about reality TV. I've never been shy about my opinion. I'm surprised you were so easily convinced otherwise." It stings, how right he is.

"Believe me, I should've known better, or at least checked with you first. I completely get that. But I hope you understand, now that I've gotten my family and a lot of the community on board, I can't just walk away. And the truth is, I don't want to. I think it's a good idea, it'll be a good show, and it'll do the community a lot of good."

"Why do you think I went along with it? I feel the same way." This gives me a measure of relief.

"So, I'm e-mailing you a link to the sizzle reel I finished this week. Craig and I had been planning to go to Reality Buzz in Manhattan Beach tomorrow to pitch it."

"I know, I gave my permission. Look, I'm in the middle of dinner and accepted the call because you said it was urgent. Is there something else?"

I take a deep breath.

"Yes, there is. I went to Craig's tonight to go over the last-minute details. He's been editing a completely different sizzle reel for tomorrow. In secret. It makes Wolf look like those trashy reality shows you hate. It's exactly what I promised everyone it wouldn't be." I don't even wait for Hogan to interject. "But we don't need that to sell the show. I don't care what Craig says. The reel I made, and Janine helped me with, shows the heart of the town. There's drama, everything we need, but without making false promises for the show. Even if Craig's version is what it takes to sell the show, I wouldn't be a part of it, and I don't think you would want to be either. And I know everyone in Wolf would be horrified to see what Craig created by manipulating it with editing—"

"Absolutely not," Hogan interrupts me. "You can't let Craig show something that butchers Wolf. I'm sure he's thinking that as long as he makes a deal tomorrow, I won't care. But that's bullshit. Pardon my French." I hear him take a deep breath. "Are you with him right now?"

"No, I left to call you." I can't begin to describe how relieved I feel.

"I'm calling him now to straighten this out. He has always known how I feel about Wolf. I can't believe he would try to get away with something like this."

Wait. He's always known?

"Sorry, Hogan, what do you mean he's 'always known' about Wolf?"

"Well, I go there every winter, Maddy. Of course Craig knows where I am and how to reach me." So Craig lied about that too. I know the next question I have to ask.

"Did he know about me?"

"What do you mean? Maddy, hon, I have to call Craig. Get this resolved."

"No, wait. Hogan, please. Did you ever mention to Craig how you knew me?"

"Yes, of course. I mean, I know you don't like to advertise to the crew, but Craig's in management. No reason not to tell him.

But I told him not to say anything to anyone since you prefer to keep it under wraps. He didn't say anything, did he?"

"No. He didn't say anything." I'm working so hard to breathe evenly that I'm probably going to hyperventilate. "Thanks for letting me know."

"Okay, hang in there, hon. Let me deal with Craig and I'll call you back."

What a manipulative, sleazy, opportunistic slimeball. I sit there at the curb outside Craig's house stewing. I am so livid with myself for trusting him. For falling for... everything. He was using me all along. That much is clear.

Before I can consider my next move, gum-smacking Pam comes charging out of the house. Clutching a backpack and her coat, she hustles past without looking at me, hops in her Beetle, and zooms away.

I take it as a sign that Hogan's made the call and taken care of the alternate sizzle reel. He has lawyers who can make sure that it's destroyed, but I have to figure out what I'm going to do about tomorrow. But first, fueled by a fresh wave of anger, I realize I've got a few things to say. Ignoring the throbbing in my toe, I march back to the front door and knock. This time when Craig opens the door he swings it wide, inviting me in with no hint of irony. I stare at him, perhaps truly seeing him for the first time.

An old adage my mom used to quote rings in my mind: *When a man shows you who he really is, believe him.* I know now that Craig was a person I'd built up in my mind, who I'd assumed (it pains me to use that word) he was or wanted him to be, and now I am seeing who he really is. Fool me once.

"I've spoken to Hogan. He should be calling you any minute. If he hasn't already."

"He has." Craig does, in fact, seem defeated. Seeing that I

have no intention of coming inside again, he lets go of the door and wanders through his open living room to the bar. "We deleted the 'doctored'"—he exaggerates the word with finger quotes—"version of the reel. It doesn't exist." He pops open a beer and guzzles.

Given that the Wolf County business seems to be resolved—Hogan has protected the town, not to mention my reputation with everyone back home—there's only one thing left to clear up.

"You knew all along. About me." I watch him. His eyes meet mine, but otherwise he doesn't flinch. "You acted so shocked about my family's friendship with Hogan. In fact, you *acted* hurt that I hadn't mentioned it to you. But that was all a lie. You'd known from the beginning."

"Yes. I knew. And for the record, I was hurt that you never felt you could confide in me."

Enraged, I yell, "I was RIGHT not to trust you with that! I shouldn't have trusted you at all, as it turns out. Was the whole thing a setup from the beginning? Did you only ask me out to further your own agenda with Hogan?" Even as I voice the question, I can't believe he would be that manipulative. But he doesn't rush to defend himself; he doesn't insist that what was between us was sincere. In fact, all he does is sigh and stick his hands in both pockets, resigned. "That's not an answer, Craig." In the silence, I've managed to regroup and state this at a normal volume. Maybe I'll pat myself on the back later for that.

"Okay, I knew. I knew how close you were—you are—to Hogan. I'm not going to say it didn't factor in."

"Oh my God," I mutter. I can't believe I am just seeing this side of him now.

"But I didn't keep dating you for that. I care about you, Maddy. I do. And I think we were really good together. But the show, my career, you know how important that is to me. Hell, I thought you felt the same way about your own career. You need this. Your dying little town needs this as much as I do."

"Not like this we don't." Somehow I don't think he's even aware of how condescending he is being.

"Look, you and I may disagree over how to do business. But I was never doing anything but trying to get Wolf County sold and help us all be successful. It would've made money for everyone involved. Potentially a lot of money. I don't know how that makes me the bad guy here. And now you'll never get this show made." It's his turn to spit out the last words.

I'm seething, but I respond with as much calm as I can muster. "If you don't understand what you did wrong, then I doubt I'll be able to explain it to you. It's not worth the effort anyway. And you know what, Craig? I *am* going to get this show made. My way."

I turn, and as calmly as possible walk right out the front door. As I hop in my car again, rev the engine, and shoot down to Sunset, I am determined to put Craig out of my mind. I have bigger things to focus on. Am I really going to let this debacle tank Wolf County's chances of being sold? I can't help but question my instincts here. Craig seemed so sure that the only way to sell Wolf was to manipulate the footage. Despite my confident exit, his words ring in my ears: *"Now you'll never get this show made."*

But then I hear an even louder voice that says, *"Well, Maddy, I always like to think there's a will and a way, but it's pretty useless if you have one without the other."*

I can hear my dad's voice as plain as if he's in the car with me, and I know he's right. There must be a way—and I do have the will.

Act Four

Scene 001
Int. Soho House, evening

HC: Finishing dinner at Soho House. Can you come by? Would like to talk in person.

Incredibly relieved to get this text from Hogan, I am sure that if we put our minds together, we can figure out how to salvage this situation. I make a U-turn and head back toward the famous club. I leave my Toyota with the valet and ride the fancy elevator up to the main lobby. *Okay, a plan,* I think. I need a plan. I could just go home and Google "How to pitch a TV show." Maybe Wikipedia has some useful tips. I can't help but overhear the two suits sharing the tiny elevator with me.

"We packaged the deal. Everything was signed tonight," the dark suit with the red tie says. He's got great hair, for an agent.

"Well, it's a great concept," says his friend. Trying not to listen, I pull out my phone and fake a text.

"I haven't heard it pitched before. And everything right now is about the personalities attached. The networks want good characters. And we have that. I think we're going to end up in a bidding war at the conference." The Reality conference? I wonder if he's talking about the same big event that Craig was supposed to pitch *Never Cry Wolf* at tomorrow.

"Who's pitching the show tomorrow? The show runner?"

"No, that guy's good at getting the job done, but he couldn't sell lemonade in the Sahara. You have to be able to sell." Hogan must know people who can sell shows ... maybe he'll have a great idea for who to send to the event.

"Pitching is just acting. You either can or you can't," the guy says smugly as he holds the door open for me to exit the elevator. *What does that even mean?* I am starting to understand just how out of my depth I am as I check in with the hostess and notice how completely underdressed I am. When I tore off for Craig's house two hours ago, the last thing on my mind was how I looked and the last place I thought I would end up tonight is Soho House. My life is full of surprises these days.

I'm not normally starstruck, but I can't help but notice that Steven Spielberg is heading up the main stairs toward the dining area. The beautiful old-fashioned décor perfectly complements the startling good looks of all the movie stars and the ego and power of the industry moguls present. As I approach Hogan's table, I see Derek Jordan sliding into a darkened booth. His companion is none other than Lola Stone, that actress Adam had bet me was making the moves on him. Seeing them canoodling at a table right there in front of everyone, I find my first smile tonight. Adam's instinct was exactly right about Lola's agenda. I guess I do owe him a whiskey. The thought helps quell my nerves as I approach Hogan's corner table.

Hogan rises to greet me, kisses both my cheeks, and waits until I've been seated to return to his seat opposite me.

"How are you doing?" he asks, first a friend.

"I'm okay. Still so shocked. I just can't believe he's such a slimeball." As the words are flying out of my mouth, I realize we're talking about Hogan's EIC. Despite Craig's dubious actions, it's pretty inappropriate for me to comment on it to him so blatantly. "Sorry, Hogan ... I just mean—"

"No need to apologize. Craig is an asshole. Pardon my French." Hogan dismisses him with a wave of his wineglass. "I fired him."

I stare at Hogan. "You did?"

"Of course I did! I don't tolerate behavior like that. He deserved to be fired for how he tried to manipulate you and the people of Wolf. There are tons of places he can go and make that kind of sensationalist, negative television. But I don't want that kind of lowest-common-denominator thinking to represent me or my company." Hogan sighs. "The bottom line is, I've felt for a while that Craig and I were at cross-purposes. It's like we say the same words but mean two completely different things. So, I'm not just letting him go because of this. You don't need that on your conscience. It's a lot of things."

I don't know why that didn't occur to me. I just thought Hogan would be mad; it never crossed my mind that Hogan would fire him. I wonder if Craig knew he was fired when we spoke. If that was why he was so resigned. Selfishly I am relieved to hear this news—it would have been very awkward for Craig and I to continue working together on *The Wrong Doctor* after everything that's happened. Not that I would have wished for him to get fired, but it does make my life easier. Besides, I am sure Craig will land on his feet somewhere. That's how the world works. So long as it's far away from me and Wolf County, I'm fine with that.

"I'm sorry this happened. That you lost an employee you trusted over all this." It's tough because while I feel badly, like somehow I put this in motion, I don't know that I could have done anything differently. "I guess I should have had my eyes open about Craig. I took him at face value, and I should've been more aware that he had his own agenda. I know why *Never Cry Wolf* was so important to me. I never got an honest answer about why it mattered so much to him."

"*Never Cry Wolf*?"

"That's the name we came up with. *I* came up with." I'm done letting Craig take credit for my ideas.

"I love that. Great title. Maddy, I know this show is important to your parents. It can make a difference to the town."

"We can still sell the show." I can't help but go for one last-ditch effort to salvage this. "Who do you know that could step in last minute for Craig? There must be someone who has reality TV experience, someone you trust to help pitch the show. I could brief them tonight." I check my watch—8:42 p.m. "And be on the way to Manhattan Beach tomorrow morning." I feel the desperation showing on my face. "We could offer someone executive producer credit if they'll go to Reality Buzz and sell it."

The idea of everything going down the toilet because of Craig seems so unjust to me. I can't stand for that to be how this ends—like one of those art house movies where everyone loses in the end. I hate those movies. I glance around Soho House, starting to feel the edge of hysteria creep up on me. "God, there's got to be someone here, tonight, who could do it."

Hogan looks at me oddly.

"There is," he says simply, taking the last bite of his entrée. "You."

What? "What?"

"You know perfectly well what, Maddy. You should sell the show. You can do it. Pitching isn't that hard, especially when you're as passionate about the subject as you are about Wolf. You'll do great. I'm not going to find you someone else with this late notice, some random exec who has no investment in the project. I know how to sell TV, and I'm telling you, you can do this. Better than anyone else."

I am still dumbfounded. "But...Hogan...I—"

"Not only that, but also when you sell the show, I'm putting you in charge of it. You're going to be the EIC. I know you don't think you're 'creative' or whatever, but you're wrong. You have a feel for this. I watched the reel you put together. It's excellent. It's got heart. Like you. Like Wolf County."

There's a burning behind my eyes that I am determined to ignore.

"I just don't want to let you down, Hogan. What if I choke?"

Hogan reaches across the table, pats my hand, and smiles at me kindly.

"Don't choke."

Scene 002
Ext. Billy Fox's mansion--night

Billy Fox was surprised to hear from me at 9:00 on a Friday night, but he was the first call I made as I pulled out of Soho House. *Pitching is like acting*, I remember the agent in the elevator saying. So why not call the best? Billy will have tips, or at least a good pep talk and a giant glass of Pinot. And luckily enough, I catch him before he heads out for the night. I give him a brief rundown of my evening and my predicament, and he tells me to come right over so we can strategize. Luckily, it's not far, but with Friday night West Hollywood traffic, it's still forty minutes before I pull up to his gated home in Hollywood Hills. I punch in the gate code he sent me and whistle as the gates pull back to reveal a gorgeous Mediterranean-style villa. It looks like a transplant off some Tuscan vineyard, not an American McMansion. I park next to a long row of bright green hedges and notice there's another car already parked on the landing. I wonder if Billy's bought another BMW or if he has a guest and I'm horning in on his plans. The door swings open as I walk up.

"Maddy. Glad you made it. Come in; I opened some wine. You could use it." He hands me a glass, kisses me on the cheek, and ushers me inside.

"I saw another car. Am I ruining your plans? I won't stay long. I just need—"

"Since he can't get invited anywhere on his own, I was going to let him tag along with me tonight." I turn around to see Adam taking off his jacket and throwing it on a chair. "But of course I canceled the second Billy called. I thought he would need help saving the day."

"If you had a thought, it'd die of loneliness," Billy retorts in full Texas twang.

The way they verbally spar reminds me of my brothers. Being surrounded by their friendly, encouraging faces, I finally start to feel like maybe this can really work.

"Did you tell Adam what happened?"

"Yeah, an abbreviated version. Why don't you fill him in?"

I sit down and with a fortifying sip of wine, tell them both the play-by-play, starting with showing up at Craig's house and all the way to Hogan's send-off at Soho House.

"We need to make sure Craig is out. For good." Adam speaks up after I finish my monologue.

"I think Hogan saw to that. I mean, he fired him. That's pretty 'out,' right?"

"No, Adam's right. But one thing at a time." Billy looks at Adam. "Let's get Maddy ready to pitch this. What do you say?"

Adam nods and focuses on me. "Okay. Have you ever taken improv classes?"

I shake my head.

"Any acting? Public speaking?"

Again, no.

"That's okay, it doesn't matter. What do you think, Billy? She should just pitch it, right? We'll be the network. Just do it once, and we'll see where we are."

They sit down on a sofa and stare at me, slightly hostile and expectant.

"Why are you looking at me like that?"

Billy laughs. "Buyers are tough customers. You'll have to win them over. Ignore the uninterested faces and do your thing."

"Okay..." I hesitantly stumble through a brief explanation of what the show would be about. I stop talking, and they continue to stare at me. "Um... should I tell you about the format too? Like the technical stuff?"

"Go ahead," Adam says formally. I guess we're still acting.

"Well, we think the show is best in a one-hour format. We have several story lines based on the people we discussed that we would thread through each episode...but uh...I think each episode would focus on one theme...whether it was a specific event or a storm or well, things like that."

"Is that all?" Adam asks, still in the role of mean network guy.

Billy hits him in the arm. "Stop being so hard on her. It's her first run at this."

"Dude. It's almost ten o'clock. We need to fast-forward this. She needs to sleep and get to Manhattan Beach. We don't have time to workshop it." Adam looks at me. "Besides, she can do this." He hops up and pulls a notebook out of his backpack. "I'm writing down the bullet points that I thought were the best parts of your first run-through. We need to work on your confidence. You know what you're talking about. You believe in the show. We just need to see that more. That's what sells people. If they're going to give you their money, trust you to make a show, they have to see that you believe in what you're doing. Here, let's start with these." Adam tears off the piece of paper where he has impressively summed up all the main talking points I had wanted to get across in my pitch.

I look over the list and start again. This time, I'm not more than a couple sentences in before Adam is on his feet.

"Hold on, hold on. This girl can memorize, right? Maddy knows our dialogue better than we do most of the time. Let's play to her strengths." Adam grabs the paper back from me and starts peppering me with questions about the show. The Gordons, Pete's

Tavern, the blasters, Mike, etc. We talk through each story line and the right way to show the variety, the drama, everything the show has to offer. And we write it all down. By the time we've polished the "script," I already have it mostly memorized. Every minute that goes by, I start to feel more confident.

"Hello? Where are you guys?" A female voice comes floating through the foyer.

"Hey! Sophie! We're in the game room." I look around. We're in a game room? I notice the billiard table for the first time. There's also a vintage Pac-Man machine against one wall. My eyes catch Adam's and we share a thought—of course Billy has a game room.

"Sophie? Your publicist?" I ask Billy.

"I asked her to come," Adam offers. "To help you present the exact image you want tomorrow. You gotta look the part, right?"

Having met Sophie Atwater several times on set, I can only imagine how it will feel to have that confidence and enthusiasm turned toward me. Sophie comes around the corner loaded down with clothes stacked up to her chin. Both guys leap up to relieve her of her burden.

"Thanks, guys. Hot male clients are good for something, after all." She laughs. "Adam filled me in, Maddy. I think we should start with the right outfit."

I don't know how actresses do it—they can have half a dozen wardrobe fittings per scene. After the third outfit change, I'm exhausted. And it's a little bit odd to come out and do this fashion show thing with each outfit. Modeling them for Billy and Sophie somehow seems almost normal, businesslike, but I can feel Adam's eyes on me as he examines each new choice. And it's not in a creepy way, just a little intense, like he's soaking in every inch of me. My cheeks heat up just thinking about it.

"Do you need help in there?" Sophie calls from the hallway.

I smooth out the skirt of an adorable knee-length fitted dress. The waist hits me perfectly, and the beige tone complements my skin. The best part is this little black detail at the waist and hem that offsets the simplicity and makes it feminine. This one is my favorite.

I walk out and stand in front of Sophie, who lights up when she sees me. What is it about trying on clothes together that bonds women? Her opinion right now is so important to me.

"Oh my God. It's perfect." She grins and pulls me into the living room, where I hear the rumbling of the guys' voices stop as we get close.

I step into the room. Sophie braces my hand and instructs me to stand on my tiptoes, so we can see how it'll look in heels. I flinch at the thought but dutifully rise up onto the balls of my feet.

"Perfect." Billy high-fives Sophie. "You did it. That's why you get the big bucks, huh?"

They laugh together but I don't hear what they're saying. I wander down the hall to take in my reflection in the full-length cut-glass mirror in the front hallway. I rise up on my tippy toes again, trying to imagine how tomorrow is going to go. I also wonder if I can really risk doing it in high heels, or will I just fall flat on my face and ruin everything before I can even get the chance to give my pitch?

"You look beautiful, Maddy." Adam leans against the wall next to the mirror, watching me. So much for not blushing.

"Thanks, Adam. I feel good about this one." I look down at myself, feeling pretty and incredibly self-conscious all at once.

"You should," he says simply. "It's exactly right." He glances down at my feet, reminding me I'm still balancing on my tiptoes.

"Thanks so much for helping me out tonight," I say, trying to subtly return to my flat-footed five-eight. I very rarely feel petite, but even separated by several feet, Adam's taller, broad frame makes me feel very feminine.

"I'm glad I got the chance to help you. I guess it's safe to say things with Craig are done?"

"Oh...I didn't know...you knew?" I stammer, caught off guard by his boldness and the fact that he knew it was Craig all along. So much for trying to be discreet.

"Yeah, Billy let it slip. Well, after I fed him a bottle of Jack. I wanted to know who my competition was." He's grinning now, and the heat in my cheeks has turned into a full-body flush. "He also told me that if I was lucky enough to get a chance with you, and I messed it up, he would, quote, 'kick my ass with the sharpest spurs on his snakeskin boots.'" Adam's impression of Billy's Texas twang is as dead-on as Billy's of Adam's Brooklyn accent.

"So? Will I be lucky enough to get a chance with you now?"

"I...um...well...it's just that..." Oh my God, I have not been able to form a complete sentence in the last five minutes. But turns out, I don't need to because Adam pushes away from the wall to come toward me. I hold still as he reaches out to adjust the necklace around my throat. It's a delicate diamond solitaire that Sophie is generously lending me since it's "perfect" for the dress. It was a gift from her husband, Jacob, so it's all the more touching she's letting me borrow it for good luck. He centers the charm on my clavicle and then gently traces his finger along the delicate gold chain to where my shoulder meets my neck. His hand spreads out there, and I feel its warmth seeping into my skin, muddling my brain. So much so, that it isn't until I actually feel his lips on mine that I catch on that he's kissing me. I can't even react right away. He slowly starts increasing the pressure of the kiss, directing it to turn into something stronger, more passionate. He now has a hand tilting my face up to meet his more fully and the kiss grows stronger. I lean into him and feel my heart beating against his chest. Every nerve ending I have is exploding with sensation as I feel him press me against him. He is still leading this embrace, and somehow my arms reach up around his neck and I am just hanging on for the ride, my body quivering and my mind complete mush. He slows the kiss, pulls back a bit, and looks me right in the eye. Then he comes close to kiss me again on the lips, a gentle "this isn't over" kiss. He's now holding my shoulders as he gives us both a bit of breathing room, which allows me to realize I haven't taken in oxygen for quite some time. Only I don't think that's the reason I'm light-headed.

One good, deep breath turns out to be a mistake for two reasons: (1) It comes out sounding like a contented sigh, which makes Adam smile knowingly, and (2) I inhale his aftershave, which only makes my head continue to spin.

"Go get 'em, Maddy. You've got this."

Scene 003
Int. Manhattan Beach Hilton--morning

Between the kiss with Adam, replaying yesterday's turn of events over and over in my mind, and the nerves about today, I didn't sleep at all last night. Finally, as the sun came up, I stopped trying to sleep and just took a long hot shower, which was somewhat calming. Then I drank a venti cup of coffee on the drive down here, thinking of everything that could go wrong, which was not calming at all. Luckily, Wanda had a great detour that allowed me to avoid the insane traffic issues on the 405, so I got to Manhattan Beach with plenty of time to spare.

The printout Craig's assistant e-mailed me of Craig's schedule for today is shaking in my hands as I stand outside the doors of my first pitch meeting. I force myself to take deep breaths and look at my notes again. Sophie told me to take five deep breaths every time I felt nervous. It was exactly what she advised her client who made an appearance on *The Tonight Show* last week, two days after being caught in a threesome on a video that went viral. If it worked for him...I'm about to take in another cleansing breath when a harassed-looking intern-type kid pokes his head into the hallway, surprising the air right out of me. "Where's Craig?"

"Um, he's not here," I choke out. "I'm here for the pitch."

"Okay, well. Whatever." He heads back into the room, holding the door open behind him, the only indication that he is expecting me to follow him into the suite. World-Weary Intern gestures for me to head through another door off the foyer. Who knew hotels had rooms like this? I can't help but look around at the expansive layout. It's bigger than my first apartment.

There are three men and one woman, all in clearly expensive suits, talking among themselves. I stand there awkwardly, not sure how to get their attention. I picture Adam last night in Billy's living room and what he would say about my current predicament.

ADAM

Take charge of the room. Make them pay attention
to you.

I clear my throat. The executives pause in their conversation and look up at me with barely disguised irritation. My stomach shrivels up.

ADAM
(wincing slightly)
It's okay. Shake it off. Tell them who you are and
why you're here.

Good advice from Adam's voice inside my head. Now I have to put it to action.

"Hi, I'm Maddy Carson. I'm here to pitch you my show."

"Where's Craig?" asks Executive on the Left, with the slick Italian hair, looking down at his iPad.

"He's not working on this project anymore." I barely avoid tripping over that vague answer.

The female executive looks confused, and I clearly see all four of them lose interest in the space of a second.

"And you are...?" she asks me.

"Oh, like I said, I'm Maddy Carson."

"Yes, I know, you said that." She looks and sounds exasperated. "I mean, who you are? What shows have you done?"

"Um, well, I work on *The Wrong Doctor*..." I see them perk up a bit. "I'm the script supervisor." Is it my imagination, or did they deflate?

"So you have no experience selling or running a show?" This time it's the guy with glasses.

"Well...no, not exactly. But I—"

They cut me off before I can even finish, which irks me at first but is actually probably a blessing since I don't know exactly how to convince them of my credentials. Even though it seems hopeless, I continue to stand in front of them. Frankly, I'm not even sure how to leave. Tail-between-my-legs isn't my style, but I can't see another way out, so I'm stuck with my pride. Standing tall but silent. *The Good, the Bad and the Ugly* theme music plays in my head. After endless excruciating seconds pass, the guy on the right caves. He seems the youngest of the four. "So, let's hear your pitch," he says in a chipper voice, as if nothing happened.

I take a deep breath and smile. "This is a show about America. It's a show about getting by when times are tough. It's a show about heart. Let me introduce you to Wolf County..." I go through my whole spiel. I pass out the handouts I made, prop my iPad up on the coffee table in front of them, and play my sizzle reel. They politely lean in to get a view of the screen, but when the video ends, they sit straight and offer semi-sincere smiles, asking no questions. After another awkward pause, one of them says, "Thank you." And like that, I am dismissed.

I keep my shoulders straight all the way to the hallway, but once the door closes behind me and I'm sure I'm alone, I wilt against a door. It took all my willpower to tough that one out. They can't all be that brutal, can they?

The next room seems much more cheery. It's for one of those female cable networks—bright pink logo and four women in fantastically glamorous outfits laughing and, if I'm not mistaken, drinking champagne when I am escorted in. As they size me up, one of them compliments my dress. I silently thank Sophie Atwater.

"Go ahead when you're ready," a woman with short spiky blond hair directs. Her slim figure is accentuated by cigarette pants and a fitted black cashmere sweater.

"Oh, okay. Well, I'm Madelyn Carson. I'm representing Hogan Chenny Productions today. And I am really proud to be here to pitch you our new reality show."

"Let's hear it," the blonde says.

"This is a show about America..." Again I get through my presentation relatively flawlessly. As I pull out my iPad, I notice the women exchanging glances. I focus on the blonde, clearly their leader, for some idea of what's going on here.

"Sweetheart, thank you for your pitch. It sounds very exciting, really. But I'm going to stop you. We don't need to see the presentation. Your show really isn't right for our network. It's just not what we're looking for at this time."

The other women nod, and as I look around, they actually don't seem bitchy, just honest. Well, okay.

"Thank you for your time."

The blonde gets up and walks me to the door of their suite. She holds the door open and as I pass through, she says quietly, "It's a good pitch, but slow down. It's not speed dating." She smiles at me and then the door shuts in my face.

And so it goes...room after room.

Some rooms are nicer than others. The reactions range anywhere from crickets—complete silence followed by a "we're not interested"—to polite applause and even one "Oh, I go skiing there every winter! I love Wolf, but it's not really the right show for this network. Sorry." The worst is when I play the sizzle reel I sweated over and worked so hard on and fought for, and I watch executives check their smartphones and even take calls while it plays.

Going from room to room, pitching these people is physically and emotionally exhausting. And having been around actors long enough, I know I'm still not doing it exactly right. I still sound too forced, like I'm repeating something I've memorized. Which is exactly what I'm doing. I take a minute and brace myself against a doorjamb near my next appointment with new appreciation for how much harder "acting" is than I realized. It's a humbling thought as I take a bite of a half-eaten protein bar I found in the bottom of my purse. It's now 3:00 p.m., and I haven't eaten since...I can't even remember when. Before the whole Craig thing happened. I couldn't eat at Billy's since I was so busy trying on clothes, perfecting my script...and kissing Adam. Thinking about Adam, that kiss, I feel the blush creeping up my cheeks. I haven't had a moment to think about it all day. I have no idea what, if anything, it means...

A head pops out of the doorway. "Craig? Are you here?"

Ugh. I wish there was some way to get ahead of this. The ghost of Craig Past is haunting me at every meeting, as I have to explain his absence over and over.

"I'm here," I call out. "Maddy Carson." I shake hands with the intern as we walk into the room and make a point to remember his name—Louis. Over the last six hours, I've learned if I give the intern some attention, some respect, they'll reciprocate and introduce me with more enthusiasm to their bosses. "Sorry, Craig's not here. I'm representing HCP for the meeting," I explain to the cute kid in a bow tie. I look around waiting for him to point me in the direction of the executives' room.

"Oh, it's just you and me," he explains apologetically. "The gang had to leave—some sort of emergency." He gestures for me to sit with him on the sofa against the back wall. "I'm a junior executive now, so I've taken pitches before."

But we both know that I've been stood up by the real decision-makers. He sits patiently and waits. What the hell.

"It's a show about America…"

I get through the whole thing and Louis hasn't said anything, which I now know does not bode well.

"Any questions?" I ask as I fold the iPad back in the case.

"It's a good idea, Maddy. I like it, I really do." His tone still has its apologetic undertones, so I'm not getting my hopes up or anything. "I'm going to mention it to Angela and the rest of the team…"

"But?"

"Well…I know what they're going to say. The stakes aren't high enough."

"What does that even mean?" I don't expect him to really answer. This isn't the first time today I've heard that—and it's just so frustrating, everyone speaking in these phrases that I just don't understand. They're speaking English, and yet it feels like I need a dictionary.

"It means that you haven't made me feel like I can't wait to find out what happens next. Especially when you pitch a show, you have to have me, us"—he gestures to the empty seating area where invisible network executives are hypothetically sitting—"on the edge of our seats, imagining the endless series of dramatic moments for every episode. It's a programmer's dream, a series filled with cliff-hanger moments, you know?" He's escorting me out the door, still talking. It's not until I'm alone in the hallway yet again that I realize I should have argued with him. There are tons of dramatic moments in the show. But it's too late.

I am thinking about what Louis said as I dash to the bathroom before my next and last meeting. I think about ways I can make my pitch more dramatic. I am nervous to leave the script I've perfected, but hey, what have I got to lose if I go off the cuff a little bit? It can't get any worse.

So in the next pitch I make sure to hype up all the dramatic aspects of life in Wolf, and how we could create very dramatic cliff-hangers. I feel my tweaks are very compelling, and I think Madame Executive of Home Living Network would agree if she heard one word I said. Her phone defeated the purpose of being on vibrate because placed as it was on the metal coffee table, the sound echoed louder and longer than a beep would have. Since it's gone off every ninety seconds while I am talking, and she is read-ing and replying to every incoming e-mail, I'm pretty sure she has no idea what I'm saying. And yet I keep going, determined to finish until...

"Oh, sorry. I have to take this one." She interrupts me right as I'm getting ready to finish. "Thank you for coming by." She doesn't even glance up as she answers the phone.

Beaten. I just feel beaten. Limping down the hall back toward the elevator, the high-heeled shoes I'm not used to wearing have rubbed identical blisters onto each foot. I am not really a crier, but the exhaustion, the sleep deprivation, and the humiliation of knowing that Craig would have sold this show and I couldn't all contribute to a weight on my chest that make it hard to catch my breath.

In the hotel lobby, the quiet bar catches my eye. The pitches are over, but I see a sign saying there's still a speaker session and cocktail hour taking place at 7:00. I have maybe fifteen minutes of quiet before everyone will be here socializing and networking, another major part of this event. I order a vodka and soda and sip silently, wondering if I have the stamina to try again. To socialize, schmooze.

"You look how I feel."

I glance over to see a slightly older man sitting down next to me.

"Um, thanks?" I reply, not caring that my sarcasm is apparent.

"Sorry, that was unkind. I just meant that this event can be exhausting." I look over at him and take in his grandfather-style argyle cardigan and kind eyes, and see he wasn't trying to be a jerk.

"No, you're right. I never knew pitching a TV show could drain everything out of you." I take a big swig of vodka.

"Any prospects?" He calls the bartender over and orders a whiskey neat.

"I heard everything except a yes. In one room, they green-lit another show while I sat and waited, but that's as close as I got. I also learned today how completely shitty network executives can be."

"Indeed." He chuckles, sipping his drink. I swallow more vodka.

"Half the time I wasn't even given the courtesy of their attention." Now I'm on a roll. "I mean, isn't that their job? The point of even being here? Why take a meeting with me if they're not going to actually listen to my pitch?" I'm twisting my cocktail napkin into little pieces. "I would. If it were my job. I'm sure you would too. You seem like the type of person who would listen if it were your job to listen."

"So let me hear it," he says casually, as he scoops up some mixed nuts from a nearby bowl.

"I just meant figuratively. You don't really have to hear about my show."

"I want to. If you're up for it."

And knowing it doesn't mean anything, except perhaps to have this random stranger agree that I'm right—everyone here are idiots for not buying my idea—I tell him about *Never Cry Wolf.*

"They say the stakes aren't high enough? Are they kidding? They couldn't be higher. This is a show about a community trying to survive. Everyone doing everything they can every single day, to not just earn their livelihood, but also to rely on each other, to keep their hearts and spirits up too.

"Someone today said 'the characters aren't big enough.'" I put air quotes around that preposterous statement. "You couldn't ask for bigger, more vibrant people. They're not just characters you can sum up or put in a neat little box. These people, like the Gordons, for example, are bigger than life. He's into taxidermy—which is only one tiny part of this huge Paul Bunyan–type guy, who also knits, makes moonshine that'll put hair on anyone's chest, and stops every night to appreciate the night sky with his wife of forty-plus years. Or Pete, who is the third-generation owner of the local tavern and keeps it open all year, even when the only people who go are teetotalers who drink water with no ice and bring their own Ritz crackers. Pete cares about his community, and it's more important to him to be there when people need a gathering place than to shut down when times are tight." Having finally found my voice to contradict every negative comment I heard, I can't seem to stop myself until it's all out. I barely take a breath before going in for the next argument.

"And talk about 'demographics'? There's a whole team of blasters who risk their lives to set off explosions after every snowstorm to prevent avalanches during the season. There are ski bunnies in bikinis at the hot springs. It's a guy's fantasy—things that blow up and hot chicks, right? And women will love watching the way everyone supports each other, how couples support each other to find their way through these tough financial times. Tons of sports advertisers would love to have a show like this to buy time on. Never mind the integrations we could organize, the clothing sponsors, the equipment we use . . . I can't imagine a sponsor who wouldn't want in on this show."

Through it all, my new friend sits and listens, his eyes widening slightly, the only give-away that my passionate defense of my show surprises him. I'm sure this is not quite what he was expecting when he asked to hear the pitch.

"I worked so hard on the sizzle. I didn't sell out and fake shit that didn't happen." I don't even care that I cursed; I don't care what anyone thinks of me anymore. "I fought for this show, and then I get here and no one even wants to see it."

"I want to see it."

"Well, sure you do—it doesn't matter to you," I say dismissively. "Here." I pull the iPad out and slam it in front of him. He has to find the video and press PLAY himself as I've turned back to the bartender to order myself another round. "You want another?"

He doesn't take his eyes off the screen. "Yeah, sure."

Our second drinks come as he's wrapping up the video. He thoughtfully closes my iPad and hands it back.

"It's really good. What's your name? We haven't formally met yet."

"Maddy. Hi. Sorry about my outburst. This has been a tough couple days. I'm not normally this worked up. I swear."

"That's okay, Maddy. I know what it's like to know you have a good idea no one will listen to."

"Yes, that's it exactly. I know it would be a great show, if someone will just give it a chance."

"I love your show. *Never Cry Wolf*? It's great. Different. And warm and exciting. I was really drawn in."

"Well, how 'bout we go back to all those rooms today and you can tell those idiots to buy my show?"

"Why would I want to do that?" He looks up as people start milling into the bar. It's almost time for the cocktail hour/ networking event, and this place is going to fill up soon. I want out of here before that happens. I'm completely burnt.

"What do you mean?" I try in vain to flag down the bartender to get the check.

"Why would I want to convince anyone else how great your show is? As it is now, I know I don't have any competition."

I stare at him, uncomprehending.

"I want to buy your show," he clarifies.

"What?" I am sure I must have misheard.

"It's perfect for my network. It's the best pitch I've heard today. And in fact, I'm shocked you weren't on my pitch list." He gets the bartender's attention while I'm trying to understand what just happened. "Put her drinks on my tab. Suite 920."

"Of course, Mr. Greenling."

Greenling? Ed Greenling? Oh my God. Even I know that he's the billionaire tycoon who invested in a struggling cable network a couple years back and turned it into the Outdoor Network, a major competitor in the adventure programming genre, a cross between Discovery and Nat Geo. In other words, the perfect network for *Never Cry Wolf*. And I was a total raving lunatic to him.

"Oh, Mr. G-Greenling," I stammer as he turns back to me "I'm so sorry. I had no idea..."

"Clearly." He smiles. "I haven't had anyone be so straightforward with me in years."

"Oh, God."

"I liked it. We do this show together, you promise me you will always be so forthright with me."

"I promise," I dutifully echo.

"Good. We'll work on the paperwork next week. In the meantime, shake my hand. I'm old-fashioned that way." We shake, and then I get up and start to reach for my things, still completely stunned by the turn the night has taken. It doesn't feel real yet.

"Well, um, thank you..."

"Where are you going?"

"Well, I just thought..."

"Stay. You must." Without waiting for my reply, he takes my coat and sets it back down on the bar stool. "Everyone is going to be gathering here. You should get to know the players."

"Well, if you think I should..." I look around at the growing sea of people drinking, talking, laughing. I had nothing to laugh about ten minutes ago. I look at Ed Greenling again, and it's starting to sink in that I have a big reason to smile now.

"That's better, my dear. Take my card; we have lots to discuss on Monday. For now, let's go share with people your good news." He takes my elbow and leads me toward a tall guy who is telling an elaborate story involving loud helicopter sound effects to an entranced group.

"There are some show-runners you should meet. Maybe someone we want to engage for *Never Cry Wolf*? You've got a show to get off the ground."

I've got a show. And now I've got *to get it off the ground?!?!*

Scene 004
Int. Nobu restaurant, evening

"To Maddy!"

"To Maddy!"

"MADDY!!"

"Yay, Maddy!!"

I am beaming as all my friends toast me. "Thank you, everyone! Seriously, I don't know how to thank you enough. Everyone here helped make this happen." I look around the table and know it's the truth. Billy is sitting next to Janine, who is seated next to Sophie Atwater, who brought her gorgeous husband, Jacob. Brian came down from Wolf with Lily, and Matthew surprised me by coming along. And on the other side of Matthew, seated to my right, is Adam Devin. I've lived in LA for ten years and never ventured over the hill into Malibu, but Billy and Sophie insisted that Nobu would be the perfect place to celebrate selling a show. And it is.

Feeling unexpectedly sentimental, I continue my impromptu toast. "If you'd asked me six months ago about doing a reality show, I would've laughed in your face. I never thought I was a creative type—and yes, Brian, I see you rolling your eyes at me. It's just that I've always been good at the numbers, the details. You know me, I could organize and make lists, endlessly. But *Never Cry Wolf*...the chance to have my own show...it's an opportunity I didn't even know I was looking for and I am so grateful to have. It's going to be an amazing ride.

"Billy, Adam, Sophie..." I lump them all together and throw Adam in the middle on purpose. I don't want Brian or my brother to see him getting any special attention from me. "Thank you for helping prep me for the presentation, for dressing me so well, and for everything else this week. I'm so glad to have you on board as the show's publicist, Sophie." She raises her glass in salute.

"Janine, thank you for your tireless work getting that sizzle reel ready. I almost passed out more times than I can count, but you kept going. Your talent as an editor is only outmatched by your Energizer Bunny endurance.

"Brian, Matthew, Lily, you all paved the way for me at home. I know you went out of your way behind the scenes to get people on board and willing to be a part of it. And I promise to never let you down. I will protect the town and the people and tell the true story of Wolf every episode."

"Of course you will, Maddy," says Matthew, always with unwavering confidence.

"Okay, enough from me! Let's eat!" The food comes out in waves, a vast array of sushi and seafood. Those of us who don't normally go to five-star ocean-side restaurants can't stop commenting on the sound of the waves crashing right next to us as we enjoy our delicious dinner.

I take a deep breath and realize it's probably the first time I've been still for this long in a week. Ever since I met Ed Greenling, my life has been completely hectic. We're powering through the final episodes of the season for *The Wrong Doctor*, and during my off hours, I've been in meetings and conference calls regarding *Never Cry Wolf*. I don't think I've slept more than four hours total all week. I plan to sleep till at least noon tomorrow. Even Ed Greenling can't work on Sundays, right?

"Great speech, Maddy. You told me you'd never done any public speaking. Liar." But the way Adam says "liar" sounds like an endearment, and he brushes my shoulder as he reaches across me to scoop up a spicy tuna roll.

"It's true, I hadn't. But spending all day pitching to strangers definitely immunizes you to speaking in front of a group."

"No doubt. Trial by fire, right? But you did it. You should be so proud." Given how absolutely crazed it's been this week, I haven't had a lot of time to talk with anyone, including Adam. Our kiss seems like a lifetime ago.

"I wasn't kidding. It was a brutal day. All those rooms. Some of those executives were even colder than your practice session. But if I hadn't prepped with you, I wouldn't have made it into room two. I would have fallen apart. So thank you, again."

"You don't have to thank me." He sets down his chopsticks and turns to look at me. "I was glad to help." I am completely lost looking in his eyes. I don't hear my brother's laugh, or feel Lily splash me with soy sauce as she clumsily tries to use chopsticks for the first time. I just stare at Adam. The spell isn't broken until the waiter clears his throat and I realize he's been standing there for a while.

"Would you like another cocktail?" Apparently, he has already gotten everyone else's drink order.

"Yes. Please. Another mai tai." Because as it turns out, I do like fruity drinks. Even though he's taking a sip, I catch Adam's smirk at my order.

"Shut up." I lean in and shove his knee with mine, feeling completely at ease with our proximity.

"You're not always right." He focuses on scooping more rice onto his plate, his smile firmly in place.

Which reminds me...

"Speaking of being right. I forgot to tell you I saw Lola the other day at Soho House. And you know who she was with?" I poke his arm. I could get used to this, touching him whenever I want.

"Mmmm...let me guess...Derek Jordan?" he says with a knowing grin.

"Exactly. And she was all over him," I say with relish. "So, I guess I should pay for your next whiskey."

"Well, that wasn't the bet, Maddy. Technically, you have to come to my favorite bar and buy me a whiskey there. I'll have my people text you what dates I'm available," he deadpans.

It takes me a second to register that he's joking.

"Isn't that what we diva actors do...have our people call your people? Just trying to live up to your expectations." Adam is laughing.

"Oh, I know you have a diva in you, Adam Devin." It feels nice that we can tease each other like this. Adam puts his arm around my shoulders and pulls me in close. Everyone else at the table is deep in other conversations, but I look up and see that Billy is watching us. He winks at me, and I smile.

"When were you at Soho House, by the way?" Adam asks as I'm taking another sip of my mai tai.

"Um, last week? The night you helped me prep for the conference. I met with Hogan before I saw you."

"Ooh, really?" Adam leaps on the information. "You've known you lost the bet all week and you're just telling me now? There should be a fine for that. Withholding," he announces as if he's a referee at a football game. "It incurs a second date penalty."

Adam and I are clearly lost in our little bubble, because suddenly all around us the group is gathering their things and getting up. Apparently Billy has paid the check and we're all going to head to the lounge area.

Lily, Sophie, Janine, and I hold down some seats near the fire

pit while the guys get drinks. Minutes later Adam returns handing me another drink, this time with an actual umbrella in it. I
smile back at him, knowing that he requested that especially for
me, loving our inside joke.

I can't tell if my giddiness is exhaustion or Adam or the
three drinks I've had, but I feel lighter and looser than I have in
months. It's a good feeling. Janine is telling us a story about her
latest date, when the guys head back to the bar. I guess when she
got to the part about how the guy said he was going to run out
for *smaller* condoms, it was TMI for them. I am still laughing as I
head to the bathroom minutes later.

On my way back, I see the guys are in a huddle, chatting just
off the side of the bar. They don't see me as I approach, but I stop
short when I overhear Billy say, "I'm just saying she doesn't need
someone else jerking her around. She's been hurt enough."

Instantly, I know they are talking about me. I am equal parts
touched and mortified.

"I'm not going to do that," Adam replies intently.

I can't see my brother since he's obscured by a row of tall
lights, but I hear his voice loud and clear. "Just because I don't
live here, man, doesn't mean I can't come down here and kick
your ass." I am relieved when Matthew cracks a laugh, which
Adam joins in on. These two are going to get along.

"Okay, guys, back on track. Let's get to the part where we get
to kick Craig's ass."

"I'm already on that, Brian. Don't worry." Billy's Texas jus-
tice system is very straightforward.

"Hey, guys, what's up?" I interrupt, stepping around the corner. I'm too embarrassed to look at Adam, so I choose instead to
stare daggers at my brother, which he knows means "I'm going
to kill you."

"Oh, hey, Maddy." Adam pushes away from the wall and puts

a proprietary arm on my shoulder. "We're just talking about how much we adore you."

"Well, some of us more than others," jokes Matthew, looking pointedly at Adam.

"What do you mean?" I suppose it's too late to play innocent, but I give it a go anyway.

"I like this one, Maddy," Matthew says as if we're alone. "But as your brother, I have to tell you, you haven't always shown the best judgment...so I had to let him know"—he jerks his head at Adam and continues in his matter-of-fact tone—"if he hurts you..."

"All right, back off, Cujo. You've made your point." Billy gives Matthew a friendly slap on the back. "Come on, guys, let's leave these two alone. I'm buying the next round." Matthew and Jacob trail Billy back to the bar, leaving Adam and me alone.

"I'm so embarrassed."

"Don't be; you're lucky you have so many people looking out for you. Your brother is definitely a trip. He challenged me to some sort of Iron Man obstacle course. I guess that means he likes me?"

"It does. You may have to let him win, though." We make our way over to the railing that looks out over the ocean.

"It's a great night, huh?" Adam looks up at the stars in the dark blue sky.

"It really is. I'm exhausted, but I'm so excited about everything that I can't even sleep."

"You mean you *don't* sleep because you're working so much. I see you, Maddy Carson."

"What does that mean?" I feel myself getting defensive.

"It's not a criticism, that's for damn sure." He leans his forearms on the railing next to me so our faces are at the same level and we're both looking at the water. "You're an amazing woman, Maddy. No question. But I've seen you on set. You are always doing nine million things at once. You think it has to all be on your shoulders or you're failing."

"That's not true." Except actually he hit the bull's-eye.

"Just take care of yourself. That's all I'm saying."

"I will." Although I really can't imagine things slowing down anytime soon.

"I'd like to help." He turns to look at me. "If you'll let me."

I think I know what he means, but I need clarity here. "You mean, you want to help me with the show?"

He smiles at my misunderstanding. I think he knows it was deliberate. "I want to take care of you, Maddy. And before you get all twenty-first century on me, I just mean..." His eyes roam my face. "Well, I guess, I just mean, I want you to give me a chance. And we'll take it from there."

There are a thousand things I could say, namely, "Yes, I'd like that," but instead, I reach over and kiss him deeply and hope that says it all. We walk back to the table hand in hand and are met by smiles all around. Adam goes off to get us a drink while Lily, who is clearly a little tipsy, grabs me in a big hug. Brian, who is standing behind her, offers an indulgent smile. I guess Lily is making the most of her rare Mom's night out.

"It's just so beautiful here, Maddy. Thank you so much for inviting us. It means a lot to Brian and I to celebrate your big news with you," she gushes.

"Of course. I'm so happy you're here. I hope I get to come up to Wolf a lot this winter with the show. It'll be great to see you all so much."

"A lot of fun, Maddy. I'm going to picture you at dinner meetings here every night now. It's just so glamorous."

"Oh, right. Yeah, this is how I roll."

"Well, you are dating a real live TV star." She giggles and then hiccups.

"What are you talking about?" Again, I try to play dumb. "Matthew told us about Adam. He's sooooo cute, and he really likes you. Brian and I are so happy. Aren't we, honey?" She looks up at Brian, who is nodding and smiling.

"We are, kiddo," he says with touching sincerity. "I just can't believe you're breaking your number one rule. Never thought I'd see the day. I guess not everyone in LA is a stereotype, as it turns out, huh?"

"I know, right? Well, I trusted my gut with Craig, and look how that turned out. Maybe I'll try trusting my heart this time instead of my gut."

Brian looks at me, and I can see the Santa Monica lights twinkle in the distance over his shoulder. "I think that's a great idea."

Act Five

Scene 001
Int. Maddy's apartment--night

Flipping through the channels in my flannel pj's and wolf slippers, I catch a glimpse of my all-time favorite movie, *The Princess Bride*, playing on TNT. I sigh with relief, happy to sit back and enjoy Wesley and Princess Buttercup instead of thinking about Adam walking the red carpet, women screaming at him, starlets brushing up against him. Ugh. My imagination needs to be reined in, but this is what it's been like ever since I officially started dating him.

Not that anyone knows we're dating. And at this point I want to keep it that way. And I have to say that the secret, stolen moments on set have been, well, in a word: hot.

Yesterday, for example, Frank told me Adam needed to change some lines. I went to his trailer to go over it with him, only to be completely swept off my feet. Literally. He was kissing me before the door clicked shut and lifting me off the ground to spin and sit on the tiny sofa in his trailer, placing me on his lap. We didn't speak for at least five minutes. It could've gone on for twenty...or forever, as far as I was concerned, except Frank didn't feel the same way. My walkie-talkie, which had fallen to the floor, came alive with Frank's voice: "Does anyone have eyes on Scripty?" Obviously, I was so distracted I missed Frank's call, so now everyone on set was searching. I should have been completely horrified by how unprofessional I was behaving but there wasn't room in my brain. (And even now, looking back on it, I don't regret it for a second.)

"I thought I was the only one who gets to call you 'Scripty.'" Clearly not perturbed by the idea of a manhunt for me, Adam didn't stop nuzzling my ear.

"Frank's going to freak out if I don't get back to him," I said breathlessly. He didn't stop me from grabbing my walkie-talkie, but he also didn't remove his hand from the inside of my thigh.

"Call him, then," he said teasingly. "Tell him where you are, that you need a ten." He slipped one hand under my shirt. "Better make it a twenty."

I laughed. I wanted nothing more than to disappear into the moment with Adam, but I forced myself to pull away and radio Frank back.

A split second later, he responded. "Maddy, you're needed on set. ASAP."

Adam reluctantly let me detangle myself from him.

"Come with me tomorrow." He'd been harping on me to go with him to the premiere of one of his friend's new movies all week, and all week I explained over and over that it just wasn't my scene.

"I would, but I swore when I broke up with Justin Timberlake that I just wouldn't do red carpets anymore." My comedic skills were clearly lacking, as my joke had exactly the opposite effect. Any hint of a smile was gone, and Adam was looking at me completely seriously.

"What is it? You've never hesitated to shoot straight with me, Maddy. Don't start now."

Collecting my thoughts, I stepped down to the door of Adam's trailer. It also gave me a hair's distance, as it was hard to think clearly in such a small space with him.

"Adam, you'll never know what it feels like to walk next

to someone who is famous. Meeting fans on the street, the one-on-one stuff is fine; I can handle it. But at a big event like that? I've been there. Done that. And the T-shirt's not worth it." I turned back at the bottom step inside the trailer, looking up at him, but with the window behind him he's a little bit silhouetted so it's hard to read his expression.

"Everyone's there to see you. It's work. You go do your thing. I would just be in the way."

"You could skip the carpet, wait inside while I do the photos and press?" One last push from a guy who probably doesn't ever hear "no."

"Lurking solo in the lobby, making small talk with the popcorn guy? Wishing they hadn't taken my phone away at the security check so I'd have something to at least pretend to occupy me until you got back?"

"I'll skip the red carpet. You're killing me here."

"Now you just don't want to lose," I teased lightly. "You should go. It's fun for you—it's your job and career, and you're helping promote your friend's movie. I totally get it. I want you to go."

"Okay, okay," he relented. "I'll swing by after, maybe?"

"Sounds good. Text me." I was out the door of his trailer before I remembered, turning back. "Were you really going to give me a line change with some advance warning, for once?" He just grinned at me.

"Whether you like it or not, Scripty, ad-libbing is not a criminal offense."

"Actors," I humphed, but couldn't stop smiling as I headed back to set. It was definitely worth the awkward questions from people wondering where I'd been.

And now here I am sitting at home while he's out in front of the historic Chinese Theatre on Hollywood Boulevard, posing for pictures that have already surfaced on the Internet. Adam and the female lead of the film in her barely-there dress. Adam signing autographs for a huge group of fans on the other side of the barricades. Adam in the middle of a throng of girls who look ready to be in the next *Girls Gone Wild* video. What kind of girlfriend am I if I won't toughen up enough to go out in public with him?

But he's right; I have been there before. Once, when I first started, and it's not like it scarred me or anything, but that's what life is, right? Learning those lessons. I learned that approaching a fancy, crowded red carpet, in a beautiful dress I borrowed or spent too much on, balancing on stupidly high heels, is tough enough without some junior publicist's assistant shoving me out of the way the instant the cameras turn in our direction. Which leaves several bad options:

1. Ducking behind the backdrop, trying not to trip on wires, cables, crew working, and security giving you the evil eye
2. Charging the gauntlet so the photographers are yelling at you to get out of the shot, which inevitably means backing into the extremely excited fans shrieking at you because now they can't see the star they camped out to catch a glimpse of
3. Waiting patiently inside the lobby area. And maybe this is what I'll end up learning to do. Standing by executives and bigwigs who drop their voices and speak in codes because they don't want me to hear who they're talking about. And listening to starlets and wannabes not-so-quietly commenting on the "nobody" parked in the corner. How did humans survive before Words with Friends for distraction?

Wesley and Buttercup take off into the Fire Swamp, and I manage to set aside my insecurities until almost the end of the movie, when there's a knock at my door.

"I'll give you one guess." I open it to Adam, who comes bearing gifts: a bag from the liquor store down the street and a gorgeous arrangement of flowers.

"What is all this?" I ask after he gives me a quick smack on the lips and then heads to the kitchen.

"I'm making you a new fruity cocktail to try. And I snuck those flowers from the after-party. That's basically what these events are...drinks and pretty flower arrangements. I figure we could do a dress rehearsal here, and then next time you'll come with me."

It's such a sweet gesture. I don't have the heart to tell him that if being by his side doesn't do the trick, liquid courage isn't enough to get me onto that red carpet. And I know he sees me as this strong chick. I'm pretty sure any how-to relationship book would advise against me admitting how insecure I feel at this stage of our...whatever this is.

"What were you watching?" he asks from the kitchen. I hear the blender.

"Oh, nothing." I switch off the TV, suddenly not wanting to reveal my childhood obsession with the silly romantic movie. I head into the kitchen. "You're out early, aren't you? I would've thought the party would be just gearing up."

"It is, but I know you have to get up early, and I wanted to have a drink with you before you go to sleep."

"You're going back?" I watch him expertly pour the frozen concoction into a glass (with umbrella). I see rinsed raspberries lined up next to the sink, so I'm less suspicious of the pink color.

"Delicious," I admit after the first sip. He smiles and opens a beer for himself. We toast. "Thank you. But you didn't have to come here just for one drink. You're right, I'm probably going to bed soon anyway."

"After your show?" he asks again casually.

"Yes," I answer vaguely. "So, was the movie good?"

"Yeah, my buddy was fantastic. It's his first leading role. And he totally nailed it." He sits on my kitchen stool. "So much of the special effects were done with green screen. That has to be so hard, acting in a vacuum like that." We spend the next forty minutes talking about everything from work to *Wrong Doctor* gossip. This is what I like best about my relationship with Adam: It's so easy. When it's just the two of us, we can chat about work or not. We can talk about politics or the weather, and it seems so honest and natural. Once he gets me going on a subject, I'm not thinking about his status, or my career, or any other stupid reason I shouldn't be with him. It just feels right.

I regret making the slurping noise in my straw that calls attention to the fact that I've finished my cocktail. He looks at it and then me, and reluctantly swallows the last of his beer before recycling his bottle and rinsing out my glass. He already cleaned my blender and put it away. Another habit he has that makes it easy to forget he's #3 on the call sheet now; #1 is, of course, Billy Fox and #2 is Alice (the female lead). But for Adam to jump to #3 in one season...he's a big deal on the show now.

"I gotta go, babe, but are you free Saturday? My buddy was telling me about this fantastic café on the boardwalk in Venice. Apparently they have an amazing brunch."

"Yeah. Sounds great. I'd love that."

He comes over and wraps me in a hug. "And I'm on set all day tomorrow, you know...so we can eat lunch together in my trailer...just the two of us..." He kisses my forehead, which makes me feel as warm and fuzzy as my slippers.

"Adam, I can't let..."

"It's your lunch break, too, Maddy."

"I know, but people will know...and I'm not ready for that."

He pulls away so he can look me in my eye. "How long are we going to pretend we're not together?"

"I don't know. But if you want to eat with Frank, Stella, and me at catering, I would love that. We'll make brunch our next date, okay? Just text me the address of the place and I'll see you there on Saturday."

"First of all, I don't need to tell you the address because I'm picking you up, you crazy girl." He rests his hands on either side of the counter I'm sitting on, so he's right in front of me. "Second, I know why you don't want to tell anyone at work, but come on... rules were made to be broken, right? No one is going to give you a hard time for breaking Rule #1, I promise. And third..." Adam caught a glimpse of my spiral notebook the other day, and he's been doing this list thing ever since. It kills me.

But now there's silence.

"Third?" I prompt, baiting him a little.

"Third..." He hesitates. He doesn't have a third.

"Third..." He grins. "So, I'll get to do this whenever I want." And he kisses me slowly, deeply. Those kisses that make me forget my own name.

It's this good night kiss I'm thinking of the next day on set when Frank catches me staring off into space.

"What's going on with you, Maddy? You've been in la-la land all week."

"No, I haven't...," I begin to defend myself.

"This is the second time *today* I've caught a line change in rehearsal that wasn't marked in your script. You don't make mistakes. Ever. I'm worried."

"God, I'm sorry. Thank you for covering my ass." I'm so glad Frank is keeping this conversation in low tones, but it's no less embarrassing to be caught. "I'm just exhausted working two gigs. Thank God *WD* wraps next week."

"Hey, don't get me wrong. Part of me is grateful for any sign that you're not actually a cyborg." Which gets the laugh it's intended to and lets me know I'm off the hook a bit with him . . . as long as I pull it together.

My phone lights up and when I see the number, I smile involuntarily, causing Frank to give me another quizzical look as he walks away.

AD: I'll pick you up at 10?

I look at Adam across the set. He's sitting in his set chair, looking through his sides with his phone casually in one hand.

Me: That sounds perfect. ☺ Can't wait.

He reads my text and replies, no change in expression.

AD: Me too. I love hearing you laugh. Looking forward to the real thing—not just an emoticon.

I know if there were a script for this moment, it would have me get up from my chair in video village, walk over to him, and kiss him in front of everyone to declare myself. But I don't. I just put my phone down and make 100 percent sure that I don't make any more mistakes at work. I know Adam sees this as just an insecurity. But it's more than that; I have to be smart about my career, my reputation. I've worked too hard to have this entire crew dismiss me as just another notch in a celebrity bedpost. With a deep breath, I acknowledge that it's just going to take time. But for now, I gotta admit, the stolen kisses, these secret moments, are pretty hot.

Scene 002
Ext. Pacific Coast Highway--morning

It's a brilliant Saturday morning in LA, bright, crisp, and not a cloud in the sky. I feel like Adam and I are on a soundstage as we drive down the Pacific Coast Highway to Venice—it's almost too perfect.

"Beautiful morning, huh?" he asks with an easy smile. It's nice to see him clean-shaven, and without the bruises and scars that are part of his character on *The Wrong Doctor*. I almost forgot what he looks like without fake blood dripping from his hairline.

"I was just thinking that!" I say with a giddy rush.

Completing the perfect picture this morning is the fact that there are so few cars on the road. Still, it was a trek for Adam to come all the way to Studio City to pick me up. Usually people in LA just meet up, since everything is so spread out.

"You know, you didn't have to come get me. I can drive myself."

"I wanted to do it," he replies simply.

"Well, thank you." I smile at him, holding my hair back as the ocean breeze whips through the open windows.

"You're welcome."

We park at a lot along the beach and walk the length of the boardwalk to the restaurant, holding hands the whole way.

Adam orders a very healthy egg-white omelet with fruit and spelt bread. If I had to take my shirt off on camera, I would probably eat like that too.

"I'll have the egg sandwich." I hand back the menu. What can I say? He's on camera, not me.

"So I can't believe we're filming the finale this week," I say.

"Hogan's crazy. I mean, you have to be crazy to think up a cliff-hanger like that." We're both speaking in low tones, as we don't want anyone to overhear the story plot points.

"But it's a good crazy. Don't you think? I mean, the fans are going to be flipping out, dying to find out what happens next."

"Well, I'm happy for what it means for my character," Adam says. "I'm grateful that my role is growing."

"Vying for number one on the call sheet, huh?" I tease him, but I know Hogan was very impressed with Adam's work this year, which is why he is getting even more airtime and an important story line in season three.

He laughs. "Yeah, I want to knock that Fox down a peg. If not on the call sheet, then at least on the tennis courts. We're playing next week—wanna come?"

"Winner gets the trailer with the stove? I still can't get over that." I can't even imagine how intense a tennis match between those two would be.

"You know I don't really care about that stuff, right?" Adam suddenly turns serious.

"What stuff?" I ask, thrown.

"Who's number one on the call sheet, who has the bigger trailer. How many Twitter followers I have. That stuff really doesn't matter to me."

"I didn't mean to undermine it. I know it all matters to your career." I match his tone.

"Yeah, it does, which is why I do it. I understand how important the fans are, and how lucky I am to have fans. But I also don't think it means more than it does. I do this because I love acting. I'm not in this for the celebrity of it." The server brings us our dishes, and Adam stops to give her his attention. "Thank you," he says with a smile. I see her blush as she walks away. That's the effect he has on women. He seems oblivious to it now, but I know he's not. I've seen him turn on the charm when it suits him.

"I just wanted you to know that." His focus completely returns to me, making me feel hot under the collar.

I dig into my egg sandwich, ready to lighten the mood. You can't take anything seriously with yolk on your fingers.

"So, thanks to you, I'm back to watching *Days* again. I've been DVRing it ever since that day I saw your last episode."

"So you're watching even though I'm gone?" he teases, mock-offended.

"Well, truth is, I was a big fan in college. My friends and I used to plan our classes around it. Our favorite character was always Kate. What's she really like?"

"She's awesome. Funny and cool. Die-hard David Bowie fan. I got along well with everyone on the set. The crew is amazing, hardworking. The actors all come to set prepared to do the work—well, the ones who last do."

We sit for a second, eating, before he asks, "Why'd you stop watching?"

"What? *Days*? Oh...I don't know. I guess after a couple years of juggling that and working on sets, I got out of the habit. And working behind the scenes, it's harder to suspend disbelief."

"Yeah?" He somehow reads on my face that there's more.

"Well, yeah, like reading romance novels. I guess I outgrew it."

"Oh yeah. You don't like romance, I forgot. You like reality."

"Exactly." My hopeless romantic status is not something I like to cop to.

He leaves a couple twenties on the table when he sees that I've finished and we head out of the café toward the beach. We take off our shoes, and the warm sand feels amazing.

"So, what movie were you watching when I came over after the premiere the other night?"

Thrown by the question, I can't think of a lie quick enough. "Um...what?" Now it's become a thing. It would be too embarrassing for him to catch me after all my talk about preferring realistic fiction over ridiculous over-the-top romance.

"Just curious, Ms. I Hate Romance. What were you watching?"

I get a sneaking suspicion he somehow knows. But how could he? I had the DVD paused on the shot after Buttercup and Wesley disappear into the quicksand. Unless he knew that movie by heart, no way would he recognize it from that.

"Nothing. New subject."

He smiles. "As you wish." He takes off, pulling his shirt over his head while running toward the surf. I take off after him. I can't help but laugh. I love that he knows the movie so well. And turning the famous line back on me? It melts my heart. So of course I have to splash him to get even until we are both soaking wet.

He ends the water fight by picking me up and gently dumping me on the dry, hot sand. He uses his dry shirt to wipe the sand from my face and then tosses it aside. I sigh and enjoy the warm sun and Adam's nearness. I am trying to soak in this rare moment of true relaxation, for once not worrying about expectations, or what Adam is thinking, or who else can see us. I'm enjoying the peace, especially since it's probably my last for a while—Monday is my first day reporting to work at our new offices for *Never Cry Wolf*. It's exciting and terrifying. I take another deep breath and nuzzle farther into Adam's chest and then... *Whap*. A Frisbee tags me right in the shoulder.

"OW!" I flinch and grab my arm.

"You okay?" Adam kisses my shoulder and moves my hand away to examine the mark. He rubs it quickly, taking the sting away.

"Yeah, I'm fine." Growing up with two brothers, it takes more than a Frisbee to bring me down.

Adam grabs the Frisbee and looks to throw it back, but the group that it apparently belongs to is already descending on us.

"See, I told you it's him." One teenage girl nudges her friend, unsubtly. Her friend giggles but just stares mutely.

"Hey, sorry about that," says one of the boys they're with. "The wind carried it off."

"Yeah, it caught the wind. Sorry," says the other boy. They're both looking at me while the girls make googly eyes at Adam. Boy #2 asks casually, "Are you on TV too?"

"Me? No." I laugh awkwardly as they don't even try to hide their unimpressed faces. The know-it-all girl speaks up. "But you're on *Days of Our Lives*, right? You're Adam Devin."

"Yeah, that's me," Adam offers gracefully.

"Can we get a picture with you?" The girl whips her phone out of her sweatshirt pocket like it's noon at the OK Corral.

"Of course." Adam poses with the girl while the other one snaps the picture, and then they switch positions and cameras. We wait while still-silent girl pulls her legit camera out of her bag, and finds focus, adjusts for the sun. She must be in a photography class in school. She's still fiddling with the settings when Adam catches my eye and we exchange a silent laugh.

"Hey, would you mind taking one of all of us?" the girls ask me after they've finished their individuals. What is this, a photo shoot?

"Um, actually, we're on a date..." Adam steps in, but I know he doesn't want to leave them with a bad impression, and neither do I.

"No, it's all right. I'll take it. I'm sorry I'm soaking wet...if you don't mind..." I brush as much sand off my hands as I can before taking the camera.

"Oh, I don't mind at all." She hands it to me with only the briefest hesitation. "Come on, everyone, get on this side so you don't block the light." Suddenly Silent Girl is a director. She gets everyone exactly as she wants and I take the picture. She's right, though; it's a great shot, the surf and sand in the background. And then right before the preview image disappears from the screen, I notice that both girls had put their hands on Adam's chest right before I snapped the picture. I look up to see that Adam has detached himself from the bikini-clad girls, as smoothly as possible. The boys have grabbed the Frisbee, done with this celebrity stuff, and are gone. So the girls have no choice but to reluctantly follow.

"Does that happen a lot?" I gesture to his chest, which he's now covering with his shirt.

"What?" he asks, buttoning up.

"Girls copping a feel every chance they get?" I ask as casually as I can, but he must know the answer is important to me.

"Well, I mean, yeah, it happens. Once in a while." He takes my hand and we start heading back to the car. "But it doesn't mean anything." He stops in his tracks and pulls me in to his chest. "You know that, right? This," he says, kissing me on the lips. "This means something to me." He kisses me right there in broad daylight, and I can't resist kissing him back with everything I've got.

Scene 003
Int. Wolf production offices--day

It's all I can do not to gasp out loud taking in the gorgeous, top-of-the-line, brand-new edit bays that Ed Greenling is showing me. All this is for *Never Cry Wolf*? I feel so outclassed as I look at all the fancy equipment. Two young editors are flipping through footage, headphones on, completely ignoring the tour that is going on behind them.

"This is, as you can see, all brand-new equipment, and I found these editors at USC film school. They're geniuses. *Never Cry Wolf* is going to get nothing but the best."

"Spared no expense?" I say, stealing the line from the tour in the beginning of *Jurassic Park*. I really can't believe that this is all for me... well, not for me, but for *Never Cry Wolf*. Twenty minutes into my first official day at my new office, and I am already pinching myself. Hogan is finding us space at HCP, but Ed insisted that we make our home here rather than cram into a conference room while we wait. He has dedicated space right smack dab in the center of the Outdoor Network headquarters.

"Exactly. You're going to have everything you need at your fingertips to make the show a success. Come on, let me show you your office." As he heads down the long hallway, I have to force myself not to whimper. As much as I love Sophie and the ultra-trendy clothes she's lending me to make a good impression here, I don't know how much longer I can stand these heels. I am fantasizing about dipping my feet into hot water with Epsom salts as I follow Ed down the hall as fast as I can, which is not that fast.

"So, take your time getting settled. We'll meet in the conference room with the other creative execs at six to go over the launch plan for *Wolf*."

Ed sees the grimace I can't quite hide at the idea of hiking all the way back to his wing of this warehouse-sized building.

"We're putting you through your paces right off the bat, but you seemed like the type to handle pressure. Was I wrong about you?"

"Oh, not at all. I'm ready for anything you've got for me, Mr. Greenling."

"Ed, please. We're going to be in the trenches together; you have to call me Ed."

"Okay, Ed...It's just that...I guess I just picked the wrong shoes for all the walking I've done today."

"Oh...of course. That's such a woman thing, isn't it? It's always about the shoes—that's what my first wife used to say." He heads to the door chuckling. "And my second wife, too, come to think of it."

He turns back at the door. "We're a casual crew around here, Maddy. Wear some flats." He winks and is gone. I collapse in my chair and immediately kick off the wedges Sophie promised would be more comfortable than stilettos. I am pretty sure I can see my bare feet swelling before my eyes. I wonder if I'll even be able to get the torture devices back on my feet when it's time to get to the meeting. I calculate how long it will take me to reach the main conference room, including time for me to get lost in this maze. I should probably leave by 5:40 to be safe.

Now that that's settled in my head, I look at the work ahead of me. There are stacks and stacks of papers and files and newspaper clippings to look through. At first it's overwhelming, but then I find a box filled with supplies from Office Depot. I feel energized by the organizational tools—there's nothing a girl can't do armed with Post-its, markers, and a fresh notebook. I put the white board up on the wall first, and pull out all the colored markers. I separate the little Post-it notes from the white note cards, and underneath the box, I discover a corkboard.

I'm knee-deep in the papers and pictures and images I brought from home, totally lost in my idea board, everything from beautiful scenic photos of the mountain to specific events. I printed out a pic of me holding my first snowboarding trophy in fifth grade so I could start painting a visual picture of the sensibility for the show. When the alarm on my phone goes off, hours later, I flinch, knowing it's time to put those damn shoes back on and head to the conference room. I really have no idea what to expect as I slowly, gingerly begin the trek to my first big industry meeting. Am I supposed to pitch them the show again, have all the details locked up? Or are we just getting to know each other? I mean, how am I supposed to know this stuff? A little heads-up from Ed would have been nice. The meeting isn't even starting until 6:00, and I have no idea how long it will go on for. I rest outside the kitchen/common area in the center of the first floor and fight the urge to take my shoes off again. Instead, I shift my weight back and forth, giving each foot a break. Then I text Adam, knowing he'll be able to calm me down.

AD: Go get 'em babe. You'll knock 'em dead.
Me: Thx. I don't know what time we'll be done here. I know we planned to finally get that whiskey I owe you... 🙁
AD: Don't worry about it. Text me when you're done. I can't wait to hear about your day. XO

His kiss and hug warms me as I walk in, shoulders squared to face the unknown.

After two and a half hours of chitchat, brainstorming, a lecture from Ed about finances that made no sense to me but had the rest of the team nodding their heads and grimacing appropriately, we are finally calling it a day. Who knew working at the development level could have as sucky hours as being on set. At this point I will have no life at all outside of work. And yet, it's exciting to see the big plans they have for *Wolf*. They are talking about a serious publicity and marketing campaign. Since it was only the initial meeting, people were just spit-balling outrageous ideas like bringing real wolves as guests on the *Tonight Show*, billboards on taxis, doing a "Wolf Week" like Discovery's *Shark Week*.

The first thing I do after saying good night to my new colleagues is take off these damn shoes and walk barefoot to my car. The risk of tetanus outweighs the thought of wearing them one more second. The next thing I do is call Adam. I can barely wait for my Bluetooth to sync up before dialing his number.

"Tell me everything." He skips pleasantries to get right to it.

"I have my own office."

"Of course you do." I hear him smiling on the phone.

"They had it stocked with all sorts of stuff for me to work on the layout and the breakdowns for the show. It was like Office Depot threw up in there."

"Which you love. You sound hyped up, not exhausted. You still want to go out?"

"Sure, I can tell you the rest in person."

"I'm just wrapping up dinner with some friends. Let's meet at your place. Go from there."

It throws me off a bit as Wanda guides me to the nearest freeway on-ramp. I didn't know Adam had dinner plans. Is that weird? He didn't mention who he was eating with and I don't want to seem all nosy and demanding and ask.

By the time we get settled at a table in one of the cool little bars on Ventura in Studio City, its 10:00 and I'm totally wired. I tell Adam all about the meeting and the publicity and marketing ideas. It's a great end to what's been an exciting day, except for right when I've smoothly brought up his dinner to see if he'll tell me who he was with tonight, we're interrupted by a rather large group of people wanting Adam's autograph and to take a picture. No, not a picture, individual pictures with each person in the group. All the guys are good-naturedly laughing as they take pictures on their phones of their spouses or girlfriends or whatever posing with Adam. I watch the photo shoot unfold patiently knowing we'll never get back to the subject of his dinner now. This is just part of the life, and Adam handles it with a lot of grace and gives each fan his time and attention. And if I'm going to be a part of his life, I'm going to have to learn to handle it as well as he does.

Nothing can dampen the rush, though, as we walk back out into the warm fall night, holding hands. I think about how great it's been to have someone to share my day with. And honestly, it scares me how much I enjoy spending time with Adam.

As we walk back to the car, there's a bunch of giggling twentysomething girls in slinky little outfits who brush past us, hurrying into a bar on the corner.

Adam sees it first, something tucked into the driver's side windshield wiper. It's not a parking ticket, but he pulls out a paper with something attached.

"Oh God." Adam laughs and goes to unlock the car.

"What? What is it?" I'm surprised he doesn't offer an explanation to begin with.

"Oh, it's nothing," he says casually. He opens his door. "Come on, let's get out of here."

I note the fact that he doesn't come around to open the door for me as he normally does. It makes me jump into the car quickly, so that I catch him before he can tuck the note out of sight.

"What are you hiding?" I laugh, making a grab for what's in his hand.

"Nothing." He shies away from me.

Now I have to know what this is. "Just let me see. What's the big deal?"

"Okay, fine." Adam reluctantly hands it over.

"'Call me'?" I read, looking at Adam. "'Hearts, Heather.'" And then I realize what's fallen into my hand with the flowery note. A pair of lace panties. I flinch and drop them into my lap like a hot potato, an involuntary "ewww" slipping out. It takes a couple of spastic movements to get it off me and back onto his side of the car. "That's disgusting!"

"Well, it's original, that's for sure."

"What? Original? Is that all you can say? Does this happen all the time?"

"I wouldn't say all the time . . . no." He starts the engine.

"Well, how often, then, Adam? How often are women giving you their underwear and telling you to call them? Once a week? Twice a week?" I tell myself to calm down, but the idea that all these gorgeous women trail Adam around just got very real.

"Maddy—"

I interrupt him. "I just can't believe someone would do that. I mean, she had to have been wearing them, right? You don't keep extra undies in your purse just in case you run into a celebrity."

"I'm not sure I understand. Are you mad at me?" We've arrived back at my house from the short drive down the block. Adam turns off the engine and turns to me.

"Well, I'd like to know why you tried to keep...that"—I gesture to the offensive note and its accessory—"from me. Why didn't you just admit what it was when I asked?"

"What do you mean 'admit'? I didn't do anything wrong. I don't have anything to 'admit' to."

"You didn't want me to know what was on your windshield. The *note* she left you." I say it with as much derision as I can muster.

"Of course I didn't want you to see it!" he says loudly. And then in a much more reasonable tone, he adds, "I knew you'd overreact."

Overreact?! I'm fuming at the implication that my reaction is anything but completely rational.

"Maddy, this isn't *real*." He holds up the crumpled note and underwear in the dark car.

"Oh my God...can you please get rid of them? Or do you have some place at home where you keep these things?!" I know I'm reaching here, but somehow I just can't stop myself.

Adam growls in frustration. "Are you kidding me, Maddy? I'm not going to keep them. I just didn't have a place to throw them away, and I'm not going to toss them out the window on Ventura Boulevard." He stalks to the trash cans on the corner and tosses them in. "Happy now?"

"No." I get out of the car too. I'm whispering so my happy, normal, suburban neighbors don't start staring out their windows. "I don't understand how you can just take that so casually. It's crazy. And maybe I am 'overreacting,' but I clearly don't fit in with all this."

"That's absurd. Maddy, you can't let a couple of crazy girls—who probably didn't mean anything by it—get to you. It was probably a bet, or a joke to them. You're blowing this way out of proportion."

"Are you really going to stand there and tell me you've never taken a girl up on an offer like that?"

"What?"

"Answer the question."

"That's so unfair." We hold a silent contest of wills, but I am not backing down on this, even though I really don't want to hear his answer.

"Yes. Okay? Yes. When I was young and stupid, I hooked up with a few fans. I'm not going to lie to you. But that was years ago. Obviously that's not what I want now. I want you. I want this."

I just look at him. I don't know what to say. I know in a rational part of my mind I'm being unreasonable, but I can't help it. I'm chickening out. How can I ever compete with all these girls, girls who are willing to do anything to be with a celebrity? For the longest time I don't say anything. And then I can't even look at his face anymore. I stare at my feet.

It's Adam who breaks the silence. "Right, never trust the actors. How could I forget?" Without waiting for a response, he gets back in his car and starts the engine. I take a few deep breaths, but he's just sitting there with his car idling, and I realize he's waiting for me to go inside. He's still there watching as I unlock my front door, but by the time I've shut the door and go to peek out the curtain, all I see are taillights.

Scene 004
Int. Wolf production offices--evening

For the last twenty minutes I've been talking with Brett, our brand-new story producer, and Joel, show runner for *Never Cry Wolf*, about the magic that was the first season of *The Real World*.

"All my high school friends had a crush on Eric Nies," I tell the guys.

"Oh, but Kevin Powell stole the show. So much drama." Brett has just moved here from New York City and hasn't even found a place to live yet. He's worn the same green shirt three days this week.

Brett, Joel, and I have had some fascinating discussions and fierce debates about reality TV in our daily production meetings. Brett worked on *The Real Housewives of New York City* and has some really good gossip about those ladies. But from our conversations over the last couple of weeks has come a clear understanding of what we want our show to be like. I have already used up three spiral notebooks on just the prep for production.

We are chomping at the bit to get up to Wolf and start filming next week. We've gotten Ed to sign off on one episode focusing on Wolf County "getting ready for winter." And then we'll hold off until the snow falls for the rest of the season.

It's a little tight, getting the crew ready and the field producers up to speed. Luckily for me, I have Joel by my side, because one of the first lessons I've learned is that I have to be careful who I reveal my inexperience in reality to. As snobby as scripted people can be about reality, the reverse is true too. Reality TV people can be total purists about their style of TV production, and I'm tired of the "Well, that's not how we do it" comments. I want to do it the way that makes the most sense for *Never Cry Wolf*.

Joel keeps telling me that I am a good test sample for him of what the people in Wolf are going to be like. "Maddy, I know if I can convince you, I can get these Wolves to do anything."

We've spent this meeting trying to figure out how to shoot the resort getting ready. My brother and dad hiring the ski school employees, the seasonal lift operators, the most interesting parts for the audience to see. We've also talked a lot about the ground logistics. The crew will be staying at The Mount Inn, which is a tiny bed-and-breakfast near the lodge. With only eleven rooms, the *Never Cry Wolf* team can take up the whole inn and effectively make it headquarters. My mom mentioned that the owner, Marybell, had told her that she bought all new sheets for all the rooms and tried a new recipe for blueberry muffins. It's like I'm bringing a dozen guests home for dinner, but I know the crew will love the Wolf hospitality.

I look at the clock in the corner as we wrap the meeting and note that this will be my fourth sixteen-hour day in a row. Every day for the last week, I've woken up, driven straight to the Wolf offices, worked my tail off all day, breaking for lunch if someone forced me to, and then come home and fallen asleep before I could even watch a minute of the news. Not that I am complaining, because the upside of this brutal schedule is that I haven't had one spare second to think about Adam.

Which is not to say I don't feel a split second's hesitation every time my phone rings or beeps a new text, but it's never Adam. Well, he did text me once, the morning after Thong-gate:

Maddy, the only underwear I care about is yours. ☺ Call me.

I know he was making light of the situation to defuse the tension, clearly he also just wasn't taking my feelings seriously. I really needed to talk to him, explain myself, which is what I was going to write back, but I knew I had to sort out my thoughts first. When I'm with him, it's hard to keep a thought in my head anyway. So I figured I would spend some time coming up with a script of sorts, and then I'd be able to explain my feelings clearly when I saw him. But then I got so busy with work and one day led to a week, and one to two, and we haven't spoken at all. There's no way he's going to come back on a white horse at this point given that (A) I'm not a damsel, (B) he doesn't even know if I am in distress, because (C) I'm the one who picked this fight. If this were a fairy tale, I'm actually more the villain, or just a fool.

And why did I do that? I had a trumped up list of reasons in my mind, but I had to cross them off, including that stupid mysterious dinner. Some fashion blog had pictures of him leaving the restaurant with Alice and her husband Tony that night. So I'm left with nothing to hide behind except the main one, circled in red at the top: I'm scared. Adam—hell, Adam's whole world—is so far out of my league, it's not even funny. He's going to realize it sooner or later and go back to dating the Lola Stones of the world, or fans with sexier underwear, who would die to be by his side at all of his fancy events. I'll remember why I had my rule in the first place. I'm saving us both the trouble. Aren't I?

"So is that a yes, Maddy?"

"Sorry, Joel, I zoned out there for a sec. What's the question?" Please let it be something easy to answer.

"We're going to the pub across the street to grab a quick drink since we're all going to be here so late. You in?"

An easy question indeed. "Yes, a drink would be great."

In the spirit of bonding with my new team, I grab my purse and follow Joel out. He has a couple of the younger producers in tow and we all file into the pub behind him like ducklings. One of the quirks about Hollywood is how quickly crews can become so close. When you're working such long hours with a group of people, you can't help but get tight, quick. It's like an adult version of summer-camp friendships. Now that *The Wrong Doctor* has wrapped, I'm glad to have this camaraderie with a new team. Sometimes, after a show wraps, it can be months before you come back from the hiatus or start a new show. When you're used to being with a huge crew for sixty-plus hours a week, it can be... quiet.

As we're waiting for our drinks at the table, I reflexively check my phone for any messages. Nothing.

"So what's your deal, Maddy?"

I look up at Kaitlin, one of the new young producers getting her first big break.

"My deal?" I ask evasively.

"Yeah, you got a boyfriend?" She looks at me sincerely, as if that isn't a totally inappropriate question to ask your boss.

"Um, no." I'm definitely not telling my story here, so I need to seem firm. "I don't."

"That's crazy," she says loudly, and then turns to include Joel in the discussion. A discussion I really don't want to be having right now. "That's crazy isn't it? I mean, Maddy is amazing. Joel, we have to find someone for her, don't we?"

"Sure, I have straight friends," Joel says. Now I'm going to die. "What's the age range you're looking for? My old roommate is a manager; he reps some good people. Totally legit."

"I'm actually not looking to date anyone right now." I swallow hard. "I used to have a rule that I don't date actors, but I've sort of expanded it. I don't want to date anyone in the industry."

"Gotcha. Once bitten, twice shy?" he replies, too knowingly.

"Wasn't that a song?" Kaitlin asks, perking up. "They play it on eighties flashback weekends. I love that song." And luckily the waitress shows up with a tray full of drinks before any other awkwardness can continue.

I ordered a beer on purpose. I don't want any of this new crowd mistaking me for the fruity-drink type. With every sip, though, I can't help but miss the refreshing cheerfulness of the fun drinks I got into the habit of ordering with Adam. But I firmly remind myself that isn't who I am, and there's no use pretending anymore.

After one drink, we all walk back to the offices. There is still tons of work to be done to get ready to shoot next week. Even the front office people are still working as we stroll in.

"Hey, Maddy. Someone's here to see you." The receptionist hails me as I head over to the employee entrance. She waves me back toward the main lobby. As I make my way to the seating area on the other side of the reception desk, I have a stupid fantasy that it will be Adam.

Int. Shiny lobby
Camera sees a blurry figure through the glass doors. They burst open and it's Adam, with a huge bouquet of expensive flowers. Looking tired and unkempt, he approaches the reception desk.

ADAM

I desperately need to see Maddy Carson. You have
to let me in to see her right away.

MADDY

What are you doing here? They called me down
saying you were making a scene.

ADAM

This has to stop, Maddy. We both said things we
regret, but there has to be a way past it.

273

ADAM (cont.)

(he hands her the flowers)

I love you...

As Adam starts to sink to one knee, right in the middle of the lobby, we go close-up on Maddy's happy tears.

I round the corner, and there he is. Not Adam, of course. Some stranger I don't know, in a suit.

"I'm Maddy Carson. May I help you?" I ask, politely covering my disappointment.

"Madelyn Carson?"

"Yes." Didn't I just say that?

"Great. You've been served." He shoves an envelope at me and darts off.

I've seen this in the movies and, I think, on an episode of *Friends*. I half expect him to come back and say, "Just kidding." I mean, it's not divorce papers... what the hell? I rip open the envelope and read the official letterhead of James Goodman ESQ, pronouncing in ridiculous legal mumbo jumbo that I am being sued by one Craig Williams for defamation of character, that my malicious lies led to his "wrongful termination" at Hogan Chenny Productions and that I "stole" *Never Cry Wolf* from him. He wants a piece of the profits and producer credit.

I read it three times before it truly sinks in. I cannot believe I am standing here reading this. And for all my bravado and tough "Wolf" skin, I am truly scared. What will Ed Greenling think? What will Hogan say? What am I going to do?

The papers are starting to get crumpled in my now slightly sweaty hands. As I get in the elevator, I smooth them out on my thigh. I go to press number 7, my floor, but my finger hesitates above the panel of numbers. What will waiting do? Nothing can make this better right now. I might as well rip the Band-Aid off quickly. I hit PH, stand back, and watch the lights tick away, taking me to Ed's office on the top floor. On the ride up, I e-mail Hogan to please call me as soon as possible. We need to collaborate on a plan of action. But I need to hear Ed's reaction and get out in front of this.

"Does Ed have a minute?" I say on my way to his door. I've learned that when it comes to assistants, the more strong-willed I am about getting inside, the better chance I have. I know if I meekly stood in front of her desk, it would be twenty minutes at least.

"Um ... Ms. Carson, I'm not sure ...," she stutters, leaving me the opening I need.

"I'll just check. If he's busy, I'll sneak back out. No problem." I don't know how I pulled off that casual voice, but it seems to have worked. She sits back in her seat.

Ed's office is huge and covered in windows. We're right in the heart of Century City, so there's a 180-degree view from downtown LA to the ocean. It's breathtaking. Ed's on a call, but motions me in while he rolls his eyes at the phone. I act as if I'm in no hurry and stroll over to look at the ocean, hoping for some serenity. A few deep breaths and I am actually glad he's still wrapping up the call. It gives me a chance to script out what to say in my head.

"Sorry about that. One of our main advertisers. Gotta keep 'em happy, right?" He chuckles ruefully as he walks over to sit in one of a pair of matching leather armchairs near where I am standing. I smile at him, but it's thin. I sit on the sofa and only for something to do, reach for a bottled water on the coffee table between us.

"Ed, I have a concern. It could be nothing really, but I wanted to bring it to your attention immediately."

"Okay." Ed remains relaxed, but his graying eyebrows furrow slightly. "Shoot."

"When I first started working on *Never Cry Wolf*, there was another employee at HCP who was developing it with me..."

"Craig Williams, right? I remember."

"Right, yes. Craig." Treading lightly, I continue. "Well, he's making some waves, and I just wanted you to be aware of it. He's crying foul that *Never Cry Wolf* was his idea, and he wants to hold on to a piece of it. First of all, I want you to know that it's completely untrue, but either way, it was in Craig's contract at HCP that all development done while working for Hogan is owned by HCP. That's clearly stated. So, to be clear, he has no legal leg to stand on...but, you know...he could still make things awkward." I finish and firmly remind myself not to ramble on as I usually do when I'm nervous. Now is not the time to chatter. But it's hard as the silence stretches on. Ed seems to be in no rush to continue the dialogue, so I force myself to sit patiently.

Finally he speaks. "You're sure the contract is clear? He can't force his way in?"

"I'm sure." Hogan spelled it out for me; obviously he was savvy enough to know this might be an issue. "Hogan can get you a copy of the deal memo if you need to see it."

"Yes, that would be good to have on file. I can give it to the lawyers to look over." He starts to get up. "Thanks for letting me know." And then he's headed back to his desk, as if we had just been talking about the weather or his golf game.

I get up but don't go to leave, not sure what to make of Ed's attitude. I watch him riffle through some things on his desk before he looks at me again.

"Maddy." He sighs. "It's business. Of course Craig is going to fight for it, even if he's wrong. He'd be a fool not to. Look at it this way: It means *Never Cry Wolf* is a good idea. Take it as a compliment." He goes back to his papers. I head to the door, determined to take his point of view to heart and not let the pit in my stomach eat me alive.

"But, Ed . . . ," I say as I'm about to leave. I remember the other element to this. "What if he goes public? Starts talking about how we stole it or something? He could maybe get some press on this."

"Good point. Get the PR department up to speed on this." I head out, about to make that call. "Maddy!" I turn back. "Cheer up. It's free publicity! Let Craig get people talking about our show. It's a good thing." I smile at his take on what I saw as a complete nightmare. Ed Greenling has nerves of steel; I could take a lesson from him.

Scene 005
Ext. Wolf Mountain--morning

Wearing brand-new hiking boots was a bad idea, and I can feel at least three blisters on my feet, but in all the chaos of getting the camera crews and production up to Wolf, I didn't put a lot of thought into packing. As a result, I am staying in my old bedroom at my parents for the week with a duffel full of mismatched flip-flops and my usual LA production clothes—shorts, jeans, and casual tops. Nothing that is right for the mountain on this very chilly morning, with my brother, his team of blasters, and a camera crew. I would be embarrassed by my mistake, but I don't have time.

We have laid out an incredibly intense shooting schedule for the week. I had no idea how stressful it would be for me to work without a specific script to follow. Joel and I worked side by side for the first two days, but with such a tight production time, we had to split up today. He's got a second camera crew doing interviews, so I'm standing here on what will be the bunny slope when the snow falls, with the guys and a camera crew, wishing I'd had a bit more in-the-field training before flying solo.

"Maddy, what do you think?" I really don't know how to answer the lead camera operator's question. Everyone is looking at me, waiting.

"Run it by me again," I say, a stalling tactic for sure, but I ignore the subtle sighs I hear because I need the minute to think.

"We've got the intro shot of them pounding through the forest here. I don't know how much light we have left to shoot the conversation about prepping the mountain for winter. Do you need that out here, or should we go back and shoot it in Mike's office?"

I look at the setting sun. My brain is telling me that it's smarter, financially and timing-wise, to reposition inside now. But I want it to be outside. That's one of the biggest selling points of the show—the beauty, the outdoors. That's what my gut is telling me and after all this time, standing here on my home turf, we're going with my gut.

"We're going to do it here. But let's set it up ASAP." I point to where I want the cameras and pull Mike aside. "If we run out of light before you're done, don't pretend it's not happening. We want this as realistic as possible. If it's getting too dark, just say, 'We'll keep talking in my office.' But if you can get it all done before sunset, that would be great."

"Sure, boss." Mike waits for the signal that the cameras are rolling and then yells out, "All right, everyone, huddle up," as if he's the quarterback. The blasting team gathers around and they get down to business.

I watch from behind the main camera, so proud of my brother who has adapted to this much more smoothly than I could have imagined. And I know he's done it for me: allowed these cameras to follow him, not even grumbled about waiting for the crew to chase him around, or when the audio guy asks him to wait to speak for a passing airplane. My love for my family and appreciation for them is indescribable, and it only reaffirms my commitment to protecting them and making *Never Cry Wolf* the best I possibly can.

My phone silently buzzes—a text from Billy:

BF: How's it going, EP?
Me: Ha. Not used to being an executive producer yet, that's for sure.

BF: I'm sure you're doing great.

Me: Thanks for the vote of confidence.

BF: Are you gonna get free from the new show to come to the WD party?

Instead of a wrap party at the end of the production season, Hogan decided to host a "premiere" party for the cast and crew to celebrate the premiere episode of season two. It's at House of Blues next weekend, and because of the Adam factor, I've been trying to ignore it on the calendar. Not sure how to respond, I look up at the scene, making sure that everything is still going smoothly before I return to the phone.

Me: Yeah. I can't wait.

Seems harmless enough, but barely an instant later his reply tells me he can read through my texts, no problem.

BF: Yes, Adam's going. No, I don't think he's bringing a date.

Me: I didn't ask.

BF: You didn't have to.

What is that supposed to mean, anyway? It's now been three weeks since I've heard from Adam. Ending things was clearly for the best, no matter what Billy, Janine, or even Sophie says.

Me: See you there.

I decide not to get into it via text.

BF: You know what they say about quitters in Texas, don't you?

BF: You don't want to find out. And wear a dress Saturday.

BF: I can tell you're reading these texts.

I hate smartphones.

Me: You are so annoying sometimes.

BF: I annoy because I care. About both of you. It's ridiculous watching him sulk around. Do something!

Like what? I ask myself. But just as I'm about to ask Billy that very question, Mike wraps up the meeting and the guys all start to head back down the hill. The sunset is a million colors on the horizon behind them.

One of the shooters, a cool chick named Katie, hasn't moved from her spot. She was shooting the conversation, but now with the guys gone, I follow her camera lens, trying to figure out why she's still filming.

She must sense me right behind her because without looking away, she whispers, "There's something in the trees over there. I think it's a coyote or a fox or something. In silhouette, it'll look great for the opening credits." I watch her work the camera, focusing, adjusting her angle slightly, panning from the creature to the sunset and then from the sunset back to the creature.

When she's finished getting every possible variation of the shot, she brings the camera down to her side, looks at me, and states matter-of-factly, "A good omen."

I'll take it.

Scene 006
Int. Carson living room--night

I miss Adam. There, I said it—or at least allowed myself to think it. The three little words I've been trying to deny for three weeks now. I've Googled him a couple or twenty times to see if the paparazzi had any recent pictures of him, only to come up empty. But that didn't stop me from torturing myself imagining Adam with a hot swimsuit model or Hollywood A-list starlet. However, finding out from Billy that he isn't dating, or at least that he was going solo to *The Wrong Doctor* premiere party, is turning into a game-changer. Now that I have some downtime before heading back to LA tomorrow afternoon, sitting here on my parents' sofa, I am lost in thought. Thoughts of Adam. Of seeing him next weekend.

Vaguely I hear my dad shout, "What is *The Big Chill?*" and then silence. I pull myself out of the *Deep Space Nine* headspace I'm in to discover that both my mom and dad are staring at me.

"Honey? Are you okay?"

"Um, yeah," I fake. "Why?"

"You didn't answer any of the movie trivia questions in *Jeopardy!*" I force a halfhearted laugh and realize I shouldn't have bothered. They are on to me.

"I'm just, I don't know...not feeling myself, I guess."

"Isn't the show going well? You said you were finishing up in the morning. Are you worried that it isn't good?"

"No, Mom. I'm not worried at all." I rush to defend it. "The show is great. Actually, it's surprisingly good. I'm really happy with everything. I think Hogan will be too. I can't wait to show him the footage."

"If it's not work, then what is it?" My dad, sipping his Waxy Sour, doesn't deviate from the thoughtful interrogation. I look at my feet.

"I broke up with someone, and I'm just not sure I made the right decision."

"You mean Craig?" My mom and dad exchange glances. "Honey, honestly, he was never right for you. I hope you don't mind me saying this, but I was so relieved when he didn't come back this trip. You are so much better off without him."

"No, not Craig. And I agree with you; I'm much better off without him." I don't bother giving them further anti-Craig ammunition by bringing up the stupid lawsuit. The last thing I need is for my dad to go ballistic over something that may well be resolved after the meeting with Craig's lawyers tomorrow. I've been dreading it all week, but Hogan's lawyers have made it clear that this is our best option.

"Not Craig? There's someone else?" My mom is just trying to follow along, but still.

"Jeez, Mom, you don't have to say it like it's a crime. Yes, I dated someone else. Briefly. After Craig."

"Of course it's not a crime, Madelyn, and like I said, we're glad you're over Craig. I guess I'm just surprised to hear there was someone else so quickly."

"I've known him at work for a while. And he let me know he was interested. I said no while I was with Craig, but afterward, he kind of just...I don't know...swept me off my feet," I say lamely. Even though it wasn't lame. It was amazing. It was spectacular. Why did I blow it?

"Why did you end it, then?" she echoes my thoughts.

Finally, the dam breaks.

"Because I'm an idiot, Mom. Because I'm scared." I start crying. I can see through my tears that my parents are frozen in place. I hardly ever cry, so they don't know what to do.

"Oh, honey..." My mom finally snaps out of it to touch my shoulder.

"Mom, I picked the stuuuuupidest fight with him," I wail. "I just couldn't take it, knowing that he's...he's..."

"He's what?"

"He's an actor," I blubber, as if that explains it all.

"I don't understand, honey. What's that got to do with anything?" my dad interjects and my mom shushes him.

"You don't have to tell us. It's your decision, your life. But if you're this upset, maybe you need to talk it out."

I sniffle and unattractively wipe my nose on my sleeve. "When I first went to LA, I just didn't want to get sucked in to the way things are there. It's all about appearances and looks and whatnot. I wanted to work hard and be real. And after Brian, yes, I've dated, but no one seems right for me. No one seems to get me. So I've just been working, and it's great because I love my job...but I want something more. And then with Craig, I thought he was right for me because he's like me. He's from a small town, too, and I thought he saw Hollywood the way I did. Adam is the opposite of all that. He's in the top fifty on IMDb, for God's sake." I am not even sure I am making sense, but now that the floodgates are open, I am letting everything spew. "And then after Craig turned out to be such an asshole—sorry, Dad—I guess it sort of showed me that maybe I could be wrong about Adam too. Even though he's so sweet to me and we have so much fun, and I think you guys would really like him...I'm not enough for him, you know? Girls, fans, throw themselves at him all the time. I'm not like that. And the paparazzi follow him around a lot. Can you imagine him in a picture with *me* in *US Weekly*?"

"Why not?" Leave it to my dad to get indignant.

"What do you mean, why not? Dad! It's...well...it's me!"

"I still don't get it," Dad says obstinately. I look to my mom for understanding.

"Don't look at me, dear. I agree with your father. Why not you?"

"I'm a script supervisor, that's why. I work behind the scenes. Even if this show takes off, I'm a producer; I'm not meant to be under the lights. The girls in *US Weekly* know the names of every (sob) new (sob) designer, and I can't even wear...high heels..." This starts a fresh wave of tears.

My parents exchange a glance that I've recognized since childhood. It's a signal I'm going to hear something I don't want to hear.

"Madelyn. Look at me." When your mother uses that tone, I don't care how old you are, you do as you're told. "Since you were little, you've been so determined to see things only one way. Your way. Your father and I wanted to pull our hair out for how stubbornly you stuck to your idea that everything is black and white. Right and wrong.

"Now, I don't know this Adam person from...well...Adam, but I know you. And I know how set in your ways you can be. If you're feeling this rotten about what you did, then I think it's time you stop thinking only with your brain. And start following your heart. No matter how determined you are to be logical and practical—that's just not the way it works with love, honey. That's how I ended up marrying a guy five years younger than me. Back then, it was a big deal—we joke about it now, but you've heard the stories. I told him no I can't tell you how many times.

But one thing you learned from your father—your stubbornness." She looks at my dad and smiles.

"I knew I was out of your mom's league," Dad adds gruffly, his words echoing my sentiments about Adam exactly. "But I also knew I'd make her happier than anyone else ever could." He puts his hand on her knee.

"Honey, you'll find that in life, there rarely are things that are done that can't be undone. You can fix this, but first you have to be willing to put yourself out there." Mom puts her hand on top of Dad's.

"Hogan has told us for years he wished you would push your way up the ladder. He said you sit there next to the director and producer and half the time he trusts your judgment, your opinion, more than theirs." Dad lets that sink in for a second. "You're the one holding yourself back. So, that's it, Maddy," he adds. "We can't tell you what to do. But life is like football; if you don't take a few hits along the way, you're not trying hard enough."

And sitting there on my parents' couch, under one of my mom's afghans, awash in my parents' love, I have a terrifying thought: They're right.

Scene 007
Int. HCP conference room--day

"We're here to discuss, for the record, the matter of Hogan Chenny Productions versus Craig Williams."

"This is ridiculous." Craig is grandstanding before the lawyer can even finish getting the formalities out of the way. "Hogan, you know the only way to make this go away is to give me a piece of this. I deserve it."

Hogan makes no move to speak, sitting quietly, politely looking at his lawyer. I don't know how he keeps his calm; I want to jump out of my skin.

"If I may proceed?" Hogan's lawyer, William Sams, the gruff, slightly heavy-set, African American man I met only hours earlier, pushes his glasses up his nose. As General Counsel for HCP, I've seen him around the offices a few times over the years but never had reason to meet him until now.

I look around the conference room table at the collection of men and two women in suits representing HCP on one side and Craig and his lawyer on the other. I am seated next to Hogan in the center of the table, surrounded by our legal team. Craig gets to give his statement first.

"I was proud to represent HCP for five years. I have been a loyal member of the company; Hogan never had one reason to be unhappy with my work until this incident. I feel I've been unfairly characterized as a villain in this scenario, when in fact,

I'm the one who fostered this idea. It seems only fair to me that I take part in its success."

As I listen to Craig go on with his version of what happened, I am partly horrified at his misrepresentation of the facts and partly in awe of his skill to manipulate the situation to make himself the victim with his righteous indignation. If I hadn't been there myself, I would have believed his account.

His lawyer jumps in as soon as Craig concludes his version of events. "Given those circumstances, we have here a figure that we believe fairly covers the contribution Craig made to the creation of *Never Cry Wolf*. This lump sum, along with a producer's credit and a corresponding fee, will resolve this issue for us."

His lawyer pushes some papers across the table to Mr. Sams, who begins to review it.

I can't keep silent any longer. "This isn't fair. I don't care what that paper says. Hogan, you can't pay him." I look at Mr. Sams. "It wasn't his idea. I swear it wasn't. He said Hogan wanted to do a reality show, which, turned out not to be true," I add with conviction as I meet Craig's eyes. "But I'm the one who thought of doing a show based on Wolf County. It's my hometown! He wouldn't have looked twice at the town if it weren't for me. He skis Aspen, for God's sake!" I add somewhat desperately.

Hogan puts his hand on mine, reminding me to pull it together.

"I hate to argue with Maddy. I know how important her town is to her." Craig's salesman's voice is in full effect now. "But even if you asked people in Wolf, like the Gordons, they will verify that Maddy and I together came up with the idea of the show. We asked them to be a part of it together."

"We'd like to provide you with the audio files and handwritten notes that show Craig and Madelyn developed this concept together on their trip to Wolf County earlier this year." The lawyer thumps a stack of xeroxed pages and DVDs in front of me. I recognize my own handwriting mixed with Craig's notes from that trip.

And now it all comes crashing back to me, how much Craig used "we" while we were in town. How I never ended up confronting him about it, and now here we are. I realize as I hear his words, that it's just his word against mine. And I never contradicted it in front of my own friends.

"I have other notebooks, ones I wrote before this even happened. Before we took the trip," I sputter, desperate to contradict the evidence in front of me.

"I love putting pen to paper too," Craig's lawyer says condescendingly. "Unfortunately, without substantiating evidence such as Craig's digital time-stamped photos and audio files, it's impossible to verify when they were written. So, as we were saying..." His lawyer speaks up again, sounding more arrogant, if that's even possible. "We feel this is a fair offer, and then we can all move on with making good TV."

Hogan, still silent, gives a barely perceptible nod to his lawyer, and Mr. Sams slides the "offer" over for Hogan to review.

"Mr. Pritt, while we appreciate the offer, and the fact that you came here to discuss this with us, unfortunately we cannot accept." My head whips around to see Mr. Sams's unapologetic face.

Craig's lawyer mockingly laughs. "What? You might want to discuss this in private before you make such a quick, and dare I say, wrong decision."

Hogan slams the paper back down on the table and finally speaks. "I trusted you with my company; you were my right hand here. And this is what it comes down to?" He looks Craig up and down. "I'm ashamed I didn't see through you when I hired you." He nods to Mr. Sams, who pulls out a thick folder.

"Regarding Ms. Carson, while handwritten notes are clearly

her preference, I do have an e-mail dated back to the beginning of September, in which Madelyn sent you her official pitch regarding the project in Wolf County," Mr. Sams says. "We had to bring in an IT expert to recover the e-mail since it had been methodically deleted from the surface files of the HCP interoffice network, but luckily, nothing digital ever really disappears. Fortunately we were able to clearly establish that you began mentioning the concept in your e-mails only after her initial pitch to you..."

Craig whispers harshly in his lawyer's ear. He nods, and they seem to be gearing up for a retort when Mr. Sams continues. "It was quite a complicated process, retrieving the deleted files in the main HCP network. In doing so, we discovered some other interesting and relevant facts regarding Mr. Williams. We have here Craig's corporate credit card statements over the last five years. If you review, we've highlighted for you that there is over fifteen thousand dollars on last month's statement that are, shall I say, 'questionable' expenses." He reads from the document with a sneer. "A weekly massage at Kim's Palace. Tickets to a Katy Perry concert. A weekend golf outing at Pebble Beach to the tune of eighty-five hundred dollars... Shall I go on?"

"Oh come on, everyone in Hollywood wines and dines. That's why we have corporate accounts. Hogan and I played Pebble together just last fall," Craig interjects.

"With one of the biggest advertisers on the network," Mr. Sams counters smoothly. "I have the names of the men you played golf with two weeks ago. I couldn't find them on IMDb, but they are tagged in several pictures on your Facebook profile of you all drinking together."

"I was with clients...," Craig starts, but Pritt shushes him before he can keep arguing.

Hogan says nothing at all, but Mr. Sams continues. "I have your employment contract here, which specifically outlines appropriate business expenses. Our accountant has tallied up the total you would owe the company in the form of unauthorized expenditures over the last five years. Let's see"—he looks down at the paperwork in his hand dramatically—"two hundred fifty-six thousand, three hundred fifty-four dollars, and sixty-two cents. If you choose to pursue this claim against HCP, we will countersue you for this amount."

Craig still looks outraged. Pritt takes the paperwork from Mr. Sams and starts furiously scrutinizing it.

In the end, Hogan offers to forgive the debt, but it is contingent on Craig agreeing to walk away from Wolf quietly and signing a nondisclosure agreement to the tune of $5 million if he violates it. I watch Craig's eyes flying through the document over his lawyer's shoulder. As if he has other options. I can't believe I thought I should be with this guy. It seems so long ago now, even though it's been only a few months. But these last few months, especially learning the truth about Craig, but also being with Adam, has taught me so much. That sometimes things don't always add up the way they should. Like Craig's credit card statements, Craig himself has huge gaps. Question marks. Meanwhile, Adam, for all his skills as an actor, has never lied to me. Has never pretended to be anything but who he really is. Adam has shown me so many times, in so many ways how much he cares for me. And what did I do? Blow it.

Scene 008
Int. Maddy's apt--evening

I'm still riding high on the victory over Craig, but now that that issue is solved, the problem of my love life is front and center. Knowing I screwed up with Adam and wanting him back just makes watching *Sleepless in Seattle* especially cruel, but I can't help myself. Tom Hanks is pouring his heart out on the radio to a distant Meg Ryan. Even if I called Adam, what would I say? Somehow I know in my gut that it's not going to be easy to make this right. And I don't deserve it to be. I was an idiot. I keep flipping through the channels, looking for something to distract me from my thoughts.

For a second I'm sidetracked watching CeeLo Green bickering with the gorgeous Adam Levine on *The Voice*. I stay on NBC, determined to put the unresolved angst from my mind. But then a contestant starts singing Jason Mraz's "I Won't Give Up." Is the universe trying to mock me?

And the answer is a clearly resounding yes, when a close-up of Adam appears on my television screen. It's a promo for *Days of Our Lives*, which shows quick flashes of what must've been Adam's final scenes on the show, and then teases the drama to come in upcoming episodes.

I stare at the TV, hearing a swirl of voices in my head. My mother's advice, my dad's concern, Matthew warning Adam to be good to me, Adam telling me he wants this. And I have what can only be called an "aha" moment. I don't know how much time passes as I sit there because now that the idea has hit me, it won't let go. I go into the kitchen and clean up from my frozen dinner. I toss the whites into the washing machine. But I can't shake it. Finally I realize that if I don't do this, I will regret it forever.

I find my phone and make two calls while I reach for the remote and scroll through the DVR with purpose.

A day and a half later, I haven't changed my clothes or showered. My only concession to personal comfort was taking off my contacts when my eyes started to burn. The glasses and the time crunch remind me of college days. I'm not letting anything distract me from my mission, even the voice mails and texts piling up on my phone.

"Maddy. It's Billy again. Seriously. Why haven't you texted me back? Give me a call when you get this. I wanna see if you want me to pick you up for the party."

"Maddy. I've left a couple messages. I'm starting to get worried. Call me back as soon as you get this."

"I'm not kidding, Maddy; I'm starting to freak out here. Billy said you hadn't returned his texts either. Call me." Janine's voice is starting to get high-pitched. I take a precious minute to text both her and Billy:

Me: I'm fine. I'll see you at the party.

Then, right on time, the doorbell rings. Through the peephole, I see that it's Stella. I open the door and yank her inside, bags and all. I look both ways like a criminal and then slam the door again, locking us both inside.

Scene 009
Int. House of Blues--night

I walk up the stairs into the House of Blues. From where I am standing just outside the main room, I can scan the crowd undetected. The place is packed. Instantly I spot Adam. He's in the middle of a crowd of actors and crew; they're laughing and toasting each other, clearly enjoying the festivities. The live band is playing loudly and enthusiastically, and the dance floor is already jam-packed. Everyone is caught up in the celebration. Except me. I look down at the softly moving bright red fabric. It drapes down to my calves in the back, but curves up above the knee in the front to show off my legs. The skirt allows for movement, thankfully, but gathers tightly at my waist to crisscross across my chest, showing plenty of skin in front and back. I know my skin is catching the light, thanks to the "body glimmer" Stella gave me. This seemed like such a good idea forty-eight hours ago. Now I hover at the threshold, undecided.

"Maddy?" I jump as Frank comes up behind me.

"Oh, hey, Frank."

He looks me up and down, taking in my unlikely outfit. "I got everything all set up the way you asked."

"Thanks, Frank," I muster, but still don't move.

"You're not going to tell me what this is all about, are you?"

I shake my head.

"Having second thoughts?" he probes as the whole party rages on behind him.

I start to nod, and then change it into a shake at the last second.

He laughs kindly. "Okay, then. They're standing by, waiting for my cue."

A few deep breaths turn out not to be enough. I dart into the women's bathroom to regroup. I stare at my reflection in the mirror, barely recognizing myself. Stella did such a beautiful job on my makeup. It's not too heavy, but just enhances my features, emphasizing my cheekbones. Thin dark eyeliner brings out the green in my eyes. I reapply the sheer lip gloss the way Stella showed me.

I glare at my reflection. *Quit stalling.*

Back out in the lobby, I wind my way toward the doorway and take another look at the crowd. Adam is still in the same place, engaged in conversation. It's now or never. I text Frank and hit SEND before I can rethink it.

I hold my phone, staring at the screen, waiting for the reply from Frank. A minute later:

Frank: Action!

And for the first time ever, that's my cue. I step out into the center of the room, going through the motions exactly as I'd pictured it in my head. The lights blink out, and the spotlight finds its target in seconds.

Adam, along with everyone else, looks around, blinking in the brightness. I am completely oblivious to the crowd's reaction as I step forward. My prop finds its way into the light. Adam sees the red rose, but he doesn't fully understand until I step all the way out of the shadows.

I'm sure the noisy crowd has lots to say about what they're seeing, but I have complete tunnel vision focused only on Adam's handsome features as he scans me up and down. Then the instant he realizes what I've done, his eyes slam back to mine just as the band switches from the intro music and plays the powerful downbeat of the tango.

Sophie had been more sure than I was that I'd fit into Megan Keef's dress from that *Days of Our Lives* scene, which she borrowed from her client, Ms. Keef. As with most things, Sophie was exactly right; the dress fits perfectly.

"May I have this dance?" I ask, extending the rose to him. The quirk of his brow lets me know that he recognizes I'm stealing his line. Time stands still as I wait for his reply. This feeling— the terror in my gut—is exactly why I've never taken a chance like this before. But now, waiting for Adam to say yes or no, to play along or shut me down, I realize that no matter how he reacts, I'm glad I did it. I'm proud of myself.

And then the wait is over. Probably only milliseconds went by, but I clearly wasn't the only one holding my breath. When Adam stands up, never once looking away from me as he takes the rose and gallantly kisses my hand like in a Cary Grant movie, a collective sigh echoes mine.

He leads me to the center of the floor. As he pulls me against the length of his body for the opening position, he whispers in my ear, "You know the moves?" And I whisper back, "I watched it on repeat for two days straight. I know it by heart." He doesn't give a lot away, but I can see the hint of a smile tugging at the corner of his mouth.

And on the next downbeat, we dance. I'd practiced until I thought my feet were going to fall off, but nothing prepared me for what it would be like to be in Adam's arms. As if he'd done the dance yesterday, Adam didn't hesitate for an instant. I feel his strong hand at my back as he guides me through a complicated turn.

The tango is a sexy dance. I never thought I'd live up to the energy, the sultriness, but with every turn, I am snapped back into the basic step, with Adam's hand on my lower back, his left hand firmly holding mine, and his eyes focused only on me. I feel myself falling more and more under the dance's spell, letting myself completely get swept away. We get to the part of the routine where I slide my leg up his thigh, and I execute it with a genuine confidence that is now coursing through my veins. And Adam is clearly affected by my assurance as his hand trails slowly, steadily, smoothly from my ankle up my thigh. And then with more grace than I could have ever hoped for, he dips me into the gorgeous final pose. He holds me inches above the ground, his lips so close to mine that I can feel his breath fanning my face.

From the moment the spotlight hit Adam, the crowd ceased to exist for me; I didn't hear them or see them. But now, even with the blood pounding in my ears, I hear the hoots and hollers, the clapping and cheering as Adam holds me still in the dip and breaks into a huge smile.

"Well, Scripty, as far as 'romantic gestures' go...this has to be one of the best ever."

I smile up at him, caught in the moment, still breathless from our dance. I can't help the awareness creeping in that we are still center stage—I even hear Billy Fox's voice loud and clear: "*Dancing with the Stars* has nothing on you guys, huh? Maddy gets a ten!" But I'm not chickening out now. My hand moves from where I've had it braced on his shoulder to slide through the honey-brown shaggy hair on the back of his head. I don't need a script to know this is the perfect moment for a kiss. I pull him those last few inches and when our lips connect, it's magic.

Adam effortlessly holds us in place, allowing the kiss its beautiful perfect moment. The next thing I know my head is spinning as he sweeps me up into his arms just as his character on *Days* did, taking me to the edge of the crowd to place me back onto my feet in the shadows. The party continues around us, the band goes back to their cover tunes, but he doesn't let go.

We pass Sophie dragging her husband toward the dance floor. She slows down to whisper, "Well done, my friend," in my ear before turning to Jacob and pronouncing, "We are definitely taking dance lessons."

Adam smiles but isn't distracted from staring deep into my eyes.

"So, now what?" he asks me softly.

"Um, I don't know," I admit unsteadily. "I only planned this far...," I begin before my voice trails off.

"You know what that means, then, don't you?" I can tell by the twinkle in his eye that he's up to something.

"No, what does it mean?"

"From here on out..." That cocky grin on his face makes him even more handsome. I love how he's looking at me, drinking me in. "We're ad-libbing."

Roll End Credits

Int. Pete's Tavern--night

It's hard to hear over the noise of the crowd gathered at Pete's Tavern, but the second the opening credits come on ("Executive Producer: Madelyn Carson"—still gives me chills), everyone starts yelling, "SHHH!" I can't help but be touched that over a hundred people go from decibel 11 to zero so quickly. I've seen the first episode of *Never Cry Wolf* so many times at this point. Now that it's finally premiering on TV, I am watching everyone else's faces, not the television hanging in the corner by the bar.

It was Pete Jr.'s idea to host the premiere party here, and I couldn't have hoped for a better turnout. Everyone is here, and even though they are all silent, it is easy to feel the energy and enthusiasm for the show. A fruity cocktail appears in front of me.

"They love it," Adam whispers softly so as not to be shushed by the entranced crowd. Where does he even find those little umbrellas in Wolf? "You can stop worrying now, Scripty."

I smile as he drops a kiss on my ear before moving to stand next to me to size up the reactions. Anticipating this moment, their response has guided me every step of the way of producing this show, especially during the sixty-plus hours in the editing booth last month. I drove myself (and Janine and Joel... and Adam too) crazy making sure that, above all else, everyone would be happy and proud to have participated.

"Look at the lovebirds!" Lily busts us as soon as the show goes into the first commercial break. The second they see an ad, the whole crowd erupts in loud applause, laughter, and some good-natured teasing.

"Maddy, it's fantastic!" Brian gives me a quick squeeze. "So, what did you end up telling your parents? Did you let them see the show early?"

It was a tough call—I even brought my brothers into the debate. My parents have been dying to see the show, and they knew I'd been slaving away, editing it. The second I had explained that I sent Hogan links to cuts of scenes, my parents began begging for a sneak peek. But it was a consensus from the Carson children that our parents wouldn't be able to resist forwarding the e-mail to their entire contact list, like they forward every semi-decent joke e-mail they get. A whole week of secrecy? No way would they keep it under wraps until the premiere.

"Of course not!" I say with such sincere determination that all three of them laugh.

"What do your parents think? You know, so we can keep the story straight," Lily asks.

"I told them it wouldn't be finished until the last minute." I do feel bad about the little white lie, but it really isn't that big of a stretch since I only got the final approval from the network last week.

The conversation abruptly cuts off as the show comes back on. All of a sudden it's so quiet again, you can hear every word. I smother a laugh, imagining the network PR team having a coronary over the very unglamorous setup we have here. They'd suggested bringing in a fancy LA party planner to throw up some massive decorations and big flat screens and have a red-carpet press event to cover the occasion. Luckily that idea was overruled by everyone, including Sophie Atwater, the show's publicist.

"It just feels wrong," I had said last week at dinner on a double date with Sophie and Jacob. Sophie insisted on treating me to a special dinner when I sent the group text that the network had officially approved the episode.

As usual, we vowed no shoptalk at dinner, and as usual we couldn't avoid it when conversation turned to the network pressure to have a big launch party.

I told Sophie how much I hated the idea.

"What makes the show work," Adam offered succinctly, "is that they're not Hollywood. A big red carpet event wouldn't make sense in Wolf."

"I'll handle the network," Sophie said confidently. "You just go have fun with your friends. Tweet a picture from the party so your new fans can feel they were a part of the celebration. Selfishly, it will help me feel like I'm there."

"I'm sorry we won't be able to join you this weekend. I am looking forward to getting Sophie back on a pair of skis." Jacob is always so formal in comparison to the actors I'm usually around, but his deadpan expression didn't last more than a second with Sophie's dramatic reaction.

"I told you, Jacob. Not in a million years! I can't even walk through the door without tripping." Before she got too carried away, Jacob's expression let her know he was teasing. She gave him an affectionate swat and then turned to me. "I'm more your snow bunny. I'm happy to wait for you in the lodge." Jacob whispered something in her ear, and I remember thinking how amazing it is that Adam and I are sitting here watching this coupley moment and it wasn't awkward at all.

"Maddy and I are so bummed we can't be at Billy's premiere. I hope he understands," Adam says to Sophie.

When I got the official airdate for *Never Cry Wolf*, my heart sank that it conflicted with the premiere of Billy's latest movie. Adam didn't even hesitate to let me know he'd be by my side.

"He'll be fine. Don't worry. He's going to tweet about the show too. Help get the word out," Sophie said with finality. "Enough work talk...we're here to celebrate *not* working!"

I'm so glad we stuck to our guns about the premiere party, because this night is exactly what I pictured: intimate, warm, and low key. I'm almost dizzy from the feelings coursing through me as I stare out at the sea of family and friends, with Adam's arm around me. Just as the second act ends, my eyes fall on the giant basket of champagne, flowers, and cupcakes with the show's logo that Sophie sent. Thank God I remembered about the picture I'm supposed to take for Sophie. Perfect timing, since there's another commercial break.

"Hey, everyone!" I shout over the dull roar that breaks out in an instant. Adam sees me pulling my phone out and gives a loud whistle that gets all heads turning. "Picture time!" he shouts.

"Come on, everyone, over here!" I have my phone lifted over my head as high as I can, but I can see on the screen that I'm getting only a small portion of the people. Before I can figure out where to reposition myself, I feel my feet leaving the ground. Adam grabs me around the thighs and lifts. My head is spinning, but not just from the altitude. Even though we've been back together for a few months now, I still get an electrical charge every time he touches me. I think I always will.

"One! Two! Three!" Everyone yells and cheers as I take the picture.

Adam lowers me back to the ground, but even with the crowd all around us, it's such an intimate moment. His hands are wrapped around me with my back pressed against his chest, his face over my right shoulder.

"I love you, Maddy." He whispers it into my ear. Simply. No fancy gestures, no elaborate buildup. It's the first time he's said those three little words, and it happens in a noisy, crowded bar in the middle of the premiere of my show. Somehow, coming from him, it's just right.

"I love you too." I can't believe how easy it is to finally say it, how wonderful it is to get off my chest something I've been feeling and thinking for so long. I turn around and bury my face in his delicious-smelling chest.

"Hey, hey, get a room, you two," Matthew jokes loudly, and then Mike, right behind him, grumbles, "Can you please not say things like that?" Mike will never let go of being the intimidating big brother, which he's made clear at every family barbeque this summer. But I know he loves Adam and is so happy for me.

"I love it, sis. You did amazing." A big Mike hug follows. As he heads back to the bar, I feel a buzz in my back pocket.

Ed: Great picture on Twitter. You did it. Congrats. Can't wait to see numbers tomorrow. Good job.

It's an incredible pat on the back from Ed. I'm still glowing, staring at the text when Adam calls my attention to the table in the corner where my parents have sat all night with their friends, beaming with pride. I see the back of a head full of shaggy, gray overgrown hair. Hogan's here.

I take Adam's hand and drag him over to say hello.

"I'm so sorry I'm late, " Hogan says, giving me a big hug.

"I can't believe you made it at all." I know how hectic his schedule is, getting ready for season three.

"I wouldn't miss this for the world."

"How do you think the show will do, Hogan?" my mom asks.

"Honestly, Helen, I don't care what the ratings say." That's not exactly something you hear every day from a Hollywood producer. Even Adam looks surprised by Hogan's response. "I'm proud the show is an HCP production. No matter how it does. I know I was right in trusting it to her."

It's too much. I swallow a huge lump in my throat as I hug Hogan again.

The show is over and someone shouts, "Hey, you DVRed it, right, Pete? Let's watch it again."

And then Brian steps up. "Great idea. But first, a toast. Maddy, get up here."

I do as I'm told, and Brian says all sorts of lovely things about how proud everyone is of me and how much the show means to everyone in Wolf. I try to take in all of his words as I see all of my friends and family around the room. Through the tears I finally can't hold back, I think: This is not how I would have imagined this script ending, but there you have it. I never thought I'd say it, but life is just better without a script.

A Note from the Author

I had such fun writing this novel. In some ways, the process is not that much different from acting. It's so exciting and rewarding to create a world full of characters that I would want to hang out with...and I'll be honest, a lot of them are based on my real-life friends and family. Is that cheating? I do have a friend whose motto is "Never trust the actors"—she says it in a joking voice, but she's *so* not kidding. I wonder if this book will change her mind...I doubt it. My makeup artist is definitely every bit as sassy as Stella is. The tight-knit dynamic I attempted to re-create among the crew on *The Wrong Doctor* definitely mirrors my experiences both at *The Biggest Loser* and *Days of Our Lives*. When you work together for such long hours, in sometimes tense, often exhausting situations, you get close quick, you learn to rely on each other, and it is very much like a second family.

I can never say enough how important being a part of *Days* has been to me for the last twenty-one-*plus* years. Adam's story gave me the chance to reveal a little of what life is like there, a bit of how we do things, and maybe most importantly, how indescribably meaningful the experience has been.

I borrowed Maddy's quirky movie-quoting habit from my own life. I love movies. I especially love quoting movies. It goes way

A Note from the Author

back to my brothers and I sitting around the dinner table making John Hughes movie jokes as kids—everything from *Planes, Trains & Automobiles* to *Vacation*. It's still one of our favorite bonding activities. On set at *Days*, we don't go a day without referencing the classics—and by that I mean *Arthur* (the original with Dudley Moore), *Dirty Dancing* ("Nobody puts baby in a corner"), *Princess Bride* (in its entirety)...I could go on and on. So it seemed only natural to make Maddy a movie quoter. I referenced lots of classic TV shows too, *Friends*, *Seinfeld*, etc. but here I have compiled a list of the movies that I referenced in the book:

A Fish Called Wanda	*Princess Bride*
Airplane	*Real Genius*
The Big Chill	*School of Rock*
Can't Buy Me Love	*Sleepless in Seattle*
The Eagle Has Landed	*Spaceballs*
Forrest Gump	*Star Wars*
The Good, the Bad and the Ugly	*The Terminator*
Jaws	*Vacation*
Jurassic Park	*Young Frankenstein*

Looking at this list, I'm cracking up at how I'm dating myself. But these movies shaped my generation. If you don't know them, you should. "If you have the means, I highly recommend picking one up"—ha, see that, I just tossed in a *Ferris Bueller's Day Off* quote for good measure. But seriously, if you've never seen these movies, or it's just been a while, add them to your queue. Rent, on-demand, download them. You're welcome.

Acknowledgments

I find it's both easy and difficult to write the acknowledgments for this novel. Easy because there are lots of people to thank, I know who they are, they know who they are, and listing them is pretty straightforward. It only gets complicated because I hope to sincerely express to every person mentioned how important they are to me and how grateful I am to have them in my life.

So, Deidre Decker-Wilson, you're first. And we both know why. "He's taking the knife out of the cheese...do you think he wants some cheese?" But seriously, I hope you know how much I appreciate working with you every day. Our jokes, your serenades, talent, and, most especially, your compassion.

Matthew Elblonk, you were the first person to meet Maddy Carson. I love how open you are to brainstorming with me and allowing me to bounce every crazy idea off you. Thank you for gently guiding me in the right direction. Thank you for championing me every step of the way.

It was such a joy to work side by side with you on this novel, Christine Pride. You kept me on track and focused. It sometimes felt like we were Maddy's friends, concerned for her love life and excited for her career opportunities. Thank you for helping bring her to life.

Acknowledgments

I have to say, Max Stubblefield, you really did come through on this one. I can't thank you enough for letting me pick your brain to make Maddy's experiences developing and pitching a show as realistic as ~~possible~~ I wanted it to be.

Hearing your initial feedback, Leslie Wells, lead to an initial sigh of relief—*Whew, she gets it!*—followed by a slew of activity. Thank you for your fresh insight into this character and to everyone at Hachette for believing in her story.

You will never hear enough from me how grateful I am to have you as my best friend, Carrie Simons. I continue to grow, learn, be inspired and challenged by you. Every reference to Sophie's saving-the-day style in this novel is the closest she gets to being like you.

I love my team at UTA, I'm so lucky to have you guys on my side. Barbara Rubin, you are a role model to strong women everywhere and an inspiration to me. When thinking of people in my corner, Stephanie, you deserve a special shout-out. Thank you for always striking the perfect balance between loyal, unquestioning friendship and objective insight and counsel. Corina, I know we will work together for the next twenty-plus years, laughing and cursing every step of the way and I can't wait.

In writing this book, I glorified the movie quoting habits that make my friends and I laugh every day. It started with my brothers, Sten & Ryan, "Happy pie..." still gets a snicker. The award for Most Accurate Quoter goes to Kyle Brandt. Dave Braun, Bryan Dattilo, Eric Martsolf, Patrick Muldoon, Lauren, Mel, MK and Lisa, all get honorable mentions here for quoting and loving movies and TV as much as I do.

I am filled with pride to be working on a reality TV show like *The Biggest Loser*. With Bob, Jillian, Dolvett, and the executives and the whole *BL* family, it is incredibly inspiring to be a part of

Acknowledgments

helping people change their lives; the contestants on the show as well as the fans who watch.

I cannot miss the opportunity to thank my parents for their constant support and guidance. Papa, your business sense is only outshone by your thoughtful parenting and wise counsel. Thank you for sharing all of the above with me. Mom, thank you for every new experience you introduced me to as a kid. The classes, especially the violin (yes, it's now officially in writing) the auditions, all the extracurricular activities helped shape my belief in myself and my ability to dream big. I try every day to share the lessons you've both taught me with Ben and Megan.

Ben and Megan, it is the most incredible gift ever to see the world through your eyes. Thank you for reminding me how beautiful, fun and surprising every day can be.

Dave, I'm so lucky to be on this journey with you. Thank you for putting up with my crazy work hours and my *sometimes* kooky artistic temperament. Thank you for making me laugh, for making our life together so wonderful. I love you.